ALL THE WATERS OF THE EARTH

A ROMANCE

GIVING YOU …
BOOK 3

LESLIE MCADAM

Cover design by RJ Creatives.

Editing by L Woods LLC.

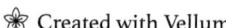 Created with Vellum

THE GIVING YOU ... SERIES

What would you give someone you loved? I would give them

The Sun and the Moon,
The Stars in the Sky,
All the Waters of the Earth,
and
The Ground Beneath Our Feet

For Erika

1

ROMANCE WRITER'S PROBLEMS

*A*nd he shifted, pressing his full male heat into her petals.
Delete.
. . . *and he gently slid his member into her secret center.*
No. Delete.
. . . *and he impaled her on his straining shaft.*
Ugh. Delete.
I rapped my fingers on the side of my desk.
What's on Facebook?
No. No distractions. Keep writing.
Or . . . take a break.

I got my ample booty out of my chair and walked into the kitchen of my duplex to pour a glass of water. Today's writing wasn't going very well. Romance novel number sixteen, I feared, was falling into the pitfalls of cliché and drivel. I needed something new. My hero wasn't making me wet. At all. I was tired of typing and deleting, typing and deleting, not getting anywhere.

The thing was, I loved being a romance novelist. I loved everything about it—the meet cute, the hot men, the secret, tragic past, the chemistry, and the sex. *Oh, the sex.* I loved all of it.

My fictional guys tended to have a few things in common.

They were all tall with chiseled good looks—high cheekbones, strong jaws, full heads of hair, and ripped bodies. Uniformly Alpha males. The type who'd fuck you hard against a wall and make you moan in pleasure. Order you around and then show you their soft underbelly. *Ooh, baby, make me quiver.* I liked them to be *men*, you know, not wishy-washy. But I liked them to have a soul, too.

For some reason, however, I was having trouble with this book. I always start with the sex. If I can't get that right, then I know the rest of it won't work either.

I needed inspiration.

And to tap into my imagination, because I hadn't gotten any in too long to admit. Since I'd had my son, my dates on my child-free weekends were of two types. Either once they found out I had a son, they suddenly got an important text and had to leave, or there was no way in hell I'd let them around Roberto. So while I waited for Mr. Right (and the Mr. Right Nows didn't measure up), the only action I saw was between the pages of a book. No wonder I wrote such steamy scenes.

Given my profession, I had this habit of always looking for the real life versions of my fictional heroes. That sexy-ass DILF in line at Target, with broad shoulders and a beard, balancing a tiny baby girl on his impressive bicep? He looked like Zack from my fourth book. That tattooed masterpiece at Home Depot, all jeans and legs and boots and body? If you grew his dark hair a little shaggier, he kind of looked like Clint in book twelve. And that artsy hottie standing by the bar with the Smith and Wesson belt and what had to be a giant cock? I was going to have to write a book about him next.

The thing was, I had banged out fifteen romance novels in seven years and I wasn't stopping anytime soon. I'd done this long enough that I knew the secret to finishing a novel—keep at it. And I kept at it, almost every day, all day. Normally, it was pretty easy for me to do. Just not today, for some reason.

While I worked from home, I certainly didn't do so in my pajamas. No manky old college sweatshirt for me to write in. A girl had to show some pride. You'd never find me without full makeup on every day and a Brazilian blow-out for my naturally frizzy hair. I had to look good to take my kid to school.

I was no writer recluse either. I got out of the house often, going for drinks with my friends. Life was too short not to play. I just made sure to get babysitters.

Still, I loved to write, and I did it almost daily. I was glad to make a living at it. To make ends meet, however, I had to supplement my income in two ways. I got child support from my ex, Carlos. And I also modeled nude at an art school.

No judgies.

My body was womanly and I flaunted it.

The nude model gig brought in a little bit of cash to spend on high heels for me and video games for Rob.

It's true that there was no way that I could be a regular five foot ten, one hundred twenty-five pound model. No way. I was what you'd call fun-sized. Five foot nothin', baby. Because of that, I never really took off my high heels when I went out.

You know those magazine articles about how to dress for your type that ask if you're an apple or a carrot or something? Me? Pear shaped. And how.

I defined the term, *junk in the trunk*. My booty entered the room thirty seconds after I did. My waist? Nothing there. Tiny. My boobs? Small, but perky. My legs? Short and strong. When I bought pants, they never fit because they were too big in the waist and too long in the legs.

But you know what? That was the problem of the clothing manufacturers, not me.

Though my body was not made for high fashion modeling, it

was ideal for modeling for art classes, where they celebrated shapes and curves. I'd decided a long time ago not to waste precious brain space wishing I had a different body. This was the one I was born with and I accepted my looks. This was how tall I was and I wasn't getting any taller. This was how long my legs were, and they weren't getting any longer. And my booty? Yeah, I showed it off in a tight mini skirt and heels when I went out dancing.

As I drank my water, I looked around my nice Santa Barbara duplex. A royalty check for my fourth novel made the down payment. Royalty checks on the fifth and sixth helped to pay the mortgage. The rest of the books paid for food for me and my twelve-year-old son, Rob, as well as clothes, taxes, insurance, and all of the other grownup things in life.

I must say, though, I was really not a fan of the grownup things in life. I'd rather be a romantic. Who had any use for the real world? That was why we had books.

My home felt cozy and lived-in. Rob had his Xbox and games out, but other than that, we kept it neat. We had a small kitchen, a large great room that was both a dining room and a living room, three bedrooms, one of which I used as an office, and two bathrooms. I'd call the decorating style early Target, with a dash of Restoration Hardware, meets *Día de los Muertos*.

The duplex was part of a larger complex. Because I was home a lot, I could probably tell you about everyone in the complex—the elderly couples who watched television together, the college kids who had one too many parties, and the newly-weds with a baby on the way. But my unit was off to the side and shared a wall and a laundry room with the unit next door, which was a rental. Someone moved in over the weekend but I hadn't met them yet. It was probably a bachelor, what with the dark furniture and big television. I'd only seen the moving truck—and the movers, jean-clad and wiry, but young, sweaty, and cute.

My patio adjoined the neighbor's, and looked out over the pool. I loved to swim—I really loved being in the water—and I used the pool often. We were lucky in California that the time of year did not hamper our ability to go swimming and I could go in the pool now even though it was early December.

Thinking about my current writer's block, I decided that maybe I just needed to get out of the house and take a break. Rob wouldn't be back from school for a while. Sometimes doing mindless, automatic things like laundry or swimming helped with the writing. Good ideas came to me then.

Downing the last of my drink, I went into the bedroom and put on a pink string bikini. As I said, I was very much a girlie girl. I lived so close to the pool, that I didn't need any cover-ups —just a towel and my oversized sunglasses.

Grabbing my keys, I slipped on my high heeled sandals and threw open the door to a man standing there, with his hand raised to knock on my door.

A very handsome man.

The most handsome man that I had ever seen.

Thick, ebony hair. Sapphire blue eyes. His face had the curves and the edges of a romance hero, with high cheekbones, hollows in his cheeks, and a shapely jaw.

He was dressed in Mr. Businessman attire—a crisp white shirt, perfect, thick, and lush; a gray and blue silk tie that matched his eyes, not too shiny, not too matte; and a dark gray suit that enhanced his frame. He was tall, but of course everyone was tall next to me. Short girl problems. That said, he was probably a foot taller than me, or more, with muscular legs, a flat waist, and broad shoulders.

For a second, I couldn't react. Or rather, I couldn't believe what I was seeing. My fictional hero at my door. I almost laughed. That didn't happen to me. I mean, really, despite the evidence, there was no fucking reason why this man should be at my front porch. He was the kind of man I wrote about in my books.

But I knew for certain that those men didn't really exist. They were just figments of my imagination. Real men have bellies and are too short or too lanky and wear cargo shorts and Star Wars t-shirts and need to manscape. They don't show up at your door looking like Gideon Cross.

He looked at me, equally startled, and then his vibrant eyes went up and down my curvy body, taking in my tiny pink bikini and high-heeled sandals. Well, *guapo*, nice to meet you too. He rocked back on his heels, bringing a hand to the back of his neck, and stared down at me. Like he wanted to say something but couldn't. I was mesmerized by his partially open mouth displaying a glistening tongue and perfect white teeth. Putting his hand down and shoving it in his pocket, he opened his eyes wider. Then he seemed to recover, took a step back, and started talking in a great baritone voice.

"Hi, I'm Jake Slausen. I moved in next door. I'm staying here while my place gets remodeled. So, I guess I'm your neighbor. Nice to meet you. What's your name?"

He was chatty. Aren't most romance heroes quiet? But *God*, the sound of his voice. Sexy chatter in a deep voice that I could *feel* in my body. He made me not want to do anything that would make him go. I wanted him to stay on my porch forever, even if I was in a string bikini. *Especially* if I was in a string bikini.

And him? He looked equally flustered—a red tint to his cheeks and a shortness of breath that told me he noticed my curves. But I answered his question.

"Lucy Figueroa," I said, shaking his hand. His hand was warm, firm, and strong. I noticed that he held my hand just a second longer than most people did. I wanted to get to know that hand better.

I wondered what it would feel like between my legs.

Probably pretty damn fine.

Shaking off my naughty thoughts and remembering my manners, I continued, "I was just heading for the pool. Have you been down there yet?"

"Not yet. I have to get back to work." Regret washed over his face. He looked genuinely disappointed that he couldn't go. "I stopped by here because I forgot my walk-through papers and I needed to return them to the management office. I thought maybe I'd left them in the laundry room because it was the last part on the list. I went to check it—we share it right?" I nodded. "Well, I went to check it and I found my papers but I also found these and I figured that they were yours."

And he held out his other hand with a funny look on his face that was embarrassed, amused, and if I wasn't mistaken, turned on. There dangling, in those hands that I wanted to meet, were a pair of my red lace thong panties.

No way.

"Those yours?" I asked, trying not to be too embarrassed. Talk about meet cute.

His cheeks burned as red as my panties and he laughed. "No. Not my style. Well, I mean they *are* my style. I mean, I like them but they aren't ..."

I took pity on him and grabbed my undergarment with a grin. "Thanks."

Then we stared at each other. I bit my lip and jutted out my hip. He ran his fingers under his jaw and then behind his neck again.

"Well, it's nice to meet you, Lucy. Good to get to know my neighbors. I work long hours but I'm sure to see you around. Let me know if you need a cup of sugar or anyth—"

"I'll have to bring you some tamales," I offered, coming up with an excuse to see him again. "Christmas is coming. My mom and I make them for the holidays."

"That sounds good," he said absently, still looking up and down my body. It made me shiver even though it wasn't cold outside. And then he took a step backwards and brushed up against the large potted ficus that sat on my front porch, tripping slightly. Pushing it aside, he turned to leave and said with a smile that made my insides get all squishy, "Well, I'll be seeing you. I have to go back to the office." And then he turned and left.

Yes, I did want to be seeing him again and I wanted it right this minute. I couldn't help but think that his job was really inconvenient, because it got in the way of me getting to know him better. I stared at him as he left and then I closed my door slowly, went down the hall, and deposited my red panties in my bedroom.

A pulse of excitement ran through my body from top to toe. Of course I was short so this didn't take too long. But this thrill that I felt? I hadn't felt it in a long time. Maybe since high school? Since my rat bastard ex?

And this guy was my new *neighbor*?

Life was about to get more interesting.

I needed to cook up a plan to get to know him better. He seemed just perfect—perfect looks, perfect manners, perfect voice. I wonder if he was perfect in bed, too.

Retracing my steps to my front door, I took my towel, sunglasses, and keys to the pool, now on a mission to think about not only the plot to my new book, but also this new romance hero, living next to me.

TAMALES TAKE A LOT OF WORK

I was up to my elbows in masa. Seriously.

Rob sat on the floor of the living room, the annoying music of Minecraft droning on, playing with his Xbox. He once tried to explain the point of Minecraft and I never got it. Endermen? Steve? But it seemed harmless and actually creative, so I let him play.

Twelve year old boys like videogames and I struggled with the tension of wanting to be a cool mom who let him do what he wanted, such as rot his brain in front of the television, versus wanting to be mom the enforcer who'd tell him to ride his bike or read a book. As a single parent, I was both, and I couldn't decide which one was more important. Sometimes he needed a friend. Sometimes he needed a parent. Although I tried, it felt impossible to do both well. Today was cool mom, since he was OD'ing on the Xbox. What can I say? I did my best.

Carlos Castro, my ex-boyfriend who got me pregnant, still lived in town and he saw Roberto every other weekend. I took full advantage of the weekends I didn't have Rob, getting drinks with the girls and dancing.

Not that I didn't love my kid. Just every parent needs a break.

Carlos worked for his parents, who owned a chain of flooring shops. He was a manager. He made decent money and normally paid his child support, but our relationship wasn't good. We were always civil in front of Rob. Sometimes we were civil to each other when Rob wasn't around. But sometimes it got very ugly when we were on our own.

I didn't really want to think about that right now. I was too busy making tamales.

My friends, Georgie and Sara, were in the kitchen, dealing with the corn husks, while my mother tended to the seasoned pork. Georgie was short like me, but she let her hair frizz, unlike me. She worked as a bookkeeper for an automotive parts dealer and told the best jokes. Sara, taller, more regal and elegant, almost always wore white. She was quiet, but when she talked, whatever she said was important and made you laugh or think. She always had the best clothes because she worked at Macy's and spent all of her money using her employee discount. My mother was just like me—same height, same high mainte-nance, same looks, just twenty years older and a grocery store cashier.

Although we chatted while we cooked, we were all intent on our tasks. Tamale making was serious business.

My mother made tamales regularly, but for me, it was a once-a-year event—only at Christmas. I tried to make a ton to freeze for later. I always enlisted help, because there were so many steps in the process. That said, it was fun. For example, even though it was barely ten o'clock, all of us were on our second margarita. It was a party! At least the type of party where you all had a job to do and needed to coordinate to make it work well. So we drank, we cooked, we assembled, we chatted, we laughed, and we had a good morning.

It was Saturday, five days after I had met Jake, my neighbor. In that period of time, I'd become obsessed with seeing him again. I mean, he was going to be the inspiration for my next book, right? So I needed to observe him. It was research.

Yeah, that was it.

I'd spent the entire week trying to come up with ways to talk to him or run into him. In so doing, I'd deduced the following.

He lived an incredibly regimented life. I heard his door open every morning at five-thirty. Then the door opened at six-fifteen. Then it opened again at seven and never opened again until after seven or eight every night at the earliest.

As far as I could tell, this meant that he went for a run every morning, first thing. When he left to go for a run, he wore a tight, white t-shirt and long, black athletic shorts. He went out looking sleepy and came back bright-eyed and covered in sweat.

That only made him look better.

Then he went inside his duplex and I presume that he showered, ate breakfast, and went to work, working twelve hours a day until he came back home. He always wore a pristine suit, even wearing the jacket, very formal, no shirtsleeves for this guy. His cufflinks winked in the early morning sunlight. And his long hours? Man, that type of schedule was so dreadfully boring.

I didn't know what he did that made him work so much, but I hoped that he loved it, or at least got paid well for it. Based on the look on his face, though, I concluded that he was tired by the end of the day and very done with life and what he was doing. He didn't look happy, the bright-eyed spark from his morning exercise gone.

I made these deductions through careful observation and analysis.

Okay, I could tell this by peeping out the little hole in my front door.

I was reduced to being a stalker.

He hadn't had any visitors the whole week he was there. I hoped that he was single. For, you know, research purposes. And he was very quiet, with no music, or even television blaring. I needed an excuse to see him. Thus my tamale delivery plan.

I really hoped he'd like them, because if I was honest, I wasn't making them for Christmas. I was making them for him.

Just then there was a knock on my door. Hoping it was Jake, I scuttled to the front door in my heels, and opened it with my elbows, trying not to get masa on the door.

There was a man standing on my doorstep.

A bike messenger man, all slim muscles, tattooed calves, and messenger bag.

He pulled some papers out of his bag and handed them to me. "Lucinda Figueroa?"

"Who wants to know?" I asked, the back of my hand on my hips.

"You are being served with this petition by Carlos Castro—" he started, as he handed the documents to me, and I screamed, "That SON OF A BITCH!" and then I clamped my messy, masa hand over my mouth because I remembered that Rob was in the room.

Wow, what an asshole. What was he trying to do this time?

I grumpily yanked the papers out of the messenger boy's hands and said, "Fine, the jerk has served me," and I slammed the door in his face.

Then I felt bad because it wasn't the bike messenger's fault.

So I gingerly opened the door again and said, "I'm sorry. I didn't mean to be rude. You're just the messenger and my ex is an asshole. I'm sorry," I repeated. "Have a nice day." And I smiled at him and then slammed the door again.

"Lucy," called my mother. "What was that all about?"

"Carlos," I muttered under my breath, and then I went into the kitchen. I set the papers down on the only clear surface, and then wiped my hands off on a paper towel. "Carlos served me with some papers. I'll read them after we are done here."

"Oh that *cabrón*," my mother muttered.

"Mom!"

"She's right," said Sara.

"Yeah, he's a *pinche* cabrón," said Georgie.

"Rob. Can. Hear. You." I hissed.

"Sorry, girl," Georgie replied, immediately.

"Don't say sorry to me, say sorry to Roberto."

"Sorry, Rob," Georgie called out.

"No worries, *tía*," he called back. Rob called both of my friends tía, meaning aunt.

I let out a breath and managed a weak smile.

"Oh, that was ugly. Okay, let's finish these up."

Two hours later, I had dozens upon dozens of pork tamales and a clean kitchen. My friends and my mom had gone home and I'd cleaned up and now sat at my dining table with the envelope from the messenger, scared to read the words on the page.

Better do it, though.

I looked at the first sheet. It was a petition to modify child custody and child support. Basically, my ex wanted to take my child from me and pay me less in child support.

Bile rose up into my throat and my hands shook. I had downed three margaritas before lunch and then had barely eaten any lunch, but this news put me over the edge. The room spun and I felt ill.

No way could he take away my child. No way could he threaten me with this. Rob and I were so stable. We had a good home. We didn't need to change anything.

Carlos worked all day. He wouldn't have time to take Rob to school or pick him up. What was he thinking?

He probably just wanted to stop paying child support, because the more time Rob was with his dad, the less child support he had to pay me. I needed to call my lawyer on

Monday. I hadn't had to use her in a while but it looked like I'd have to since Carlos made this move.

I tossed the papers on the floor and stamped out of the room, flinging myself on my bed. I didn't need this. Everything had been going so great. I didn't want a legal battle and I didn't want Rob to have anything to do with his parents fighting.

Goddamn fucking Carlos. He'd ditched me when I had Rob and left a scar so deep it hadn't healed. Even though I'd just had a house full of my closest female confidantes, I still felt like the unsupported single mom who, because of a single choice in high school, now had all this responsibility.

I took a deep breath.

After I lay there for a while, I calmed down. I'd call my attorney Monday morning and until I talked with her, I didn't have to think about this. It was time to chill and enjoy the rest of the weekend. Actually, it was time to give Jake the tamales that the four of us had slaved over for hours this morning. That would cheer me up.

I'd heard Jake leave that morning and I had heard his door open while I lay on my bed. Time to make a delivery. For research purposes.

I checked my hair and makeup in the mirror, and put on fresh lip gloss.

Calling to Rob that I'd be back in a second, I slipped out of my house, a dozen still-warm tamales wrapped in foil. My high heels clacked on the concrete as I scooted over to his door and knocked.

After a second, the door opened and Jake stood there looking godlike as ever, in jeans and a black t-shirt. His blue eyes bored into me and I saw a flash of surprise and, I hoped, delight. He held his cell phone to his ear with one hand and the other rested on the doorknob.

"Hang on a sec," he said into the phone. "Hey, Lucy, how are you?"

"Good. I made you some tamales." And I handed them to him.

"Uh, thank you," he responded in a friendly, but distracted tone, and then said, "Yeah, I'm back," into his phone and closed the door in my face.

Seriously?

What was up with that?

YOU NEED TO GET SOME ... MANNERS

I stood on Jake's stoop fuming, apoplectic, while a million thoughts ran through my head. Amidst all of my rampant thoughts was one rational truth: he didn't have to give me anything other than a reasonably polite thank you, which he did. I'd made the tamales out of the goodness of my heart and he didn't need to invite me in and fuck me in his shower, which was what I really wanted.

Wait, no. I just wanted more research for my book.

Well, anyway, I knew that the world didn't owe me anything. Jake didn't owe me anything, either. And I couldn't control any other person's responses to my actions, I could only control what I did in a situation.

The other part of my brain, perhaps irrational, perhaps not, ran me over and left me motionless, outside his door, thinking the following. I was pissed. I'd spent all morning on those. I invited a crew over to make them. I ignored my son to make them, letting him rot his brain on videogames. I even got served by a process server while I made them. While covered in masa!

I wanted the homemade food—a care package—to be my

excuse to get to know him and to talk to him. Anything other than having him just take them and close the door in my face.

Jerk. Maybe my impression about him was wrong. He didn't deserve any more attention from me. And as I stood there, I realized that it *hurt* to be rejected like that. Based on the way he looked at me before, I'd thought he liked me.

Fucking rejected by a man, again. Just like Carlos.

I turned to walk back to my home and paused.

No.

I was going to tell him that he was a jerk and that I deserved better. I turned back toward Jake's unit, raised my hand in a fist to pound on his door, and it opened before I could make contact. I dropped my fist immediately and Jake stepped out, closing the door behind him.

"Hey," he said, running his hand behind his neck, stretching his well-defined arm. His eyes looked weary, and such a distracting, intense shade of blue. But I saw kindness in them and something hotter. We both stared at each other and then I remembered to talk.

"Hey," I responded, looking up at him, sidetracked, and trying not to drool. Then I remembered that I was angry at him and I put my hand on my hips, sassy-Lucy style. "You know, you need to get some manners. I worked hard on those and you don't have to like them but you didn't have to slam the door in my face."

"I didn't mean it," he said immediately, walking towards me, backing me against the wall. What was this? "I was on the phone with someone from work and I got distracted." He looked sheepish. "Work gets in the way of everything and runs over my life. I'm sorry. I was coming over just now to tell you that I appreciated you bringing them to me."

"Yeah, well, acting like that? I thought you were a complete tool," I said, now hitting the wall. I couldn't help it. It was true and I deserve to be treated better. I'd learned from my past.

"So tell me what you really think," he muttered and his blue eyes danced. I shrugged in response, twirling my long brown hair around my finger. He let out a breath and put his hand on the wall next to me. Damn. That was close. I liked it. He looked me in the eyes, apologetic. "Look, I'm sorry. I didn't mean to be rude. I wasn't expecting you and I was in the middle of a conference call. I finished it just now and like I said . . ." and he trailed off and started looking at the top of my head.

And then I started looking at his mouth and I started really wishing he would kiss me. So badly. I wanted to feel him. I wanted to smell him. I wanted to run my hand along the back of his neck like he did, rubbing out the tension. Poor workaholic.

He stepped forward, towering over me, and put the other arm against the wall next to me. Then he leaned in and I knew he was going to kiss me. I closed my eyes, and . . .

I felt a peck on my cheek.

My belly dropped to my toes, which wasn't a long journey. I let out a breath. Ugh. I was so disappointed.

"Thank you," he said, and turned to go into his unit.

No. This was not the way he was supposed to act. He was supposed to kiss me and sweep me away. He was not supposed to give me some cheesy, chaste kiss and leave. I needed to fix this.

"Wait," I burst out.

He stopped and looked at me, his brows raised in silent question. Oh, he was so fine.

"That's not the way to kiss me," I whispered, turning my face toward him.

Jake smiled, a dazzling smile that made me want to buy his brand of toothpaste. "No, I suppose it isn't." He ran his finger under my chin and I went up on my tiptoes and looked him straight in his dark blue eyes. He leaned down and kissed me on the mouth, this time for real. A lovely kiss, his mouth heated and wet, his tongue velvety, his strong hand behind my neck, holding me to him.

Now that was the proper kiss that I'd wanted from him ever since I laid eyes on him a week ago. And now that I had it, I knew that I wanted more.

I invited him into my mouth, loving this, loving kissing my hot neighbor. I wrapped my hands around his neck and felt the back of his soft, thick hair. He smelled clean, like he was just out of the shower. Yum, yum, yummy, yum, yum.

He took his time with this kiss but it was still too soon when he broke apart. He ran his finger down my nose and I melted a little more. The way he looked at me was analytical. He seemed to be taking me all in, studying my face like he was memorizing it as if there would be a test later and he'd have to recreate it. It didn't make me feel uncomfortable.

It made me feel wanted.

And, seemingly satisfied with what he saw, his jaw ticked and then he asked, "Can I take you for a drink, Lucy?"

"Yeah, that would be good," I answered a little breathlessly, attempting to be nonchalant, but still feeling his lips on mine, his finger on my nose, his taste in my mouth.

"When? Tonight?"

I loved that he was eager. It was goddamn awesome. But I couldn't do it.

"No, I can't. I can go next Saturday night, though," I said, thinking about Rob's custody schedule. Carlos would have him next weekend and I was free to go out. I had a new art class to model for, though, so I wouldn't be done until about three o'clock. That was still plenty of time.

"Saturday night it is," he responded. He looked me up and

down, in my high heels and my white capris and pretty pink fluttery top. "You like to dress up?"

"Of course."

"Then dress up, honey. I'll take you someplace nice." And he smiled his glorious smile again and leaned in, and it looked like he was going to kiss me again.

"Okay," I whispered, and as he leaned down, his goddamned cell phone sounded, and he looked at me apologetically, straightening up again.

"We'll set it up," he said, and then answered his phone. "Jake Slausen." He walked back into his duplex, giving me a little wave this time as he shut the door.

4

YOU ARE GOING TO GET WET

I didn't see Jake the rest of the weekend. What I did do, however, was clean my house, take my kid to the park, and shop for Christmas presents. Normal mom stuff. I tried not to think too much about my next door neighbor. I failed. He was always there, just below my thoughts.

Hmm. What was going on? He was more than just a research project.

It was easy not to see him, though, because he was gone the entire weekend, probably working. Right?

First thing Monday morning, still pissed about Carlos and his legal papers, I called my attorney and made an appointment to see her at the earliest time I could get, which was in a week. Great. One more week to worry and get pissed. After calling, I spent the morning and early afternoon writing. I liked most of what I wrote. I especially liked the kisses between my characters, for some reason. Then I picked up Rob from school—again, normal mom stuff. He did his homework, we ate dinner, and I cleaned up. After dinner, at about eight o'clock, there was a knock at my door.

Would it be a hunk or a process server? I was seriously hoping for the former. The latter never needed to come again.

When I opened the door, I found Jake, rumpled in his suit, his tie undone slightly and his hair roguish. One exhausted businessman.

"Hey," he said, those sapphire eyes regarding me. God, he smelled good. Even tired, he gave off an energy, pheromones. All I wanted to do was touch him.

"Hi. Are you just finishing up work?"

"Yeah," he said, resting an arm against the doorjamb over my head, making me react with a throb in my heart and other places. He gave me a crooked smile. "I worked all weekend too. I wanted to bring you this, one of my clients makes it." And he handed me a jar of salsa, a very good local brand.

"Thank you. I love this brand, it's delicious." He'd thought of me. Nice.

"I'm glad." He looked at me, then glanced over at his door and let out a breath. "Well, I don't want to keep you. It was a long day." He looked like he wanted to say more.

Who took care of this guy? It didn't seem like he had anyone looking out for him. "Did you get dinner?"

"I picked up something at work. My usual. There's takeout next door."

"No, no, no." Eating out all the time wasn't healthy. "You need to start eating good food, home cooked, you know."

"It's hard when I work so late all the time. I loved your tamales, Lucy."

Yay. The effort was worth it if it nourished him. I had to sass him, though.

"You should try my *chile relleno* casserole. It's a recipe from the Dairy Council of America, but it's the shit."

"MOM!" yelled Rob.

"Sorry, *mijo*," I called back.

"Don't swear, Mom," he called back.

I ignored him and looked at Jake who had been observing me with amusement. Then I took the next step, the one I normally avoided. "You want to meet my son?" I'd never kept it from people I dated, but it definitely was a damper on relationships. *The* test to see if a guy could handle me.

But right now I didn't hesitate or feel weird introducing Jake to my son or vice versa. We were neighbors. He was bound to find out that I had a son.

Love me, love my son. That's the way it worked.

But also with Jake, well, I wanted to get to know him and I wanted him to know me. So I hoped he'd say yes.

Jake nodded. I let out a breath. So far, he passed. "Sure. Can I come in?" I stepped back and let him come in my home for the first time, his elegant but athletic frame dominating the front area.

"Roberto, come here and meet Mister Jake, our new neighbor."

Rob came skidding up in his socks and slid right in front of Jake. Skinny, with bony knees and gangling arms, he hadn't yet grown into himself. He had cheeks meant to pinch and dark brown eyes like his father. I ruffled his short, spiky hair. "Whoa," he said, when he looked up to Jake's height.

"How do you do?" Jake asked formally, extending his hand.

"Uh, fine," said Rob, shaking his hand limply. Then he looked at me, big-eyed, panicking as to what to do next.

I laughed. "Okay, enough torture. Go back to the television." Rob slid off in his socks and Jake's eyes followed him, then returned to me. He whispered.

"Good-looking kid. Polite, too."

Now the way to melt the heart of a mama is to compliment her kid.

"Thanks" was all that I managed in response.

"I'd better get in," he said. "I'm beat. See you tomorrow?"

I nodded. "I hope so. Goodnight."

"Goodnight." Looking around to see if Rob was watching, he bent over and kissed me, not slowly, not quickly, but enough to matter. I again felt the pulse through my body. Then he kissed my nose and opened my door and left.

What was I going to do with my neighbor?

The following evening, after Rob went to bed, I sat outside on my porch in the dark, looking at the lights making the pool water dance and drinking a Skinny Girl margarita. Early winter in California meant a slight chill in the air, but I'd wrapped up in a sweater and enjoyed the peaceful evening. When I'd almost finished my drink, Jake's sliding glass door opened and he came out, holding a bottle of 805 beer and wearing a tight, dark gray t-shirt and plaid pajama pants, barefoot. Even his feet were attractive. He headed to the edge of the patio to look at the pool, not noticing me.

"Hey, neighbor," I called out quietly.

"Lucy," he responded, and walked over to me. He glanced at my drink, said "Cheers," and leaned over the low wall that separated our patios, clinking his bottle with my margarita glass. "How was your day?"

"I got a lot of work done." I had and it felt so satisfying.

"Me too," he said. "But now I need to unwind. You go in the pool, right?" I nodded, secretly laughing, thinking of how I'd met him in my bikini. "How's the water?"

"It's great. They heat it so you can swim all year long. You should try it."

He looked at me. "Only if you come in with me."

Okay.

"Now?"

"Sure," he answered. "That is, if you want. It's a nice night, you know?" Even better with him. "We should take advantage of the fact that we live in Santa Barbara." He looked at me like there was more that he wished he could take advantage of than just the amenities of the complex.

I nodded. "Okay. I'll change and meet you down there in five minutes."

I went back inside, set my glass on the kitchen counter, and checked on Rob, who was fast asleep. Gotta be a mom first. I taped a note to his door that said, "At the pool—Mom." Then I quickly changed into my white bikini with red hearts all over it, piled my hair on the top of my head, grabbed a towel and the key to the pool, and tiptoed down to the pool in the quiet night. Although units surrounded the pool, some with lights on, some without, it felt like everyone had gone to bed and we were all alone outside.

Jake paced on the coping at the edge of the pool, wearing his t-shirt and long, dark blue swim trunks. He didn't see me approaching.

As I walked toward the pool fencing, he reached behind his head and pulled at the neck of his t-shirt, taking it off, and I responded physically.

Oh my.

My neighbor looked dapper in his suits. But out of one? Now that was really something to talk about. A fit guy, his chest muscular, his stomach flat, he didn't so much look like a body-builder, but rather a guy who simply kept in good shape. I gaped at his soft-looking skin, not as tan as mine. I wanted to touch him, everywhere. He turned toward me and saw me, his dark eyes catching mine in the half-lit night. My eyes went to his chest. A little bit of hair, not much, a little bit of hair below his belly button, extending into the low waistband of his swim trunks, not much. Just right. His broad shoulders and narrow waist formed that classic triangle. Toned arms and broad pectoral muscles rounded out the view.

Yummy.

All I wanted to do was nestle myself into his arms and see what his chest felt like against my cheek, what his nipple felt like on my tongue, what his back felt like when I clawed at it.

Instead, as he watched me, I set my towel on a chaise lounge, took off my heeled sandals, and dipped a toe into the pool, which registered as a comfortable, warm temperature.

Then I turned around, away from him, and walked to the shallow end, feeling his eyes on my ass the whole time. I grinned to myself. If you got it, flaunt it. I wiggled in, and dog paddled over to where he stood on the side of the pool.

"Are you going to come?" I asked, blatantly embracing the innuendo.

"Yeah." He smirked and dove into the pool next to me, splashing me and making me squeal, surfacing at the other end of the pool. He took off underwater and came right next to me, under the surface, pulling me down by my ankles.

"Jake! No! I don't want to get wet!" I protested, wiggling around. He breached the surface like a mer-god in the middle of my squeals and grabbed me by my waist. He was so much bigger than me, but having him so close, wet and muscular? And playful? Hot damn.

"You're in the pool," he laughed. "You are going to get wet." Yeah, that had already happened every time I thought of him.

"My hair!"

"It's beautiful."

"But I don't want to get it wet." I never put my face in the water either, not wanting to wash off my makeup.

"Okay," he relented, taking pity on me. Instead, he pulled me in close to him and kissed me, our bodies wet and close together, those muscles holding me tight. With only a thin layer of clothing separating us, I could feel him on my belly and I could tell that he was starting to get ideas.

More yummy.

He broke apart. "You are so fucking pretty, Lucy. I don't know what comes over me. I can't keep my hands off of you."

"You don't have to," I gasped.

He held me in the water by my waist. I wrapped my legs around him, feeling his hardness against me, reveling in it, and he groaned. "You share custody of Rob?" he asked, sucking on my neck.

Rob, Rob who? Then I chastised myself. God, what kind of mom was I? But Jake absorbed all of my attention when I was with him. "Yeah, every other weekend his dad gets him." I ran my hands through Jake's thick, wet hair. He kissed my nose and looked at me.

"Then I'm looking forward to this weekend."

Me too.

5

THAT'S PART OF THE REASON

The following evening, after dinner, dishes, and Rob's bedtime, I heard the knock and opened my front door to Jake in a dark blue business suit paired with a sober red- and blue-striped tie, holding a bottle of wine. Since it was past his newly usual seven or eight o'clock visit time, I'd dressed for bed in a white tank top, with no bra, and cute, pink pajama short shorts. I hadn't wanted to admit that I was waiting around for him, so I had gone about my night as usual.

Though I still had my makeup on. So okay, I wanted more than just research for my book. I liked the guy.

The night before, after swimming and making out in the pool, we somehow tore apart from each other and ended up back in our separate homes, in our separate beds. I didn't know what he did in his bed, but I sure know what I did in mine.

Tonight, tired, leaning against the doorjamb, his coat swinging, he gave me that thrill that he was taking the time to see me, even though he worked so much. As much as this excited me, however, I still felt the need to be cautious. I didn't know him and I was wary to invest too much in pleasing a guy. I got so epically burned pleasing Carlos. While I leaned against the doorjamb under him, he noticed my scantily dressed body, then shook his head and blinked.

"I have a lot of clients who bring me samples as gifts," he said in his low voice, "but this one I thought you would like." He handed me a bottle of Santa Barbara chardonnay.

"Thank you," I said, happily cradling the wine.

"I was thinking that you could chill it and we could drink it tomorrow night," he continued. "I should be able to get out of the office earlier tomorrow. By earlier, I mean earlier than," he looked at his watch, "nine forty-five."

"That sounds great—" I started and his fucking phone sounded.

He let out a breath, pulled his phone out of his pocket, looked at it, and muttered, "Fuck." He gave me an apologetic look. "I have to take this but I'll see you tomorrow. I'm sorry." Leaning in, he brushed his lips against mine. Then he kissed the tip of my nose and closed the door behind him. I heard him answer the phone as he crossed the way over to his unit and unlocked his door.

The sound of his door shutting made my brain click into place.

What was I doing?

I didn't want to be second place to a phone call. No way in hell would I be a convenient booty call for a guy with no time for me. Alarm bells rang in my head because I did not want my self-esteem hanging on whether a man thought I was worthwhile. I knew I was worthwhile. I'd spent the last twelve years building my own self-esteem about my body and my choices so that I knew this deep down in my soul. I wasn't going to sit around all day and wait for him to come to me when he thought it was time to see me.

That said, he was just so goddamned pretty and playful when he wasn't working, it was hard not to. I felt really, really,

really pulled to him. And he said he felt the same way. Otherwise, why was he even making the attempt to see me?

So apparently I *was* just sitting around waiting for him to come to me, under the circumstances.

I padded down the hall, turning off lights, and started washing off my makeup, thinking it had been *never* since I let a man see me without makeup. I got into my bed to read, but I put my e-reader down and thought about it.

I liked Jake. I also saw how little time he had for me.

If a man is into you, he makes time for you no matter what he does and no matter how busy he is.

But Jake seemed to be trying hard to make time for me, despite the fact that he was phenomenally busy. And I liked it.

So I didn't know how to take this. I decided to sleep on it. I turned my e-reader on, face clean, hair up, and started reading.

The following morning, no brilliant conclusion had come to me overnight. As I showered and dressed, I realized that I had to proceed with caution, not get overly attached to responses or attention from Jake, and have fun and see what happened.

That evening, Rob sat on the porch with me, drinking milk, while I sipped a sparkling water in a glass, looking at the lights on the surface of the pool.

"How you doing in school, mijo?"

"Good," he answered.

"Not good enough of an answer for your mama," I returned. "What's that mean?"

"I got a ninety-three on my spelling test, a ninety-five in math, and an eighty-nine in social studies."

I nodded. "Those are good grades. But numbers and data aren't everything. How are your friends?"

"Good," he answered.

When I looked at him, he kept going. "Cody is fine and he likes to play Minecraft too. So does Ramón."

"And your teacher?"

"She's nice."

I nodded. "What do you have coming up in school?"

"Winter pageant and then we have to get started on our science fair project."

With kids, sometimes you had to press them, otherwise you would just get yes/no answers. But when they started talking, that was where you could find the gold.

It was time for him to go to bed and I went inside and tucked him in. I decided to get out Jake's wine, and, feeling optimistic, I got out two glasses to go with it. If he didn't come by, I'd still have a drink by myself.

I sat out in the dark night, looking out and listening to the quiet noises of the complex and the occasional car driving down our street.

Jake's patio door opened and he stepped out, wearing dark blue jeans and a tight, white t-shirt, looking immediately for me, and walking right over. In that getup he looked like he should be leaning against a muscle car, with a pack of cigarettes rolled up his sleeve, his jet hair spiky and his eyes so blue they were almost black in the low patio light.

"Hey, there you are," he said pleasantly.

I hopped up from my perch and walked over to the waist high partition between our patios, where he was standing, bracing his arms on the wall. I gave him a slow kiss, our noses mashing, our tongues meeting.

"Want a drink?" I asked after I pulled back from our kiss.

"Yes, please."

I went over to the table and poured him a glass of the cold white wine, handing it to him. He dragged his patio chair over by the wall and put his feet up on the front railing, talking with me. "This is a much better way of ending a day than at the office." He took a drink of the wine. "The wine's good too." He looked out at the pool. "So how long have you been a single mom?"

"In other words, how old am I?"

He laughed. "Yeah, I guess. I'm thirty-five."

"Twenty-nine. I had Rob when I was seventeen. His dad was my boyfriend in high school for a short period of time. And then we did it and he left me." Jake's face twitched. "It's okay, he showed me who he was and I deserve better. I deserve a guy who will watch out for me, not one who will leave me."

"You're right about that."

I sipped my wine. Then, because I couldn't help myself, I asked, "Why do you work so much?"

He let out a breath. "That's a long answer. I guess part of it is ingrained in me from my dad. He worked really hard and he wanted me to do so. He pushed me in school, he pushed me in my career. I always wanted him to think that I was, you know, up to snuff. Sometimes he was a real taskmaster. I guess that's a longer story. It's complicated. I love him and I resent him at the same time. Well, that's one part at least."

"And the other part?"

Jake looked at me. "I don't know the reason," he said quietly. "I'm not balanced. I work a lot. Probably too much. I don't have time for relationships. I've always drowned myself in work." He paused. "I mean, I exercise. I do a couple other things. But other than that, I'm at the office as much as I can be. I've always picked work as my escape from, I don't know, life."

"That sucks. You need to live."

"I know. I think that's part of the reason why I'm so attracted to you. I keep thinking of reasons to come see you. I want to know every single thing about you. I want you to talk to me for hours. I want you to get me out of the office. So that's part of the reason why I can't stay away from you."

"Part of the reason?" I had to know the other reason.

"The other part is that you are so fucking sexy, I can barely stand to be near you. You're some sort of J. Lo lookalike. You are a knockout. I have to keep this wall between us otherwise I would be all over you. And you have a kid asleep in there and I can't do that."

Holy shit. It appeared that the attraction was way mutual. My next words reflected the see what happens part of my earlier decision.

"You can come over," I whispered.

Jake stared at me, then slowly set his glass down on the ground. Before I could process, he moved. Like a gymnast, he vaulted over the low wall and pulled me out of my seat by my armpits. In a quick move, he sat down, then set me into his lap so that I was straddling him and pulled me down to him, crashing his lips into mine, kissing me breathless.

I responded by exploding as well. My hands rubbed up and down his torso, then made my way to his back. I ran my fingers through his thick, dark hair, under his jaw, behind his neck. My tongue explored his mouth as much as his tongue explored mine.

And his hands went roaming, over my clothes, along the curve of my waist, down my ass, pressing me into him, feeling my breasts over my bra.

We broke apart, breathing hard, staring at each other. I leaned in to kiss him.

"We can't take it farther right now," he said against my mouth, "but I really want to."

"Me too. But you know Rob's dad has him on Saturday night."

"Yes. I'm taking you out." He kissed me again and I thought that he was being too much of a gentleman to complete the thought—that he looked forward to what came after taking me out even more.

6

LIFE DRAWING

On Saturday morning, I arrived about fifteen minutes early to the art school, greeting the professor in the otherwise empty classroom. The first session of a new life drawing class began today, and the professor had booked me as a model for the whole eight weeks. I'd arranged for babysitting for Rob during the times that the class met when I had him on the weekends, but today I was free to do whatever I wanted because he was with his dad.

The huge, airy room had an empty space located in the center of the room for the model to pose, circled by easels staggered all around. Every art student would have a different view and be drawing from a different angle. I'd been to this classroom before, so after I chatted with the professor, I headed to a small room off to the side to undress and wait until it was time for me to model. I always brought a white, waffle pattern robe to wear.

Even though I'd done this before, I felt a familiar sense of nervousness and anticipation about the public nudity that this job required. In some ways, having dozens of pairs of eyes on me was nerve-racking. But in other ways, I felt incredibly liberated when I modeled. Free. There I'd be, standing before them, naked as a baby, allowing them to look at me, to record me.

Art students trained their hands to record what their eyes saw. They focused on lines and curves, on spatial arrangements and on proportion. They didn't really see me as a person, but as an object to draw with pencil or charcoal. A beautiful object, perhaps, and one with the flaws of humanity. But still, it did not feel personal. I felt separate from them.

Normally, the class would do a series of quick sketches while I held various positions for as long as I could. Projects might be to draw the inside of me, the weight, not focusing on the outer lines. Other times, the professor would have them draw my movement, in scribbled lines.

And sometimes I'd recline or sit on a chair and stay still, often with my eyes closed, while they drew me for lengthy periods of time. The professor had requested this work today.

Again, I felt a freedom and a beauty being part of this process. I rarely saw the finished products, although occasionally the students would show me. I'd experienced every emotion in seeing myself as a nude, from gasping at how accurately they captured me, to cringing at the focus on a flaw, to trying not to laugh at particularly amateur art. But still, it was lovely to see people engage in creativity.

It was important to me to create something or assist in the creation of something that did not exist before it came out of me, whether it was a phrase on a page, or here, as the subject of a drawing or a later painting. If I really thought about it, all of nature is creating all of the time—children are growing inside women's wombs, plants are dividing cells and creating new growth, and mountains are being built up, as in the lava in Hawaii, or eroded down. All around us are creations. Allowing the artistic process, without judgment, without critique, to me, was essential to the experience of being human.

While I waited in the anteroom, wearing my white robe, I heard the class file in and get settled. After a few minutes of instruction by the professor, she came over and opened the door.

Walking to the center of the room, my eyes down, I stood in front of the students, and took off my robe, draping it on the chair that was now in the center. Then I sat down sideways in the chair, twisting elegantly in the seat so that my front pressed up against the back of the chair, my knees were together, my legs bent, my toes pointed and together. I rested my arms on the back of the chair and set my head in my hands. And then I held this position, letting them draw the curves of my spine, the hourglass of my waist, the flesh of my ass.

After a long time, the professor asked me to get into a different position, and I adjusted my body, spinning the other way in the seat, staggering my legs as they curled off to the opposite side, resting my face in the crook of my elbow. I tried to concentrate on breathing, on elongating my spine, on staying still.

The thoughts that ran through my head during these sessions were so random. Not sexy, at all. More like oh, I need to get milk from the grocery store. But occasionally I got into the restful space where I could think about my books, and I found myself thinking about my new novel.

I'd completed more writing and I was happier than I'd been a week ago, but the story still wasn't gelling. It was funny, the more that I wrote, the more that my hero was veering away from my standard issue Alpha male billionaire playboy and more into well, Jake.

While Jake looked like a classic romance hero, he didn't act like one. At least, not that I could see. He was too off-kilter with work, a little clumsy, and a lot of a talker. But I liked how he kept after me.

He was real, he wasn't some guy with a tragic past who needed to be taught a lesson. At least I hoped not.

Still, my imagination ran away from me at times, and I found my new hero looking more and more like Jake, sounding like him, and talking like him.

My thoughts carried me through the end of the class, when I was excused to go to the small adjoining room and get dressed. I took my time getting dressed, not really wanting to interact with any of the students, and when I got out of the room, only the teacher was in the classroom. She told me about the next week's class assignment, I shook her hand, and left.

I walked down the hall of the school and outside, heading for my car, when I heard a "Lucy" called out to me.

Jake loitered on the steps, wearing jeans and a button down shirt.

With a huge pad of paper under his arm and a pencil box in his hand.

My eyes widened.

No.

My stomach plummeted.

No.

Was he?

No.

"Jake?"

He had a strange look on his face. "Why didn't you tell me what you did for a living?"

"You never ask— Wait a minute. What? I'm a novelist. This is just for some extra spending money. You never told me you were taking an art class." I felt heated, pissed, and confused. And very turned on. All these *things* coursing through my blood.

"I don't talk about it. It doesn't mix well with my business."

We stared at each other.

"You mean to tell me that you just stared at my naked body for an hour and a half?"

"It was an hour and twenty-two minutes."

I didn't know what to think of all of this.

"The longest hour and twenty-two minutes of my life," he continued, "because *goddamn* Lucy, you're smoking hot. I couldn't handle being in there and I couldn't leave. I couldn't touch you, I couldn't acknowledge you, and I knew that you couldn't see me because your back was to me the whole time and besides, your face was buried in your arms." He paused. "Are you going to be the model for this class the whole time?"

"Yeah."

"Holy fuck."

"What do you mean?" I asked, starting to get a little insulted. "Is that a bad thing?"

"You know that's not it at all," he said, and his eyes sizzled. "I don't know how I can keep from dragging you out of there. I barely managed it today."

I had absolutely no idea that he was in the class. And now that I knew, the whole event had an erotic overlay that wasn't there while I was in the moment. We had just compressed an hour plus of foreplay into a minute of talking outside. Now I thought about his denim eyes—artist's eyes, why didn't I know that before?—studying my curves and restrained from touching me. Damn, that was hot.

"Are you going to show me what you drew?"

He looked up at the sky and then back to me, very intense. "Yeah. Not now. But I will." It seemed like it was hard for him to agree to this.

We stared at each other some more, neither one of us wanting to move, both of us wanting to go.

"Let's go back and get ready."

He nodded quickly. "Yeah. Do you want to go early and get a

drink and watch the sunset? This time of year, we should go before five if we want to catch it."

"That sounds great."

His arms tightened around his notepad and his fingers gripped his pencil box. He leaned over and kissed the hell out of me, but with our arms restrained, his holding his art supplies, mine holding my purse and robe.

And then we headed to our separate cars to go back to the same place.

7

A UNIVERSAL TRUTH

Question: What happens when you ruminate about a date the whole week?

Answer: When you go to get dressed for it, you get really fucking nervous and completely over-think it.

I tore apart my bedroom, trying on everything I owned that was suitable for a night out. And trust me, I owned plenty of night-out clothes—miniskirts, little black dresses, wrap dresses, fifties-looking dresses, slinky dresses, dresses with illegal v-necks cut down in the front, dresses cut so low in the back that you can almost see the top of my ass, high necked, long-sleeve dresses that hugged every curve, sequined dresses, babydoll dresses, and one pair of black pants that actually fit.

So, I had nothing to wear.

I did, however, have fabulous shoes. They were shoes that Oprah would wear for five minutes only, but I was used to wearing high heels. No problem. They had one teeny strap over the toes and one around the ankles, and were otherwise held on by luck.

Desperate, I called Sara, hoping that her Macy's experience

would help. "I've got a date with my neighbor, who is straight out of a book that I'd write, and I don't know what to wear," I panted out in a rush, pacing in my messy bedroom, wearing black lace panties and a matching bra.

"Slow down," she ordered. "This is tamale guy?"

"Yeah."

"And he apologized?"

"Yeah."

"He's worth your time?"

I paused. "I think so. He works crazy hours. I don't know what he does, some sort of advertising or something. He's always bringing samples from clients. But the thing is, he goes out of his way to come see me every day, even when it's late."

"That's your answer," she said. "A universal truth is if a guy is interested, he'll show you he's interested."

"I think he's interested. He told me as much."

"But mama, you're such a romantic. You haven't dated in so long."

"That's because I swore off real men. Book boyfriends are better."

"You see? That's why you can't forget that he's a real flesh and blood guy. He's no Franggy. I know you know this. But because he looks good doesn't mean anything unless he treats you good. And he might have some issues."

"We all have issues."

"True." She paused. "I love you, mama. Take good care of yourself."

"I do."

"I know. Okay, so then have fun and let me know how it went."

She went to hang up and I cried into the phone, "Wait, what do I wear?"

Chuckling, she asked, "Where are you going?"

"I don't know. He said somewhere nice."

"Go with classic and elegant. Sparkly top and pencil skirt."

"Shit, you're right. You're the best. Love ya."

I hung up, pulled on a sequined tank top that was between blush pink and bronze colored, a black pencil skirt, and my little strappy black heels. With my hair down around my shoulders and my lip gloss on, I grabbed my clutch purse. Then, leaving my room a torn-up mess, I closed my front door, locked it, and headed over to Jake's.

He answered the door, wearing a charcoal gray, long-sleeve, button-down shirt with the sleeves rolled up, revealing his gorgeous forearms, and black slacks. He smelled like he just got out of the shower, his hair damp. He held a coat over his shoulder and stepped out, locking his door.

"Ready?" I asked.

"No." He stood, looking at me, keys dangling in his hand.

I put my hand on my waist. "No?"

"I don't want to go out anymore."

"But why not?" I asked, feeling indignant, having put all this work into what I was wearing.

"Because you look so hot . . . I . . . shit . . . I don't want to . . . well . . . We'd better go or we won't leave," he stuttered out.

Oh.

That made me feel better immediately.

He grabbed my hand and led me to his car, a new black BMW, holding the door for me as I sat my booty in the leather seat and slid my legs around, the only way to get in a car in a pencil skirt. Opening his door, he got in, started his car, and took off.

"What kind of music do you like?" he asked.

"Dance, R&B, hip hop."

He turned on the radio and it was set to my favorite station. "Guess we have the same taste."

"Where are we headed?"

"The Four Seasons Biltmore. We can have drinks in the lounge and dinner by the ocean." The Four Seasons sat on the beach in one of the most exclusive parts of Santa Barbara, almost in Montecito, near where Oprah lived. You could cross the road and be at the beach. Those Jake-thrills coursed through me again. This was going to be a special night.

"You know, I would go anywhere, but I'm so glad you picked the Biltmore. I've only been there once and I've always wanted to go back."

After a short drive, we pulled up to the valet parking and the attendant helped me out. Jake handed over his keys, then came over to me and gave me his arm.

Like everything in Santa Barbara, the hotel was Spanish style, with a red tile roof, white stucco walls, and black iron accents. The hotel had obviously been redone and we walked into the chic bar and sat down at a little table that overlooked the ocean. Because it was getting near the shortest days of the year, the sun started to set earlier and earlier. Jake ordered a beer and I ordered a margarita on the rocks, which a friendly waiter served with a flourish.

"Tell me about your son," said Jake.

"He's shy and quiet, but smart. He likes to read, like me. He's nuts about Minecraft."

"What's that?"

"A videogame."

Jake took a drink of his beer and I watched his Adam's apple move. God, glorious. "I've never heard of it. Never played much videogames as a kid."

"So what do you do for fun?" I asked, sipping my margarita.

He laughed but it was the kind of laugh that had no humor. "I don't."

"What do you mean you don't?"

"For the past eleven years, I've worked seventy to eighty hour weeks every week, sometimes more. I go to work. I come home and crash. That's it."

"That's no way to live." God, what a workaholic.

He got a funny look on his face and paused. Then he looked around at our opulent surroundings and lowered his voice. "When I was young, my family didn't have money. Like any money. I mean, I grew up using ketchup instead of spaghetti sauce on pasta." I cringed. "My mom divorced my dad when I was a teenager, saying that she deserved better than my dad, who worked all the time, and she left me . . . Sorry, this is kind of heavy. I guess where I'm going with this is that when I was young, all I did was draw. I wanted to be an artist. But once I was a teenager, my dad, knowing how hard it is to make a living, pushed me into doing something more. And I guess that's it. I work all the time now."

"Your dad didn't support you being an artist?"

"No." He didn't elaborate.

Well, if he didn't have any family support, no wonder he was in advertising. That could be artistic—another outlet for creativity.

"But you like drawing."

"I can't not do it," he said earnestly. "So I take classes when I can. Photography. Painting. Drawing."

"What did you think of the life drawing class?"

He looked at me with a sexy stare that did things to my whole body. "It had a great model." He continued, even quieter, "Actually, I was wondering what it felt like to be up there, naked, with everyone looking at you. Drawing you."

"It feels disembodied. I know all these art students are objectifying me, making my body into lines on a page."

"I didn't objectify you," he said, intently. "I knew it was you, Lucy, my beautiful neighbor, the whole time." My margarita glass got really interesting to me all of a sudden and my cheeks grew hot. Yeah. We liked each other. But could anything happen?

I had to ask. "So with all this work, do you actually have time to see anyone?"

He barked out another mirthless laugh and shook his head. "No." Great. Stomach in my shoes. Not the right answer. But he continued, "That's not the thing to tell you on a date, but it's the truth." He took my hand across the table. God, I loved his hands. Artist hands. Strong and warm and intelligent hands. "Listen. I'm always at the office. I know it's unhealthy. But I want to see you. I want to get to know you. Will you give me a chance?"

Was there any question? Of course.

I nodded. Yes, I could give him a chance. He was trying. He was so sweet and I just felt compelled to be with him. When I wasn't around him, I was wondering what he was doing. I don't know if that was healthy or unhealthy, but it was how I felt.

I also knew that I wanted to be in bed with him by the end of the night.

And I knew that it would be the first time I'd been with a man since Carlos.

This romance writer had a way more active imagination than active sex life. For a really, really, really long time. Yes, I'd been on dates. Yes, I'd messed around. Yes, I'd done things. But I hadn't been all the way with a guy since Carlos.

Pathetic.

It just hadn't worked out. Either the guy was wrong or I was wrong and I wanted Mr. Right.

Explanation? Romance writer.

I didn't know if Jake was Mr. Right. He seemed kind of *not*. But there was something about him, something complicated to him, that made me trust him.

He'd opened up to me. Given his fancy import car, I couldn't believe he'd ever been poor. But we all have pasts and we all have things we aren't proud of.

I did pay attention to how he treated me, however. While he was clearly a workaholic, he was clearly into me and I felt a connection with him that I'd never felt with another person. Everything felt right when he was around.

The way he talked, I think it was the same way for him. Otherwise, why would he even bother stopping by my house when he got home from work so late? Even though his body wanted to do nothing more than crash, he still made sure to stop by and check in on me. I loved that.

As we drank our drinks, we watched the sun go down into the horizon over the ocean. The sunset turned the sky a brilliant shade of pink, fading to purple, fading to gray, the water gray-blue and dark. When we finished, we went to a heated outdoor patio and had dinner at their Italian restaurant.

"So I have to ask this," he said.

"Anything."

"Were you ever married?"

"No. My ex-boyfriend Carlos dumped me after he got me pregnant. Actually before we found out."

Jake looked pissed. "Fucker. That's no way to treat you."

I shook my head. "You? Have you ever been married?"

He looked amused. "No. Again, not a good first date topic, but I've never dated anyone long enough for that."

"Big guy like you probably has no problems getting a date."

He looked sheepish. "The problem has been me, not them. My work life is untenable. It runs over my whole life." He sighed. "Always so much to do in the office."

"So tell me what you like to paint."

Raising an eyebrow, he said, "You, for starters."

"Aww, that's sweet," I said, touched. "What else?"

"Anything, really. There's no shortage of inspiration if you really pay attention. I like photography, too. There's an amazing exhibit right now at the Getty, I saw it online. I'd love to go . . ."

As I listened to him talk, I realized how much I loved hearing his ideas. What a loss it would be if this creative man couldn't draw, and I was so glad that even though he was a workaholic he took the classes to tend his passion. Animated, lovely, he wasn't so slick. There was something almost sad and wistful underneath. Someone who had been missing out on life. Someone who needed care and attention.

And I kept watching him. Watching his athletic frame move in his chair and the graceful way he held his silverware. Then in return, feeling his eyes on me, studying me. Enjoying him asking me questions—about Rob, about the people in our complex, about my childhood—and listening to the answers. I studied the way his neck moved, the way his eyes crinkled when he laughed. The little glimpses of his chest that I got from the unbuttoned neck of his shirt.

Oh, yes, desire had been stirring in me for a long time. And now I had it bad.

He'd been hands-off of me, other than giving me his arm.

But now, as we finished the last bite of tiramisu, he reached over and touched my hand and I loved it and he looked at me in a way I could feel between my legs.

"Let's go back."

Yes.

8

I DREW THIS CURVE TODAY

We didn't even make it out to the Biltmore parking lot before we were joined at the lip.

Holding hands, we'd walked through the chic lobby of the hotel to the patio entranceway, lit with fairy lights wrapped around the palm tree trunks, making it look magical. We'd been serenaded by the crash of the ocean right beside us in the dark and the clink and murmur of dinner guests in the restaurant patio.

Leaving me by a lush, bright purple bougainvillea vibrant in the low light, Jake had strolled to the valet booth, handed the ticket to the attendant, and now came back to me, eyes on mine, intent. He bent down and kissed me hard. His scorching mouth, chocolatey from the tiramisu, invaded mine, our noses smushing together. I kissed him back with fervor, loving the crush into his body, loving the way his arms wrapped around me and held me to his firm body, loving the way he smelled and the way he tasted.

He didn't kiss like a distracted, workaholic businessman. He kissed like he'd never heard of a cell phone. Like this was his way of creating art and he didn't care who saw. It felt like there was nothing around us, nothing in existence except him pressing his body to me, his lips and tongue to mine. I was completely in his world and he was in mine and it was a heart-stoppingly romantic place to be. All of creation existed in that moment. At least until he bit my lower lip gently, and he pulled back and looked at me, heat in his eyes.

The young, pimpled valet standing next to us cleared his throat.

I stifled a giggle. Who knew how long he was standing there watching us make out? Jake looked at me conspiratorially, kissed my nose, then took my hand and walked me over to his car. He opened my door and I slid in.

When he took off back home, he drove faster than he did on the way to the hotel. In no time at all, I was out of the car. I fumbled with my keys. Then my door was open and Jake followed me inside my home. I turned and closed my door. He boxed me into the back of the door, arms on both sides of me. His mouth came down on mine again, and this time it was even more frenzied because we didn't have any chance of an audience.

Teeth knocked, tongues touched, he even growled against my throat. I moaned when he started nibbling his way down my neck, sucking and caressing.

I pressed his jacket off of his shoulders, struggling with it, and finally getting it off. Then I started unbuttoning his shirt, crazed to touch him, wanting to feel his athletic body. As he leaned over to kiss me, he helped, and his shirt came off and fell to the floor. Shoes kicked off. I kissed his broad, muscular chest, licking his nipples, sucking my way up to his neck.

"I want you right now," I said against his soft skin, and he groaned and then picked me up, carrying me down the hall while I squealed and kicked in his arms. I was finally going to get some. From the guy of my dreams. God, I loved it.

"Where's your room?"

I laughed. I was loving this being carried thing, which surprised me since normally when you made me feel small I got fierce. But with Jake, I delighted in his arms, feeling protected, dominated, cared for. And thrilled. This beautiful man would be mine.

"No, this one, there." I pointed at my door when he almost went into Rob's room.

Then he stepped inside and looked around.

My room looked like the day after Christmas at Macy's.

His eyes widened as he took in my room.

"I kind of didn't know what to wear." I winced in embarrassment.

Shaking his head, he chuckled. "Lucy. You are wonderful."

He set me down. With a swoosh of my arms, I swept all of the clothes strewn across my bed onto the floor and pulled Jake on top of me. But as he headed down, he slipped on a silky dress on the floor and grabbed me, twisting. We both fell to the floor, me on top of him, laughing.

"Get this off of you," he said, tugging at my skirt hem, feeling my booty, "I can't wait to touch you. After that class today? Fuck me."

"That's what I want to do." I giggled. God, yes please. Finally. A man not thrown off by my son.

"Up," he commanded. "Take it off."

I got up and pulled off my sequined top, exposing my lacy black bra.

I may have chosen my underwear specifically with the knowledge that it would be viewed. Lying on the floor, shirtless, shoeless, propped up on his elbows, his eyes were on me, focused.

So I took my time, enjoying the tease. I reached behind me, unzipped my pencil skirt, and wiggled it off of my hips, leaving my strappy five minute only shoes on.

He seemed to like the way I looked in lingerie and stilettos, judging by the way he didn't look anywhere else. With athletic grace, he stood up, pants tented, which distracted me. I leaned down as he got up and we knocked foreheads.

"Sorry," we both said at the same time. He gently kissed my forehead, and then I kissed his.

He started walking me backwards to my bed, kissing my neck, insistently, running his fingers down my side. The back of my knees hit the bed, and I fell back. He fell on me, his hot, athletic body feeling so, so good on mine, settling between my legs.

He traced his fingers down my arms. "I drew this curve today." He moved to my fingers. "And this one." Back up the underside of my arms. "And this one." Then his fingers traced down my side. "I drew this curve." And over my hip. "And this one is especially beautiful."

Even though I was comfortable with my body, I felt shy with the attention that he gave me. No one had ever touched me this way. He affectionately caressed the curves of my upper thighs, my hip bones, and my belly button. I grabbed his ass, pressing his erection into me, feeling the hard muscle against me, making me wet.

I reached down to unzip his pants and he stood up, slipping again on the pile of clothes on the floor. He unbuttoned and unzipped, exposing classic chambray boxer shorts that made him look like a hot model in a catalogue.

"I have a confession," he said, standing, staring at me, his hard cock at attention, barely constrained by his boxers.

"What?"

"It's been a long while for me. I don't think I'll last."

My heart melted. "The workaholic hasn't gotten some in a while?"

He raised an eyebrow. "That's closer to the truth than I care to admit."

Since he was brave, so was I. "Me neither."

Now he looked surprised. "The romance novelist hasn't gotten some in a while?" I shook my head.

"A really long while," I whispered.

Then he said, "So. Your turn first."

And then my heart stopped.

I'd previously written lines about a heroine almost coming from words alone and it was bullshit, right? But I almost came from his words alone.

He leaned over and unbuckled one of my shoes and then the other. Gently, sensuously, he traced his fingers up my legs, which was not a far journey, and hooked his index fingers into my lacy panties, tugging them off, exposing my neatly waxed landing strip. And his eyes got even bigger, which was adorable. I reached behind me and unhooked my bra and he pulled the straps off of my shoulders.

So, I reflected, he was the hottest guy that I had ever had in my bed. And, almost the only guy I'd ever had in my bed. He was definitely the hottest guy that I'd ever seen in real life. And here he was, nestling between my legs now, his neck bent, head down, sucking my neck, kissing my collarbone, playing with my nipples, running his tongue over first one then the other.

He looked up at me, a glint in his blue eyes, and he trailed his nose down the middle of my torso. "I want to draw you, again, Lucy, I want to paint you, but this time, with my tongue." And he dipped his tongue in my belly button and then ran it down to my pussy, where he took a lick and I moaned.

Jake flattened his tongue and ran it along the whole area,

and I could feel myself swelling, reacting to his touch. It felt so fucking good to have him down there, hot, giving. "You gotta tell me where, honey, where do you like it?" His tongue darted and licked, sucked and explored. "Here? Here? I can't read your mind, tell me. Tell me what you really think."

I writhed on the bed, thinking that it all felt pretty damn wonderful, and he held me firmly by my hips. "How about here?" He took one hand off of my hip and put two fingers into me, licking my clit at the same time. Rubbing and stroking, everything wet, looking down at his shoulders between my knees, I came quickly, quicker than I'd ever made myself come before, and I came hard, my body clenching and shuddering, satisfying the hunger.

"You ready?" he asked after I came down and back to life, and the next thing I knew, his boxers were off and he was holding a condom.

I nodded, unable to think properly, but whispering, "I can't wait anymore, come here, guapo."

After a moment to adjust, condom on, he climbed up and nestled between my legs. Jake hovered over me, broad shoulders over my shoulders, his large, pretty cock between my legs. He scooted back and slid into me, and my body received him gratefully. Time expanded. We looked at each other, him hovering over me, connected at the root, me relaxed from an orgasm and wildly turned on for the prospect of another.

I wrapped my legs around his hips, although they barely made it around, and he began to move, very slowly and carefully. He would pull out almost the entire way, then ease in. A blessing.

He was being gentle.

He was taking his time.

He was making love to me.

Over and over again, he thrust into me, slowly, but with a rhythm that was all him. Focused, devoted to me, his eyes on mine. And then I could see his eyes twitch and I could feel his cock swell. He was going to come, I just knew it. I could tell that he was holding it back, trying not to.

I was so close to another orgasm, but maybe not.

"It's okay, *nene*, come," I whispered, and with a gorgeous shuddering over me, he released and collapsed on me, breathing hard.

I'll admit that I felt disappointed and slightly greedy. The first orgasm was so good. I wanted to come again.

After a moment, he asked, "Did I leave you hanging?"

I nodded.

"I was afraid of that. Sorry. Here, I'll finish you off. Let's try this." And he pulled out of me, then gently grasped my hips and flipped me over. "Hang on a second."

He stood up, got a Kleenex, discarded the condom, and came back. Then he traced his finger down my spine. "This curve, Lucy. This curve." He ran his finger down my ass to my pussy, and pulled my hips back so that my ass was in the air and I was on all fours. With his artist's hands that I'd admired from the start, he massaged my ass, made his way down, and went between my legs. Like I'd wanted him to do when we first met.

"Head down, honey. Ass up." So, face down, on my knees, with my head in my pillow, he proceeded to finger fuck me to another orgasm.

And this one was glorious. It built and built, and I tensed—all of the muscles in my pelvic floor and my hips and my ass and my shoulders and my arms all clenched, Jake chasing my orgasm with his fingers, rolling and making me shake until I came, hard, and collapsed my hips to the bed.

Okay, that was much better.

After a moment, he slapped my ass, just a little sting, then flopped down next to me and I curled up next to him, thinking that it was wonderful to be with a guy who talked and who communicated. He wasn't my perfect romance hero. He didn't do everything exactly right.

But it was really, really fantastic anyway.

9

SOMETHING FROM NOTHING

"What made you start writing novels?"

Later that night, Jake, chambray boxer-clad, no shirt, enveloped me in his arms. I couldn't get enough of him, enough of feeling his skin, enough of smelling his clean, spicy scent, of feeling his stubble against my cheek, my shoulder, my back. I'd slipped on a cami and pajama pants, and spooned against his big body, my face clean and makeup-free.

A little scared of letting him see me without makeup, I nonetheless allowed him to follow me into the bathroom and watch me take it off. This felt very intimate, letting him see me as I washed my face. He leaned against the counter, and chatted with me. After I toweled off, he lifted my chin with a finger. "I didn't think you could be more beautiful, but here it is. The evidence." And he leaned in and kissed my bare lips, running his finger along my cheek. "I love the way you look, Lucy, but without makeup? You are stunning. You are truly a natural beauty."

Praise was difficult to take, because like many of us, I was conditioned by society to be modest, to deflect, to not celebrate myself. I'd fought those thoughts before—to accept my curvy body, my short stature, my skin color, my hair. But I'd always had to *try*, too. I mean that's why I was so high maintenance, with makeup, hair, and clothes just right. To some degree I'd beaten the bad thoughts that said that because I didn't look like the girls in the magazines I didn't have value. I did have value. But still, I'd had a layer of defense—dressing up to show off so you couldn't see what was under. Now I was letting him in, and I tried to allow in the compliment, to let myself accept that he thought I looked good, even without makeup, fancy clothes, or hair done just right. It made me glow from the inside.

Without talking about it, we'd decided that he was spending the night. There was no reason for him to go back next door. I'd ache for him. Now that I knew what he was like in bed, how generous and how honest, I didn't want to get more than a few inches away from him at any given time. I wanted to touch him constantly.

But for now, curled up with him in my bed, warm and comfortable, I answered his question.

"I don't remember when it started because I always wanted to be a writer. Stories touched me when I was a kid. It's funny. By reading, I felt listened to. I realize that doesn't sound quite right, but I mean it. I felt like by reading and understanding the people in the story and the author, I was understood, especially when they reflected something that I was thinking. There was someone who *got me*, who thought things that I thought, and who wasn't scared to put them down for other people to read. So it was like the author heard me and put *my* thoughts down for me. Or gave me new thoughts to think about.

"I love losing myself in books. I love connecting with the characters or the situations in the stories. And I love telling the stories, coming up with a different, but honest, way of saying something that I think or feel and hoping that it resonates with a reader.

"And I think the creative process is amazing. Something from nothing. Without me, my fifteen novels would not exist. And there is something to be said about allowing the creation to come into existence. Kind of like having a kid."

I didn't know if I should talk about kids with Jake or not. I'd no idea what he thought about them. I was scared to ask him if he wanted any. Two reasons. I didn't want him to reject my son, for one. But also, deep down, I wanted more. I loved being a mom. I did it the tough way the first time around, but I'd be willing to do it again. For love this time.

A lawyer once told me that you should never ask a question that you don't want to know the answer to. I didn't want to know the answer to that one, not yet, not while things were so new, so I stayed quiet.

"What do you write about?" He nudged his nose in the space between my ear and my shoulder blade and kissed my back.

"Romance." He pulled his face away and turned me to look at him.

"Real life isn't romantic."

I flopped over all the way, fully facing him, and looked at him, perplexed, upset, and concerned. "How can you say that? We just had the most romantic date. There's plenty of romance in our lives."

He smiled his sad smile and kissed my nose. "I have to go back to work tomorrow."

"Tomorrow's Sunday."

"I know. Taking today off means tomorrow is gonna be painful. And it means I have to work and won't see you."

God, why? He didn't seem to hurt for money. "Why do you do that?" I asked, burrowing under his chin.

"What are your parents like?" he asked against the top of my head, not answering my question, running his finger up and down my arm.

Why didn't he want to talk about it?

Still, I answered. "They're great. My mom's a clerk at Ralph's grocery. My dad's a mechanic. I have a sister, Celia who lives in Los Angeles and a brother, Gabriel, who lives in Dallas. What about you? Your parents? Any siblings?"

Jake stiffened and stopped the travel of his finger. Then he let out a breath. "My little brother Ethan died when I was fifteen."

"Oh no," I breathed.

"He was in a car accident. He was twelve." Rob's age. "My mom left my dad because of it. After that, I never saw my dad because he worked all the time. So I became a latchkey kid. My teenage years sucked. I went to school and got out of the house as fast as I could. And I learned to work. I learned to spend all of my time doing what it was I went to school to do. Because it can all be taken away and you have to work hard to keep it."

What? No. Was I lucky because my work was my passion and it came easily? I put my hand on my hip. "That's not true. The things that you are supposed to do come easy."

"That's not been my experience. I have never been allowed to do the easy things. I've had to do the hard things."

Oh, Jake. "Who took care of you after your brother died? After your mom abandoned you?"

"Don't say abandoned." He didn't seemed pissed, but he was defensive.

"Well, she did, didn't she? And your dad escaped by working his ass off?"

Jake didn't answer. Finally, after a pause, he said, "We do what we have to do to get by."

I didn't know what he meant by that, but I couldn't imagine

not having the support of my family and friends. They were my community. "What did you do when you were in high school? *Who was there for you?*"

"No one."

I wanted to keep asking, to keep pushing him on this. But something made me pull back. I believed that I got more out of him than he gave anyone else and I wanted to tread cautiously. Here was this dreamboat guy who was so artistic and romantic. And he seemed so unhappy with what he was doing every day. He went about it automatically, like he was forced to do it. Like he didn't know that he had a choice in life. That he could do whatever he wanted.

And why hadn't someone hooked up with him yet? He seemed so giving. He took time for me. What were his other relationships like? But I didn't want to ask him about them right now, so instead, I just asked, "You sleepy?"

"Yeah." He pulled me close. "Goodnight." And he kissed me, warmly, and it got carried away. I kissed him back, he ran his hand down my side, and then he rolled so that he was nestled between my legs again.

"Are we going to—" I started, breathless again.

"In the morning," he muttered against my neck. Then he rolled off of me, tucked me into him, and I drifted off to sleep.

I awoke the next morning, in Jake's arms, him sleeping peacefully behind me. Wiggling around, I took advantage of this unprecedented chance to study him up close like an artist would.

His dark, ebony hair was the sexiest bed head I'd ever seen. He had tiny wrinkles around his eyes that made him look distinguished. His full lips were a little pouty, the softness counteracting the angles of his cheekbones and his jaw, which was now covered in stubble.

God, even his neck was erotic, angled so that I could kiss it, with his Adam's apple going up and down as he breathed. I started tracing his shirtless torso very lightly with my finger, feeling his light hair, his soft skin.

My fingers started exploring, and I couldn't help myself. I found my fingers tracing the edge of his boxer shorts, tentatively, playing with the elastic, teasing him, even though he wasn't awake.

Then I decided to really explore and my hand went lower, feeling for his cock, starting to rub it under the thin cotton material, taking advantage of his morning wood. This play was arousing me. I wanted him awake.

I rubbed his cock, at first gently, very gently, then a little bit more firmly, and he groaned, opened his eyes, and looked at me.

A happy look grew across his face. "I thought I was dreaming, but it's better than a dream." And faster than I would have thought he could move for having just woken up, he tugged at the hem of my cami and whoosh, it was off. And then he pulled off my pajama pants. And before I knew it, his hand, flat and broad, rubbed my pussy, spreading the wetness, gently, but rapidly. I could come from that alone, my feet burning up, my hands warm, and my ears pounding. He kept going and going, until I came, hard.

Looking at me with a naughty look on his face, he took one of his fingers and stuck it in his mouth, sucking on it. "You taste mighty fine for breakfast."

I giggled, then I reached over to him, tugging at his boxers. He raised his hips to help me take them off and his cock sprang free.

Last night, I'd just felt it but I hadn't really made its acquaintance yet. Now, on my knees, straddling him naked, I started to shimmy down his body, kissing my way between his nipples, down his belly, down, down, down, until I was looking at his cock.

It was really pretty.

I mean, I'm a romance writer and there are all sorts of euphemisms for the penis. Shaft or member or whatever. But Jake's? It was a fantasy. The head was large, yes, but also smooth and not too purple. He was thick, but not too thick. Long, but not too long. Some veins popped out, but not too many. He was groomed and his balls were proportionate. All in all, it looked like the kind of cock that you wanted to lick or you wanted to be fucked by.

I picked licking.

Looking down as I straddled him (short girl taking note of the view from above), I bent and stuck my tongue out, then ran it, wet, the entire way up the underside of his cock, from the base to the tip, and he gasped. Then I moved and brought as much of his cock as I could in my mouth, getting him all wet. I could almost make it to the base if I relaxed my throat, which caused him to utter a guttural, "Christ, woman." Then I repeated the move, licking him all the way up, then taking him all in, enjoying him moaning, enjoying him enjoy it, enjoying him writhe under me and try to stay still.

"I don't want to come in your mouth," he groaned, "I want to come in you."

"That can be arranged." I hopped off of him.

I got a condom out of the bedside table (I'd bought some this week just for us) and ripped it open, putting it on him, rolling it slowly down, then flopped on my back on the bed.

He held me by my waist and scooted down. "I just want to make sure you're wet," he said, and he licked me. Now it was my turn to moan. "You are."

Then he pulled me up by my waist as he rolled onto his back. "Ride me, make yourself come."

I immediately climbed on to him, straddling his hips, and lowering myself on his big cock. I loved how I could control everything from this position—how fast, how deep, how much I bounced around. I explored. Then I decided to give him a show.

My perky breasts going up and down as I moved my body, I raised and lowered myself on his cock, enjoying the fullness, enjoying the pleasure, enjoying the thrilled look on his face. He reached out and fondled my breasts in his big hands roughly, but it felt so good. My hair fell in my face, my breathing increased, and his cock hit me in the right spot for the tightening to happen.

And then it did, and I came on top, all over Jake as he started moving his hips up into me, in rhythm with me as I crested over the waves of my orgasm.

Then it was his turn and I leaned down, eager to make him feel as good as I just did. I started running my body up and down the length of his. "Holy fuck, Lucy, that feels good."

I kept at it, up and down, up and down, until he grabbed my hips and held me still as he thrust his hips up into me, his neck thrown back, his mouth open, as he came.

He looked like a Roman statue come to life when he did it.

After a moment, I collapsed onto his broad chest and he wrapped his arms around me, still connected at the root.

"Good morning," I said, and he laughed.

After our breathing regulated, we got up, took a shower together, at which time he gave me two more orgasms, and ate breakfast. Then he excused himself to go to work.

"Do you want to come over for dinner tonight?" I asked as he stood in the open door, in between kisses. I wanted to feed him, to take care of him.

"I do, but I don't know what time I'll be back."

"Okay, so I won't make the chile relleno casserole yet," I sassed.

"Probably best. But I like being asked." And he kissed me one last time and closed the door behind him.

The romance writer in me loved my romantic weekend with my imperfect hero and wondered if it would stay that way.

10

THE BEST INTEREST OF THE CHILD

"I have an appointment with Amelia Crowley," I said to the receptionist, who sat at a desk at the front of the law firm. She looked like Pink, with short blonde hair. Tough, like she could bend me in half and break me. Muscular, like she spent all of her time at the gym. Her name plate said Neveah.

"I'll tell Ms. Crowley you are here," she said politely. "Have a seat. Would you like some coffee?"

"No, thank you." I perched in a chair in the lobby. God, nerves. I dreaded being here. It wasn't that it was a bad place. The law firm was nice, very Santa Barbara-ey, with the stucco walls and the red tile roof. But like going to the dentist or the doctor, it was better just to not have to go to a lawyer's office at all.

The receptionist paged Amelia, and as I sat, a tall, handsome man in a dark blue suit strode through the lobby. My jaw flopped open as I recognized him.

"Jake?" I called, astonished.

"Lucy?" The look on his face said, *what the ever loving fuck?*

But then he went to seriously pissed in an instant. "What are you doing here? You're not supposed to be here."

The fuck? "I have an appointment with my lawyer. What are you doing here?"

"I *am* a lawyer. I work here."

What? I was so confused. "I thought you were in advertising."

"No." His eyebrows knitted together. "Why would you think that?"

"All of the product samples."

"Clients bring me gifts all the time." He looked at me, perplexed, a finger raised, head cocked, and I stared back at him.

So he was a lawyer? *Why*? That wasn't artistic. I thought that he used his art skills for designing ads. But a lawyer? That didn't make sense, given his artistic personality.

I felt the need to justify myself. "It's rude to ask someone what they do for a living."

"Are you serious?" he asked, incredulous.

I nodded.

"I asked you—" he started, then shaking his head like he couldn't believe me, he grabbed my hand and pulled me out of the seat. "We're using a conference room," he said brusquely to Neveah. Well. No manners. He whisked me into a nearby room and shut the door. I leaned up against the table, not understanding why he was acting this way and needing space I'd not wanted over the weekend. He stood by the door.

"What are you doing here, Lucy? Why do you need to see a lawyer?"

"My ex is trying to take away Roberto. He filed papers to modify child custody and child support."

He looked angry. "Fuck. Who are you seeing?"

"Amelia."

He nodded, satisfied, but I could almost see his brain

working as he kept talking. "She's excellent. But listen. There are ethical rules about attorneys seeing clients. Fuck. If I don't work on your case . . . Fuck." He seemed to be talking to himself. "It shouldn't matter. But that will matter. No. I can't. We can't. Christ. Listen. You can't tell anyone anything about me or us. You can't . . . I don't share. I don't . . . My private life is my business." His voice got harsher. "No you and me, no art class, no weekend, no nothing, you hear me?"

What was up with him? After we had such a perfect weekend, why was he being such an ass?

All of the emotions that Carlos normally brought up in me now transferred to Jake. Abandonment, loss, aloneness, not being wanted. Another man ditching me after he'd fucked me. I thought I'd healed that scar.

But no. My wound was gaping open and bleeding out. I'd been rejected again.

No wonder I didn't do relationships. I'd been so worried about hurting Roberto. It turned out that I was the one to get hurt. I started, in a whisper-shriek, "Jake, what is wrong with you?" but was interrupted by a knock on the door. It opened and my attorney walked in wearing a professional, black skirt suit. Amelia, a dark haired, curvy beauty with brains, helped me a few years ago when Carlos stopped paying child support. After two strongly-worded letters sent by her on letterhead, Carlos paid all of the arrears, with interest, plus her fee. I adored her.

"Lucy, how are you?" she asked warmly, shaking my hand, but she looked crestfallen when she saw how upset I was. "What's wrong?" Then she noticed Jake and looked back at me, confused. "I didn't know you knew each other."

"He's, uh," I started.

"We're neighbors," he interrupted. "Until I get my remodel done."

"Oh," said Amelia brightly. "How lovely."

"I'll let you be," said Jake, and he hustled out, leaving me rejected, alone, and with my lawyer.

Amelia sat down at the table and I tried to arrange my thoughts so that I was thinking about the court proceeding, but I was really wondering why on earth Jake acted so badly. She pulled out a file.

"I reviewed the petition that you emailed last week, and it looks like Mr. Castro is seeking to have greater custody of Roberto. The proportion of time that he is requesting is such that given your incomes, he would not have to pay any child support."

"I just can't believe this," I whispered, indignant. To hear it out loud from another person made it seem real. Before, just reading the words, made it seem like it was a story, not my real life. A novel. Someone else's story.

And then to my horror, tears started welling in my eyes. I never cried. But apparently, now I did. And I found myself telling everything to Amelia. I think that being served with the papers was the start, but Jake acting so weird was the trigger, and I couldn't take it anymore.

"Carlos dated me for three months in high school, until he talked me into having sex with him. He got me pregnant the first time we did it. In his Toyota Camry. Not very romantic. And then he dumped me for another girl who was a cheerleader." I wiped at the tears streaming down my face. Amelia handed me a Kleenex, listening.

"That's the short story, at least. I felt like complete shit. He just used me to get off his teenage hormones and then once I said yes, he was on to the next. I was young and stupid and I didn't use any protection. Or *we* were young and stupid and *we* didn't use any protection. So a few weeks later, when I started feeling weird and realized that I missed my period, I was like, *no.* I couldn't be pregnant. My parents would kill me.

"So there I was, pregnant with Roberto, and was Carlos there at all during my pregnancy? Did he go to any doctor's appointments? No. He'd moved on to a girl on the dance team. And was he there when I was in labor? No. He was then dating a girl who used to sit next to me in math class. And did Carlos come to see his child? Not until he was a month old. And that was only because I went over to his house and pounded on his door, demanding that he meet him."

I started sobbing in earnest, all of the old thoughts of the past coming to me now as I relived them.

"I was flat out abandoned and rejected by Carlos. He left me by myself, all those pregnancy hormones, all those feelings, all those changes. He didn't care. And I couldn't make him care. But it scarred me. It fucking scarred me. That bastard hurt me and now he's doing it again. He doesn't care about anyone except himself.

"So was it too early for me to have Roberto? Absolutely. Do I love him with all of my heart? That and more. But he's *my child*. Carlos didn't do anything. I had to chase him for child support.

"I had no money. When I had Rob, I was trying to get my GED and then go to community college. I lived with my parents. I worked at Taco Bell. I did anything just to get an education and to get money for my kid because there was no way in hell I was going to be another unwed, Hispanic single mother," I spat. Amelia reached over and patted my hand as my sobs subsided. I dabbed my eyes, noticing all of the makeup coming off on the tissue. I took a deep breath.

"And yet, that was exactly what I was. What I am. And I've had to accept that, had to accept that I'm a stereotype and I've had to fucking pick myself up and do the work to make a wonderful life for me and Roberto.

"I knew that I wanted to be a writer and in between everything, in between school and studying, in between work and trying to make money, and in between taking care of my son, I wrote. I wrote in the middle of the night. I wrote because I had to. And I've managed to make a living out of it, but it was through a lot of hard work. Carlos needs to pay the damn child support to take care of his son and leave us alone. He doesn't really want to be around us anyway—he doesn't want to be tied to anyone or anything. He likes the rush, the good time. He always goes for the next thing. He doesn't have the attention to be a dad.

"When Roberto turned three, Carlos decided that he wanted to start having a relationship with Rob, so he started with evening visits once every other week, and then the judge gave him every other weekend. I understand that fathers have rights. But I don't believe that Carlos cares. This is just a ploy to get out of paying so much in child support."

Amelia nodded, agreeing with me.

"And what's going to happen to Rob? How is he going to get to school? Do his homework? Get everything taken care of? Carlos doesn't do that. He'll probably make his mother take care of Rob. My poor son. This is all about Carlos, this is not about Rob." I sniffled.

"Well, you are touching on something very important," said Amelia, handing me another Kleenex from the tissue box. "The legal standard in California is the best interest of the child. That is, the court looks at what is in the *child's* best interest to do, not either parent's. So it is our job to show that it is in Rob's best interest to stay with you, his mother, and to keep the custody arrangement as it is. It's very stable for him. He goes to school regularly. And he sees his father every other weekend. We can argue that there is no reason to change it."

I nodded.

Amelia continued, letting out a breath. "Now you know, this could get ugly. Mr. Castro could try to argue that there is something that you're doing that is not in Rob's best interest and he's going to try to dig up dirt on you. He's going to argue that he should get even more time with Rob or even that you should pay him to care for Rob."

"That's crazy! I'm his mother. I've cared for him his entire life."

"I know, Lucy, I know." She looked at me seriously, analytically. "I'm sorry, but I have to ask, as your attorney. Don't keep anything from me because I can't protect you if I don't know about it. Is there anything that he could use against you? Anything that wouldn't look good to a judge?"

God, I hated this. The lack of privacy. The fact that some person who didn't know me, the judge, had the right to look at my life and determine what would happen with my child. It wasn't fair. And the thing was, if I took a look at my life objectively, I did have some things to worry about. I didn't have a steady job with a steady paycheck. Royalties came in when they came in, and on an uneven basis. I modeled nude for money and I'm sure that would look bad.

And Jake. I didn't know what to do about Jake.

I sighed and told Amelia about my work situation and the modeling. Her eyes got a little wide, but she didn't say anything.

"Are you seeing anyone right now?"

I stared at her. At this moment, I didn't know how to answer that. A half hour ago, I would have said, "Yes." But what had happened with Jake? Why was he so cold and distant and demanding? Why had he rejected me? What had happened to my generous, artistic lover?

I wanted to lie to her. I wanted to tell her no. But I needed to tell her, because I was not going to do anything to jeopardize Rob.

"I'm kind of seeing Jake. I think. I don't know."

Amelia looked surprised. "Really?" Then she recovered.

"He's a nice guy, but he works way too much. I've never seen his personality except for being totally and utterly a lawyer. Around here, he lives and breathes the law. I don't know anything about him other than he's here, all the time, working."

But then she continued. "Courts pry. It would look bad to a judge if anyone, including Jake, for example, comes over all the time and is around your son. We need to show that your son's living situation is stable. I don't want to tell you what to do in your private life, but a new relationship doesn't scream stability to a court."

I nodded. "Okay." I didn't know what to do with this. I felt like a wrung-out washcloth.

We discussed the next steps that she was going to take and I gave her information for my declaration. But I was not looking forward to having to testify in court. Ugh.

I was also curious about what she said about Jake. Why were his public and private selves so different? Why was he so kind to me at home, but treated me like total shit here? He said that he was a workaholic, but that was no reason to pretend that you weren't who you really were. I couldn't figure it out and it totally pissed me off. I was already upset from him and then from all of the emotions that were dragged up by reciting my history to Amelia. I just wanted to go home and hug my son.

Amelia walked me out, and we walked by Jake's office. He sat at a desk, working on a computer, and looked up when I passed by, calling, "Lucy."

"I'll call you later," said Amelia, shaking my hand.

Jake had gotten up, and when I walked into his office he shut the door. His walls had nothing on them except two framed diplomas. The stark room had no personality, just papers and file boxes everywhere.

"Did you tell her?" he asked, accusing, pacing.

God, Jerk. My anger flashed. "Yes. I had to."

He closed his eyes and opened them, looking pained and said in an angry hiss, "No you didn't. I told you not to. My private life is personal."

No more. No more of this bullshit. I had too much pride to put up with this treatment from this workaholic loser. I walked to the door and put my hand on the doorknob, turning to him. "This is about my son, you jackass. This is not about you. I'm not going to lie to my lawyer." He got a strange expression on his face. And I couldn't help but sputter, "How come you're being like this? After we had such a fantastic weekend."

He reached for me and then put his hand down. "You don't understand, Lucy. You're so . . . but I can't . . . I want . . . I want you," he finally finished lamely.

"You're not going to have me," I whispered. "If we were together, it would hurt Rob. And me. You just showed your true self. You're an asshole. I can't believe I wasted my time with you." I left his office and shut the door as hard as I could. As it closed, I caught a glimpse of the anguished expression on his face.

I went out to my car and cried harder than I had in twelve years.

11

LIFE ISN'T MEANT TO SUCK

"So let me get this straight. He slept with you once—"

"Twice."

"—Twice, and now, while you'd never say this out loud, because you're a woman, you think he's in love with you and you're wondering why he was an asshole when you saw him on his turf when he wasn't expecting you."

"Well, if you put it that way—"

"He's a guy. He's going to want to sleep with you. Don't confuse it with emotions. He didn't. You're being a romance writer. Knock it off."

I glared at Georgie, who sat on my couch, munching chips and queso dip and sipping a margarita. Sara had tucked herself elegantly in the arm chair, quiet as usual, nursing a glass of chilled white wine. After dinner, Rob had retreated to his room to do his homework. I'd called my friends after I got back from Amelia's office, needing to talk and get all of these thoughts out of my head. Too much had happened since I'd last seen them.

"It felt like it was more than a booty call."

"I know," said Georgie. "It always does."

Her sympathy wasn't helping. Jake had opened up to me and then he just shut down. And whatever it was that made him work so much, whatever it was that made him lose himself that way and forget that he was a caring, artistic guy, whatever it was that made him close himself off, well, I guess it wasn't my job to figure it out.

That sucked, though. I wanted to figure him out. He was a puzzle. A dazzling, generous, complicated puzzle, who'd treated me like shit not eight hours earlier.

But I wasn't going to do it.

For Rob, I wasn't going to have anything to do with Jake. I wasn't going to do anything that put Rob's status with me in jeopardy, and if that meant no new relationships and stability all the way, then I would. I'd smile pretty for the camera.

Okay, not having anything to do with Jake was for me too. I needed to forget him.

It'd be different if I trusted Carlos or if I thought that Rob would like spending time with him. But that wasn't what was going to happen. Carlos would surely leave the job to his mom while he worked. She was nice enough, but she had a lot of medical issues. She wasn't going to be able to really take care of Rob. This was selfishness on Carlos's part.

"He told me some things," I said. "His childhood was bad."

"Everyone has a bad childhood."

"No," I said. "Not everyone. I didn't. Rob didn't."

"Don't get so defensive, mama," Sara said in a chillax voice. "But there's a point where you have to grow up and learn emotional maturity. It doesn't seem like he has that. I don't care how old he is."

"I just don't think that anyone told him that life was what he made it. It seems like he thinks that life is meant to suck."

"It does suck sometimes," said Georgie.

"Not all the time," said Sara.

"He seems to think that if it feels good, he's not allowed to do it," I mused.

"Don't we all?" asked Georgie.

"What, you mean the guilty pleasure thing? I know all about guilty pleasures. I write them. And you know what? They aren't guilty. There is no reason to feel guilty about pleasure."

"Preaching to the choir, mama," said Georgie. "Calm down." She looked at my glass. "How many margaritas have you had?"

"Three."

"Listen, half pint, you're getting drunk."

"Wouldn't you, if you finally met your dream guy, your Mr. Right, and he did what Jake did?"

"I'd be drunker than you." Sara smirked.

"Is there a chance that you are overreacting?" asked Georgie.

"No!" I said, a little louder than I had intended.

"Oooh-kay," she responded. "Just asking."

But was I overreacting? He'd been trying to tell me something.

At this point, who cared? I was going to follow my lawyer's advice. No new relationships until this court ordeal was over.

Okay, I *did* care. I liked my neighbor and was upset that he freaked. I found myself explaining myself, yet again, to my friends, not wanting to accept that my fledgling relationship had been terminated.

"He's just a little sad. I wanted to take care of him. He took care of me. The whole weekend, he was so open. It was a really awesome weekend. I don't know what happened."

"You may never find out," said Georgie.

"That's what I'm afraid of."

A few hours later, my friends had left, I'd cleaned up the dishes and put on my pajamas. Although my friends had not solved anything for me, I felt better having talked it out. And I was so tired.

When they'd left, I'd noticed a man sitting in a car across the street. Totally suspicious. I wonder if Carlos was having me watched. Well, nothing was going to happen.

I'd tucked Rob in bed and went to go turn on the television, when there was a loud pounding at my door.

"Lucy. Open up." Jake's voice.

No. I wasn't going to talk to him.

A thud.

It sounded like his forehead was against the door.

I could ignore him and he'd probably go away, eventually. But I'd learned that it was better to just deal with people than to hide. I opened the door to Jake, still in his blue business suit that I'd seen him in ten hours earlier.

"Can I come in?" he asked.

"No."

He sighed. "We need to talk."

"No we don't. I don't need to talk with you. I don't want to see you."

"Give me a chance," he whispered. Dammit. No. No puppy dog eyes. No lovely face. No. I wasn't going to fall for it again. I was angry and I didn't want to hear it.

"No. You had your chance." I went to close the door.

"I fucked up today."

"Yeah, you did. And you showed what you're really like. So no, go away."

He looked like he was going to reach for me, his hands twitched, but he restrained himself. Those artistic hands. He spoke quietly. "You're the only one who knows me. The office? That's not me."

God, strike me in the heart. But no. *No.*

"Whatever. I'm not going to find out. I'm not going to be with you because it could hurt my son, one. And I don't want to be in a relationship with someone who has to hide the fact that he's in a relationship from people he spends most of his time with every day, two. So no. And no. This is now bigger than me and you. I am not going to give my ex any ammunition."

I went to shut the door in his face, and he put his hand out, stopping it.

"Let me explain—"

"Nothing you say could change anything at this point. So just go." The look on his face hurt my heart. But no. I couldn't let him in because it would hurt even worse. "Go home, Jake."

"I don't have one," he said. "But I'll leave you alone."

And with that, he turned and left.

12

A PLACE OF CREATION

Over the work week that followed, two things happened.

First, my writing productivity exploded. *Finally.* My male character came to life, bringing a set of complex issues to solve and a distraction from my real life and legal problems. If I was going to be honest, the male character was based on Jake, but the Jake of my dreams and fantasies, not the real life Jake who lived next door. Real life Jake didn't measure up, but in my book, I could make him just right.

By Friday, I'd exceeded my word count goals, getting caught up for the past two weeks, and then some. Satisfied with the quality and quantity of my work, I spent a lot of time swimming while Rob was in school. The downtime for my brain was healthy and it kept my body in shape. While I was in the pool, I concentrated on moving my arms and legs, counting laps, and staying focused on the exercise. Swimming also tired me out so that I didn't sit around when I wasn't writing and think about my sexy but sad neighbor, and it made it so that I fell asleep quickly.

There was something incredibly soothing about being in the warm water of our pool. It felt womb-like, comforting. A place of creation where my ideas came to me. I loved the sensation of being suspended, feeling weightless, existing temporarily in a different environment. Feeling relief, pleasure, relaxation. Home.

Second, I began to freak out about going to model for the life drawing class on Saturday. The last class had been like any other assignment—I was an anonymous model, posing for anonymous art students, and I did my job and left.

This week? It was more.

Now I had to disrobe in front of a man who had made love to me. It'd felt like it had meaning, like the start of something big. But then when he wouldn't acknowledge our fledgling relationship? God, now it hurt to think about him. But I wasn't going to put up with a guy who was ashamed of me. That didn't make it any less awkward to think about going to class, however.

Saturday, I left in the morning to get to class early. Georgie watched Roberto for me this time. As I drove away, Jake's BMW lurked in the parking lot of our complex; I halfway wished that he wouldn't show up.

Truth be told, though, the other half really wanted to see him. And the real, God's honest truth be told, I missed him in a way that I didn't know was possible. I'd been waiting for him all of those evenings. I wanted to see him. As the days of the week dragged on, I thought more and more about what had happened. He'd been so romantic. I hated this. I was starting to think that I had overreacted.

I didn't know what had been going on with him at the office. I hadn't let him talk. I wondered if I'd get the chance to let him explain it, or if I'd lost my chance forever.

Maybe I should give him a second chance. I really liked him.

I scolded myself. I'd written a book about a second chance. Some person I was if I wouldn't do it in real life.

Still, I had processed some emotions with the passage of

days. I felt strongly that no one was going to walk all over me. It mattered that people treated me with respect. I felt like I had proved to myself that I had a backbone and could stand up for myself. I wasn't going to put up with bad treatment. But something more was going on. There was something below the surface, I could feel it. And I felt like I was now hurting myself—and him—by not talking to him.

Searching down deep, I was still attracted to him. Not just his body, though I was attracted to that too, but *him*. I wanted him in my life. I wanted to disassemble him, find out what made him tick. He seemed like he needed someone to love—he didn't have anyone and that made my heart hurt.

I didn't feel like I could give him a second chance right now, however, because of the court proceeding. It was better for me not to be in a relationship, especially a new one, for Roberto's sake. So the decision was easy for now. Yet seeing him today was going to be hard.

Walking into the classroom early, I was relieved to see that no one was there. The anteroom was empty, and I went in, undressed, put on my white waffle robe, and waited. After a few minutes, I heard the noises of people arriving, chairs scuffling around, and people taking their seats. The professor knocked on the door and talked with me for a moment. Today, I was to move around, and they were to sketch me in motion, going from pose to pose.

God, what a day to make me parade around naked. I tried to remember to breathe.

Last time I'd come into the classroom, I didn't look around. Instead, I'd looked down. This time, I wanted to hold my head high and look him straight in the eye.

But I couldn't.

I strolled to the middle of the class, dropped my robe, and began a series of poses, holding each until the professor said,

"Next pose, please." Each pose had movement, like swinging an arm or turning a head back and forth. Because of this constant movement, this class session, I got a lock on where Jake was seated, at an easel in the back. His eyes were on me, and every time I looked at him they seemed to have a different expression. At first, they were blank, studious, an artist flicking his eyes up from his paper, to the model, then back again. But as I moved and the poses changed, his eyes went to anguished. Then pleading. And then, worst of all, his sexiest stare, intense, unblinking heat, his hands down, not drawing, just watching me naked, moving, for the other art students to draw.

Before, I found modeling for an art class to be almost asexual. I'd thought about my Target shopping list. But this time, all I could think about was Jake's hands on me, his lips on my skin, his fingers making me come. The caresses he gave me, the way he was thoughtful and honest.

Dammit.

I had to give him a second chance. Once this case was done, I was going to do it. But I needed to figure out a way to tell him.

In what seemed like no time at all, the professor called time, and I went back and changed. This time I hurried, and when I was done, half of the class, including Jake, was still putting away their art supplies. I walked straight over to him as he was putting his pencils in the box and packing up his bag.

"Hi," I said, not knowing what else to say.

"Hey," he responded, looking at me with an unreadable expression. I felt a little hopeful.

"Can we talk?"

He looked at me with heat and longing. My heart leapt. But then he shook his head and let out a sigh, picking up his art pad and his supplies. "It's not a good time, Lucy." And then he walked away from me.

13

IT WAS FUN PLAYING WITH YOU

When I returned from the art class, Georgie took one look at my face and knew what had happened. In an instant, she pulled her cell phone out of her pocket and called Sara for emergency backup, and the two of them sat on either side of me while I cried.

Yet again. Dammit, now I was crying all the time. But I allowed myself this day of wallowing.

And then I tried to seal off my heart and move on. I'd done it before. I would simply toughen up again and set my emotions aside.

But I couldn't help but hope that Jake and I would still get a second chance.

A week passed. I bought Christmas presents for Roberto, my friends, and my family. I saw things that would be wonderful for Jake—a blue scarf that would match his eyes, art supplies, books of photography of Santa Barbara. I didn't buy him anything, but I kept thinking about him. Rob and I put up a little Christmas tree. We decorated. I went to Rob's Winter Pageant, where he wore a Santa hat and sang "Jingle Bell Rock."

But I never saw Jake. Each day, I heard him leave, following his regular routine of early morning workout, then early to work. But he came back later and later, and he never knocked on my door. I made sure never to go out when I heard him coming or going.

I missed him.

The guy in the car outside my house stayed parked there, watching my door most days. I was almost used to him now. It had to be pretty boring watching my door. Still, Carlos could spend his money however he liked, as long as he paid for his son.

About one o'clock on the Monday of the first day of Roberto's winter break, my phone rang. I was sitting at the computer, writing, while Rob read a book. It was Amelia.

"Lucy, is there any chance that you can come in today? Carlos's attorney set an emergency *ex parte* hearing for tomorrow, and we need to prepare."

"What?"

"He filed a request for an emergency order that would give him custody of Rob over Christmas break."

Why? Why would he do this? That asshole. "He goes twelve years without having him on Christmas and he wants him now? You can't be serious."

"I am. Can you come in?"

I thought for a second. I needed a babysitter. Yes, Rob was probably old enough to watch himself. I didn't care. My kid, my rules.

But I couldn't call my mom. She was at work and this was the busy season for grocery stores. Sara would be busy at Macy's, working overtime. Georgie was going crazy at work doing year-end bookkeeping for the auto parts dealer. "I don't have a babysitter. Can Rob come and wait in the lobby?"

"It's probably going to be most of the day and into the evening. Let me see if Jake can do it. He just finished up a case." Before I could stop her, she'd put me on hold. I stewed about my legal troubles with Carlos. I didn't have time to think about Jake right now. I trusted him with my kid for a few hours. I just didn't trust him with my heart.

"He'll be over in a few," she said. "I'll see you when you get here."

And before I could protest, she hung up. Shit.

About a half hour later, there was a knock on the door and Jake stood, dressed in jeans and a t-shirt.

"I hear you need an emergency babysitter."

I nodded. "Thanks. Come in."

He walked in my home. I didn't know what to say. The last time he was in my entranceway, I'd kicked him out. The time before, I'd fucked him.

I let out a breath. "You had time to change out of your suit?"

"I figured I shouldn't watch Rob in a tie."

After a pause I said, "Well, let me show you where things are." I walked him around and showed him the cabinet with snacks for Rob, the paper with emergency phone numbers, and how to work the television, just like any other babysitter.

Unlike any other babysitter, however, he still looked like he belonged in an underwear ad, and worse, he'd hurt me.

"Roberto," I called down the hallway.

He came padding out, wearing socks and sweatpants and a Minecraft t-shirt with a creeper on it. "Mister Jake is going to watch you while I go to a meeting, okay?"

"We'll be fine," he assured me. Then he turned to Rob. "Why don't you show me what you like to do? Your mom says you like Minecraft. Why don't you teach me how to play?"

I needed to get going. I had no time to worry about this. "Listen, call me if you need anything. Either my cell or, well, I'll be at your office."

Jake nodded. Rob looked uncertain.

"Okay, I'm going to go now," I said uncomfortably, and picked up my purse and keys and walked to my car, past the guy sitting in the parked car.

He didn't follow me. Weird. Maybe he wasn't watching me at all. Maybe he was following someone else. I saw him talking on his cell phone as I took off.

When I got to the law firm, Amelia greeted me warmly and handed me a stack of papers. "Mr. Castro has petitioned for the Court to allow him extra time with Roberto over winter break because he says that since Roberto is out of school, he has more time to spend with his father."

"That's ridiculous. Carlos is working. He just wants to get a precedent set so that it looks like Rob spends more time with him."

"That's what I think, too. We need to prepare your testimony for the hearing tomorrow and plan our defense."

Four hours later, we were still going through documents. We'd ordered food and worked in a conference room, practicing my testimony, coming up with new strategies, and preparing my case. No wonder Jake worked such long hours. It took a lot of time to get it right.

Another hour and a half later, I pulled up in my dark parking lot at home. No PI in a car.

I opened my door, figuring that Roberto had played Minecraft the entire time and Jake was bored out of his skull wanting out of there.

My living room looked like a hurricane had hit it. A complete disaster area. Cushions piled up on top of chairs and propped against each other, all over the place. Jake sat on the floor underneath the table, doing something with a blanket. Rob kneeled, surrounded by cushions in another part of the room, connected to Jake with pillows and blankets.

They'd made a fort.

Jake was playing with my son.

The top of the table was covered with construction paper, crayons, scissors, tape, glue, and drawings. It looked like they had created all of the characters of Minecraft in three dimensional paper sculptures. There were several pizza boxes next to it and a two liter bottle of soda.

Rob was building, playing. In heaven.

I'd never felt more relieved. And like the Grinch, my heart grew several sizes.

Jake clambered up from underneath the table, looking sheepish. "I'll, uh, just help clean up. We were making a village in Minecraft."

"Stay. Have a drink with me." Then I said to Rob, "Time for bath and bed, mijo."

Rob nodded. "Thanks, Mister Jake. It was fun playing with you."

And my heart grew another size.

Rob padded down the hall, and I heard him turn on the shower. Jake and I put the living room back together, setting cushions back on the couches and folding blankets, putting them back in the hallway closet. He took the pizza boxes outside and threw them away, and I put the craft supplies away. I left the art projects out, though, displaying them on the mantle next to the Christmas stuff. So my house wasn't going to be in a magazine. Who cared? My son was more important.

I heard the shower turn off. I went in, and once Rob was dressed, I tucked him in bed.

"How was your babysitter?"

"So cool. We played Minecraft, then made the village, and made the zombies and the creepers and Steve and everything."

I leaned over and kissed him, pulling up his blanket. "Good. I love you, mijo."

"Love you, Mom."

Turning off his light, I paused in his doorway and looked at him, all cuddled in his bed. Then I went back out to Jake, who was now sitting on the couch, which had returned to its normal status.

"Want a drink?"

"Yeah."

I went into the kitchen and opened a beer for Jake and poured a Skinny Girl margarita for me. I may have kept Jake's favorite 805 beer on hand. Then I went out to the living area and handed the bottle to Jake, sitting in the arm chair next to him. I took a sip of my drink.

"How was watching Roberto?" I asked, trying to be casual.

He smiled, but it was his sad smile. "It was fun."

I looked at him, questioning.

He took a drink of the beer and leaned closer to me. "Here's the truth. I see a kid like that and I think it's Ethan. So it's hard for me to be around kids. When I first got here, it was a little weird. He reminded me of my brother. I'm never going to get over that."

"Oh, Jake."

"But then I realized that I had a living, breathing kid here now and we had fun."

Yay.

Just then there was a knock at the door.

Since Jake was in my house, it had better not be a process server. I opened the door. It was the private investigator-type guy who'd been sitting in his car for days looking at my door.

"Is Jacob Slausen here? He wasn't next door."

"Who's asking?" I said, my hand on my hip.

"I'm here to serve him with a subpoena to testify tomorrow at an *ex parte* hearing in the matter Carlos Castro versus Lucinda Figueroa—"

"Give me that," Jake interrupted, grabbing the papers.

Shit.

14

IT IS SO ORDERED

The Santa Barbara courthouse, a historic, 1920s Spanish-style edifice, took up most of an entire city block. It was built with the traditional red tile roof and white stucco, but very grand, not humble. You walked on large, terracotta tiles to your courtroom, heels clicking and echoing in the corridors. The ultimate indoor-outdoor building, with virtually no security because many of the downstairs hallways lacked a wall on the inside, instead opening to a courtyard in the middle. In keeping with the style, heavy, dark wood furniture, massive doors, and signs painted in the distinctive Santa Barbara font served as decoration. Centrally located, tourists visited to see old murals and tapestries or walk in the gardens with lush landscaping. This was all very nice.

But if your fucking ex who didn't care about the welfare of your child forced you to go here during Christmas break, it sucked balls.

I walked up to the courtroom with Amelia, who was pulling a wheeled black briefcase behind her that clacked over the mortar of the terracotta flooring. She looked tough, no nonsense, in a dark skirt suit. I felt proud and confident that she was my lawyer, but I was still fearful of what was going to happen today. She gave me instructions.

"No matter what happens, I don't want you to have any reactions to what Carlos says. I don't want you to roll your eyes or sigh or do anything like that. Remember that the judge is watching you and you want to be on your best behavior."

I nodded, but it was going to be difficult to do what she said. The challenge arose immediately because Carlos stood outside the courtroom, to the left of the door, presumably waiting for his attorney. Jake stood to the right of the door. The league of men in my life.

Thirteen years after we'd dated, Carlos remained very good-looking, although now he gave off the aura of a used car salesman. He had always dressed nicely and today was no exception. Clearly wanting to impress, he wore a shiny, light gray button-down shirt, with a matching tie and black slacks. He reeked of cologne, with a sharp haircut and a slim physique.

Following Amelia's instructions, I ignored him. That was hard to do. I really wanted to tell him that he had no right to do what he was doing. That I thought he had an ulterior motive. That I didn't believe him. That he had not shown one iota of interest in Roberto until recently, and that this was just a ploy to stop paying child support. I held my tongue, though.

While Carlos looked like a snake, Jake, on the other hand, was really imposing. He always wore suits as if he'd been born in them, but today, he was a statesman. Cufflinks shiny, stylish watch exposed, just the right amount of cuff showing at the sleeve. He shook Amelia's hand grimly, but barely acknowledged me. Amelia had made me sign a written consent for Jake to testify, which I'd done early that morning. But it felt so strange to have him here when I'd hardly talked with him. I took a deep breath and crossed my fingers, hoping that it would turn out well, reminding myself that I had my excellent attorney and my regal neighbor on my side. I wasn't alone.

At least I assumed Jake was on my side. I hadn't talked with him about the testimony. Last night, Jake took the papers, stared at them, and then muttered, "Goodnight," closing the door behind him before I could properly thank him for watching Roberto. I went to bed dreading the next day. While if I lost, it didn't mean that I lost Roberto forever, it would mean that this Christmas, I wouldn't have him with me and my heart could not take any more bruising. And it could be precedent to losing him forever.

No. That couldn't happen. I wouldn't think that way.

The bailiff unlocked the courtroom and we filed in. Our hearing was the only matter that morning so we immediately sat at the tables in front of the judge. Since Jake was a witness, he did not come in with us. Carlos sat at the other table with his attorney, an older man.

And the clock ticked.

Carlos whispered in his attorney's ear and his attorney whispered back.

The clerk shuffled papers.

Amelia sat, calmly waiting.

My heart rate went up.

I didn't want to cry. I didn't want to cry. I wouldn't cry. I would not let him see me cry.

After an eternity, the judge, a woman thank God, took the bench.

"Castro versus Figueroa. Are the parties ready to proceed?"

"Yes," said Carlos's attorney.

"Yes, Your Honor," said Amelia.

"Proceed," said the judge. "I have read the parties' briefs. I am not convinced that this is an emergency requiring *ex parte* notice, but I understand that the holidays are coming up. Do the parties waive opening statements?"

Both attorneys said yes. I had almost no idea what they were talking about. After the first few minutes that felt like an eternity, now it felt like an eternity in a few minutes. It was all going so quickly now. The judge continued, "First witness, counsel?"

Carlos's attorney spoke. "We would like to call Carlos Castro to the stand."

I didn't want to have to listen to him. But I did it.

For the next half hour, Carlos told the court how much he wanted to be with his son, and how he had rights as a father, and how he just wanted to spend some time with his son and I wouldn't let him. Guided by his attorney, Carlos testified that he was employed but he wanted Rob to spend more time with his family.

If any of that were true, I wouldn't have a problem with it. The thing was, it was complete bullshit. Carlos didn't care about Roberto. If he had cared, he would have been there when Rob was young. This was about money, not about Rob.

God, exes. If only they would go away and you never had to see them again. But Carlos just kept ripping the wound open again and again.

His attorney asked him about the years that he'd not spent with Roberto. Yeah, I wanted to know that, too.

With crocodile tears in his eyes, Carlos said, "After years of not having it all together, I'm now, you know, in a place where I really want to see my son. I want to be a part of his life. And I think he wants to be a part of mine. And it's in his best interest to spend more time with me. Because his mother is nothing more than a nude model, which is not wholesome for my son in any way."

An indignant squeak came out of me and I wanted to stand and give him a piece of my mind, but Amelia put her arm across my chest like she was bracing me for a crash and said, "Objection, nonresponsive, move to strike."

My heart pounded. Seriously? It was art. They couldn't use it against me. What if the judge believed him?

"Sustained."

What did that mean?

The judge asked Amelia if she had any questions for Carlos, but she said, "No questions at this time, Your Honor."

Finally Carlos got off the stand and his attorney said, "Petitioner would like to call Jacob Slausen to the stand."

The bailiff went out to the hall to get Jake.

Not looking at either me or Amelia, Jake strode confidently to the witness stand, was sworn in, and sat down.

"Mr. Slausen," said the attorney, "isn't it true that you are Lucinda Figueroa's neighbor."

"Yes."

"And isn't it true that you are dating Ms. Figueroa?"

"No."

"Isn't it true that you have a sexual relationship with Ms. Figueroa?"

Amelia stood up. "Objection. Irrelevant."

"Overruled," said the judge.

What did overruled mean? Did it mean we won?

Jake answered. "No." I guess we didn't win. But what did he mean, no? Well, I guess we had a sexual relationship but that was in the past. So Jake was telling the truth.

"No?" asked the attorney.

"No," said Jake firmly. "I answered the question."

"Mr. Slausen, have you ever had a sexual relationship with Ms. Figueroa?"

"Objection. Irrelevant," said Amelia, standing up again.

"Sustained," said the judge.

Amelia sat down. I guess that means he didn't have to

answer the question. She looked a little smug. She whispered in my ear, "That didn't go the way Carlos's attorney wanted it to go. The judge agreed that your past relationship with Jake doesn't matter. And it doesn't. So we don't have to go there. His plan to smear you backfired. I'll explain about the art class. He just got shut down. That's what that means."

I let out a sigh of relief.

"No further questions," said the attorney.

"Your witness, counsel," said the judge to Amelia. She stood up, a notebook with a list of questions in her hand.

"Mr. Slausen, have you ever spent time with the minor child, Roberto Figueroa?" Jake's dark eyes, previously focused on Carlos's attorney now bored into me, then turned to Amelia, answering in a matter-of-fact tone.

"Yes."

"In what capacity?"

"I babysat him."

Amelia closed her notebook, not needing it. "Did you have the opportunity to observe Ms. Figueroa on any other occasions with Roberto?"

"Yes."

"Did you form an opinion of Ms. Figueroa as a mother?"

"Yes." No hesitation. Confident.

"And what is your opinion?"

Jake let out a breath. Then he looked straight at me, blue eyes blazing. "Lucinda Figueroa is the finest mother a child could want. Her child is well-cared for. She loves him and he loves her. She does everything she can to make sure that her child's needs are put before her own. She's raised a respectful kid. Ms. Figueroa has clearly done everything she could to make sure that her child was raised right."

Hearing Jake praise my son to me sutured a small portion of the gaping wound that this process had reopened.

"Did you have the opportunity to speak to Roberto about his father?"

"Yes."

"When was this?"

"Yesterday." Really?

"What did he tell you?"

Jake paused. "He told me that he wants to stay with his mom. He told me that when he's with his dad he doesn't see his dad that much because he works on weekends." This was news to me. "He says he's mostly watched by his grandmother. He told me that he was worried that he was going to have to choose between his mom and his dad. I tried to reassure him that California courts don't make children choose between their parents anymore."

"Anything else?" asked Amelia.

"He told me that he loves his mother more than Minecraft."

Mijo. My son.

"No further questions."

Jake stepped down from the stand.

"Any further witnesses?" the judge asked Carlos's attorney, who looked annoyed.

"No."

"Rebuttal," said the judge to Amelia.

Amelia called me up to the stand. In a blur, I answered all of the questions that we had practiced yesterday. About how Carlos had not been around for Roberto's birth or early childhood. About how I had to fight him for child support in the beginning. About how I didn't think that it was in Rob's best interest to be uprooted at Christmas. And about how Carlos and I tried to keep it together in front of Rob.

"Is it true that you model at an art school here in Santa Barbara?" asked Amelia.

"Yes. It's for art students who want to learn anatomy and life drawing."

"Are you in any relationships with a significant other right now?"

"No." And then I couldn't help myself, "I haven't been in any serious relationships since Carlos in high school." And I glared at him.

When I was done, I let out a sigh of relief.

Then the judge started talking and she was angry at Carlos. "You mean to tell me that after all this time, you want to take Roberto? This is not an emergency hearing. It should not have been brought on an *ex parte* basis right before Christmas. The evidence shows that the minor child has been cared for by his mother, almost entirely, for his entire life. The test is best interest of the child. The Court finds that it is not appropriate for the father to be awarded custody for the entire winter vacation. I will award one day of visitation extra on the day after Christmas. But the remainder of the holiday, except for the regular weekend visitations, is to be unchanged. It is so ordered." One more day with Rob was fine. I'd have given him that if he would have asked.

Carlos lost.

Thank heavens. I couldn't even manage the strength to think, *yay*, I was so mentally exhausted.

I let out my breath that I had been holding. I needed to go home so that I could let out the tears, too. Damn all this crying lately. I looked at Amelia and gave her a hug. "Thank you so much," I whispered. "Thank you."

"You're welcome," she said. "Not to be a damper on things, but this is just an emergency hearing. We still have a later hearing to handle, but we will have time to prepare. Jake and I came up with a strategy to protect you last night."

"I didn't know how you knew all that about Rob and him."

"He called me," she said. "We worked on it until really late last night. Or actually this morning."

Oh my God. He had been helping me. Protecting me. Shielding me from himself to protect Rob.

"Excuse me," I said. I ran out of the courtroom. Jake waited in the hallway looking at his cell phone, immediately turning to me and putting it away at seeing me emerge from the room.

"What happened?"

"Basically, we won," I whispered, excitedly. "Carlos gets one extra day with Rob during Christmas break. That's it."

"Excellent," he whispered back. "Listen, can I talk with you?"

I nodded.

He pulled me aside, down the hall, and down into a corridor out of the way, and kept walking until my back was against the wall, his hand on one side of me. He started talking fast, quietly and sincerely.

"I tried to stay away. I knew this was going to happen. I wanted to protect you and Rob. I know how these family law things go. They look into everything and ask you all kinds of questions about your personal life. Anything could have been twisted and used against you. I wanted to be able to answer the judge honestly. If I would have done what I wanted to, pound on your door every day since we had that fight, then that private investigator hanging out all the time would have had a lot more than innuendo. There was no way I was going to jeopardize you and Rob. So, I stayed away."

My eyes widened and my breathing stopped.

"But I can't do it any longer."

15

SHOW ME

"Jake," I breathed. My voice sounded whispery, even to me. I'd just transported myself into my own romance novel and I could care less. I could talk to him again. I could hold him again. Maybe. If he'd let me. I looked down at the ground, unable to process what he had just told me.

The mass of thoughts and emotions swirling around inside me coalesced into a few discrete thoughts. He'd been acting noble, staying away from me for my own good, for the good of my child. He had sacrificed for me and I didn't even know it. And these thoughts warmed me. I had believed that he'd been an asshole, but there was a whole lot more going on, things that I had no idea about. He'd taken care of my child so that I could properly prepare for the custody battle. Not only was he on my side, but he was also on Rob's side. My child adored him. Basically, Jake had made sure we'd won my custody battle by testifying truthfully. I had never been more grateful to another human being.

Now, all I wanted to do was get to know him better, get to know what was beyond the wall that he had put up, that kept him from letting anyone else in. I wanted him to be mine.

He moved closer to me and gently put his hand under my chin, lifting it up to look at him, trailing his finger, caressing me.

"I don't know if the PI will be around watching us still," he said in a low voice. "I don't want to hurt anything you have with Rob. But I can't leave you alone. I can't—"

"You're good for Rob." The words came out in a rush, my body leaning in. It was my turn to get closer to him. "You pay attention to him, real attention. And you're a steady, honest, loyal man with a great career. This *what will the judge think* stuff is bullshit. Carlos looked like a snake oil salesman up there. I mean, I'm scared, but I think that the truth will win out. Don't you?"

"There is nothing certain in a courtroom." Jake took on a lawyerly tone that matched his business suit. He stepped back from me, dropping his hand and turning away. "This proceeding that Carlos brought is a big deal. You can't lose. Rob needs you—"

"I think Rob is going to be just fine. I can't believe that a judge would take him away from me. I mean, I raised him single-handedly his whole life." Then I remembered something and got mad and hissed, "And I can't believe that Carlos works on weekends when he is supposed to be taking care of Rob."

"I know. I would have told you once I found out but I didn't get a chance."

I shook my head in anger. That was a topic to bring up with Amelia. But he and I had more to discuss. Like how hot and cold he was with me. "I want to talk to you. What happened that day in your office?"

"I fucked up," he said immediately.

"Yes. You did. But why? What was going on with you?"

"The short answer is that there is a big difference between what my office sees and what you see."

"I want the long answer."

He paused.

I kept going. I needed to know this. I needed to press it. "You have to explain things to me. I can't read your mind. I can't be with you if you are going to shut me out for no reason. I can't handle it. It's on-Jake and off-Jake. You don't have to be always on, but I want to know what's going on inside your head—"

"It has never been okay for me to be an artist. That is not a part of my life that I share with anyone. Before he was a workaholic, my dad was an artist and he was the kind that was completely irresponsible. My childhood was very bad. I know how to dumpster dive. I had to panhandle. After my mother left us when my brother died, I did anything I could to get out of there. I worked as many jobs as I could to go to college and then to law school so I would never have to live that way again. The thing is, I've always drawn and I've always wanted to be an artist. But it's never been okay for me to do so. No one knows that I take classes or draw or anything. So when I saw you, I handled it badly."

"You did. Not badly. You treated me like shit."

"And I'm sorry." Eyes on me, he radiated intensity, but sincerity. I still didn't know what he was talking about. But I couldn't handle not knowing any more.

"Show me," I whispered. "Show me your art. Show me what you're hiding."

He stared at me and I stared back, hoping that he would let me in. Even though he had his quirks, every indication to me was that there was something in him, beyond the wall he had built, that was worth getting to know. Second chance? Third chance? I still thought it was worth it.

"Okay," he said finally. "I'll tell you everything, shit I've never told another soul. I don't care anymore, I just want you to trust me. I just want you to be mine." His voice lowered even more. "You remind me of some dreams I had."

I took a deep breath. "I'll give you another chance. I've wanted to for a while. I want you too, Jake." I pushed his chest at his intake of breath. "But don't fuck it up."

He looked very serious. "I can't promise that I won't fuck it up. That's the truth. But I can promise that I don't want to fuck it up and if I do, I will do anything to fix it."

Those were not the most soothing words. But they sounded like they were honest. Oh, what was I going to do with my sad, noble, artist-lawyer neighbor?

Kiss him, of course.

I got up on my tiptoes, reaching behind his neck. He looked at me for a second, questioning, and then stepped forward, collapsing his plush lips into mine, grasping me tightly in his suited arms, kissing me hard. I kissed him back equally forcefully, holding his head to mine, running my fingers through his hair, mussing it up. Oh, he smelled good. He felt good. He felt like home. I loved his lips, his tongue, the inside of his mouth, his neck, the way he held me.

I'd missed him. And all I was thinking about was how good this felt to be held by him.

But then I heard a familiar male voice call out, "Lucy?"

Jake and I broke apart.

"God you always were a filthy slut. What's up with this?" Carlos was standing there, glaring at us.

I lost it.

"And you were always an asshole," I snarled back at him.

"At least I didn't perjure myself. You fucking liar," he said, pointing at Jake. "You totally committed perjury."

"No, Carlos, he didn't. We were broken up."

"Whatever. I know what I just saw. It didn't look like you were broken up to me."

And with that, Carlos gave me a nasty smirk and said, "See you here again soon." Then he walked away.

Fuck.

16

YOU ARE AN ARTIST

Jake and I watched Carlos saunter down the hallway, Jake super pissed. "He knows about us. I was trying to avoid that exact thing. *Fuck*."

I shook my head and put my hand on my hip. "You know what? I'm glad." He looked at me, surprised. "I don't like to hide things. With me, what you see is what you get. I am who I am and I'm proud of it. And I'm proud of being with you. You're good for my son. So screw him."

Jake smiled his wan, sad smile. "I suppose it's too late now, anyway." He pulled out his phone and looked at the time. "I guess I'll go back to the office."

I shook my head and grabbed his hand, pulling him to me. "Oh no you don't." I stepped way into his space, putting my finger on his chest. "This is the day you get a quickie before you go back to the office. And you're going to show me your house because I've never seen it."

His eyes flashed. He nodded, not saying anything. Unusual. I guess I'd stunned him into silence. I went to go and leave, but before I could turn to go down the halls to find our cars, he grabbed me, hard, slamming me into him. Hand on my ass, hand on my shoulder, he kissed me like it was his life's work. Like he was creating a moment with me.

And for the second time in that historic courthouse hallway, heels on the terracotta tile, I lost myself with him. In him, the taste of his tongue, his seductive smell, the feeling of his hard, athletic body. People walked up and down the hallway, clattering their rollaway briefcases and their shoes. These sounds barely registered in my consciousness. I got lost—or maybe he was lost—but we both found each other.

He might be mine now.

Suddenly propelled to get a move on, we split apart, kissed again really quickly, and then with a hand squeeze to say goodbye, breathlessly headed to our cars.

We drove in separate cars to the same place. As I drove home, I called Amelia and told her. Again, I wasn't going to keep anything from my attorney if it would hurt Rob. I told her that Jake had testified truthfully, but we might have gotten back together afterwards and Carlos saw. She gasped and said she would do damage control. I wasn't sure what that would be, but I was grateful for her help.

Once I parked in front of the duplex, no private investigator in sight, I got out of my car, feeling electrified and turned on. As in, really fucking heated. Wet. Wanting to be naked with him.

But I had to be a mom first.

Jake pulled up right after me and I went over to him. "Let me check in on Roberto and I'll be over."

He nodded and looked like he was feeling about the same way I was, like he was going to explode if he wasn't touching me. But he didn't touch me anywhere except my hand, holding it. He walked with me over to the duplex and then let go of my hand, looking at me.

"I'll be just a minute."

"Be fast," he ordered, and then he went and unlocked his home.

I walked into my house and called in to Sara, who'd been watching Rob during the hearing, so grateful for her help. She was the only one available at the last minute. I'd lucked out that she was going to work late tonight at Macy's, so she could help me. Holiday hours.

When I walked into the living room, Rob was sitting on the couch reading a book and Sara was reading something on her tablet.

"Hey, guys."

Despite being interrupted from his reading, Rob smiled at me. "Hi, Mom."

I looked over at him. "You good, mijo?"

"Yep. Tía and I went to the park and came back and now we're reading."

"Sounds good," I responded, grateful for the awesome free babysitting.

"How did it go?" Sara asked in a low voice, getting up. She walked with me into the kitchen before I started talking.

"Carlos basically lost," I told her, "and Jake and I made up. But then Carlos caught us in the hallway so he thinks that Jake lied on the stand."

"Huh?" She had a look on her face of utter bewilderment.

I realized that I hadn't told my friend everything that had happened in the past twenty-four hours.

"I'll explain, but right now, Sara, can you watch Rob for just a little bit longer?" I was begging. "Like less than an hour? Jake has to go back to work. I need to go talk to him."

"By talk you mean—" she started, suggestively.

"I hope so," I giggled.

She laughed. "Go get him, mama. I'll watch Roberto."

"I'll be back in a little bit, mijo," I called to Rob. "Just a little bit more."

"Uh-huh," he muttered, his nose back in the book. Clearly he was my kid, lost in his reading.

I knocked on Jake's door, feeling tentative, because I'd never been inside his place. The door opened. He stood there, hot, still in his perfect suit.

"Come on in, Lucy."

He opened the door the whole way and I stepped inside, looking around. His place was basically the same layout as mine, except reversed. As I expected, there wasn't much in the way of furnishings, just a table and chairs in the dining area, a couch and a coffee table in front of the television, and not much else. Clean and orderly. Nothing on the walls. This made it seem light and airy, though, rather than depressing. Minimalist to the utmost degree.

But this was his space. Even temporary, it was him. More so than his depressingly stark den of an office. He stood in the room and shrugged.

"Looks the same as yours, no? I only moved what I needed here and put the rest in storage."

"Tour, guapo. I want to see it."

He grinned. "Well, this is the living room."

I nodded. "Duh."

He took my hand, holding it lightly, his hand bigger than mine. I pulled his hand up to my lips and kissed it, noticing how long his fingers were, how sensuous his artist's hands were. Nails well kept, prominent veins. God I wanted them on me again.

"I sleep in here," he said, pointing to the master, "and paint in here."

We stepped into the second bedroom.

Two large tables, one bare but paint-splattered, the other stacked neatly with large pads of paper, jars with paintbrushes sticking out, paint tubes, colored pencils, charcoal, markers, and other art supplies made it clear that yeah, he did paint.

This was more than just another room to him. He made a place for his art here.

He walked me past canvases stacked against the walls and an easel, to the table with the art supplies. Pausing for a moment, he fingered the cover of a large pad of paper on top.

"These are my drawings of you."

Then he handed it to me, his eyes piercingly blue.

For a moment, I just stood there, grasping it with both hands, looking down at it, wanting to open it and unwilling to breach his privacy.

I knew how it felt as a writer to show someone something you create. Would they judge? Would they shame me for thinking this way? Would they make fun of it? Of me?

It took trust to show someone else your art. Trust that someone would connect with it and not rip it apart. And when you stood there, next to the person who created the art and looked at their eyes and saw the breath escape their lips as they had that delicious pain of *being seen*? Well, *that* was intimacy.

Letting someone know you, all the parts of you, not just the parts that you want them to see. He was giving me a piece of himself that he didn't even know that he had to give. I wanted to accept it, to allow him in. I gently set the tablet on the empty table, perched on a stool, and opened up the cover. Then I reacted viscerally.

The first picture depicted my face. Just my face. With very few lines, he'd captured the curves of my jaw, the angle of my nose, the line of my brow. My hair was suggested with just a few quick strokes. I looked calm, reposed.

And beautiful.

I turned the page.

The second picture illustrated just my lips. My full bottom

lip, slightly pouting. My upper one separated from the bottom. The hint of my teeth beneath.

Page flip. My eye. Just one, at half-mast, alluring, upturned, with full cat eye makeup.

Page flip, my face again. More detail this time, and from different perspectives—in profile, looking to the right, straight on.

Page flip. The first one of my body—my back, head, neck, and arms while seated. My waist flared in from my hips. He'd taken the time to draw my spine in intricate detail. I could probably count the vertebrae.

Page flip, just my hips, from the side, my hip bone jutting out, and showing the tops of my thighs and the curve of my waist.

Another picture, my arms.

Another, my hands, different poses.

I turned the page again. This one was my whole body, nipples on display, my curvy thighs, my shoulders covered by my hair.

Another one, my ass.

And another page of my ass.

And yet another page of my ass. I stifled a giggle.

The sketches were all utterly realistic, but also better than realism. Because while it was me, clearly, he had made me look better. Like there was a light emanating from me.

This was how he saw me.

And he had piles and piles of sketchbooks, canvases, and papers.

I looked up from the drawings and he stood near me, uncertainty radiating from his striking face.

"They are just sketches," he began, "I drew them quickly, you know, they are just to get the idea down."

"Stop."

He looked perplexed. "What?"

"Don't minimize them. You have unbelievable talent. You are an artist. You create loveliness. They are amazing. I love them."

He still looked uncertain.

"What do I have to do to convince you that you're an artist?"

"I don't know," he said heatedly, "but I'm going to let you do that. You can look at all of them if you want. Whenever you want. Right now, though? I can't wait anymore to have you naked."

"Okay," I whispered, and walked to the door, looking back at him over my shoulder. "You coming with me?"

17

STARTING TO LOOSEN UP

In two loping steps, Jake bounded across the room and grabbed me by my waist, picking me up. I squealed and he carried me across the hall into his bedroom. Before I could look around the room to check out my surroundings, I was on my back, on a Craftsman-style bed with a dark blue comforter, and he was on top of me, between my legs, still wearing his suit jacket, tie, shoes, and everything else.

"You're going to get your suit rumpled," I exhaled, in between kisses.

"Don't care," he muttered against my lips.

"*Yay*," I whispered. "My businessman is starting to loosen up."

He pulled back from me and smiled his white toothpaste smile. "But I can't fuck you wearing all this, so I'd better take it off." He got up off of me, and I scooted back on my elbows to watch the show. I snuck a glance around the bedroom, though. Monastic, like the living room. Just a bed, chair, and dresser. Nothing else. No pictures.

Really, the other bedroom was the sanctuary.

But Jake undressing was way more interesting than this

room. He took off his jacket and set it on the wooden chair, his polished dark shoes next, hitting the floor. Then he pulled on the knot of his tie, loosening it, and taking it off over his head. He gave me a look while holding the tie and said, "Ever use these in your books?" I giggled and nodded as he unbuttoned the collar of his shirt.

Now it was time for the good part.

Fuck yeah Jake striptease.

Looking at me with a mischievous look on his face, he started unbuttoning his shirt, slowly, one button at a time, exposing his trim physique.

"Is this weird? Do you like this?" God I loved that he was willing and brave enough to ask questions like that. I could never write a book boyfriend like him because he wasn't all Alpha perfect. That said, was he serious?

"Um, *yeah*," I answered immediately. "Keep going. And a little slower."

He bit his lip. Then he grinned a shy, sexy half-grin, and looked down, unbuttoning his shirt all the way.

Then the shirt was on the floor and his upper body, all obliques and pecs, was on display. He leaned over to take off his socks. As he did that, I scooted off of the bed and came down to the floor on my knees.

"Let me help you," I whispered, and I undid his pants, easing them down his long legs. He stepped out of them. He was wearing classic boxers again, this time black.

Yeah, he was hard.

I nudged the elastic down and his cock sprung out. Looking up at him, eyes on mine, I opened my mouth, taking his cock in as far as it would go, enjoying the feel of him, enjoying the scent of him. I softened my lips around him and sucked, pulling back, and he made a noise, like a whine.

"Can you do that again?" he rasped.

I nodded, on my knees, totally submitting to him. I loved doing this, feeling like I was giving him something, pleasing him. He deserved a good blow job and I let him know it, stroking him with my tongue and my hand, my attention absorbed only by him.

I kept going and at one point, when I pulled back with a pop, he groused, "What are you doing still dressed? Clothes off."

So I stood up, backed away, and took off the gray dress that I'd worn to court, unzipping the side and stepping out of it. Again, I was standing in front of him in panties and high heels, this time cheeky turquoise panties with a matching lace bra, and sober, corporate black pumps.

His eyes raced up and down me, which didn't take that long, given my height.

"Tell me honey, what kind of love scenes do you write in your novels? What do you secretly think is hot?"

He stepped toward me and reached around behind me, unhooking my bra with ease. His fingers at first skimming lightly over my breasts, and then got more insistent. Then he bent down and started nibbling on my neck. "Tell me."

"Against the wall," I started naming my secret favorites that I wanted to try. "In public. Tied up. In the shower. In a hotel room. In the bath. All sorts of naughty things. Sometimes it's slow and sensuous. Sometimes it is just base fucking. But it has to tell the story."

"I'm compiling a list," he said against my shoulder, whisper-kisses on my bare skin.

"Jake, you're not a character in my book."

"Nope. But being with you reminds me that it's okay to be creative. And it could be fun."

"Have you ever done it against a wall?"

"Nope. You?"

I shook my head. "I've barely done it at all, remember."

"That's first, then," he decreed, and he hooked his hand in my panties and pulled them down. I stepped out of them, still wearing my shoes.

"Keep those on." He pushed me onto his bed, stepped back, and took off his boxers. Leaning forward and wrapping me in his arms, he recommenced kissing me, licking my breasts, sucking on my nipples, making them hard, while I felt his soft skin. He trailed his nose down my middle, into my belly button, and between my legs. "Holy shit. You are so fucking wet."

"Yeah, guapo, get going. This is supposed to be a quickie."

In response, he put his tongue on my clit and started rubbing it, licking it, nudging it. As much as I loved it, I wanted him inside me. Now. "Where's your condom?"

He went to the dresser and opened the top drawer, pulling one out. "We need to deal with birth control at some point."

"I'm on the pill. Get tested and we're good, okay nene?"

"Yeah, fine," he said, as he put the condom on. "What does nene mean?"

"Honey." I watched him roll it down his length and the sight of him stroking himself made me even wetter.

"That's what I call you," he whispered, amused.

"I know."

"What does guapo mean?"

"Handsome."

He smiled and then gave me a chin lift. "Let's try this."

I got off of the bed and walked over to the wall, still in my heels, which helped with the height difference. In one move, he hoisted me up by my ass, entered me, and pressed me up against the wall.

Oh my fucking Lord.

That felt so amazing.

I wrapped my legs and arms around him tight, and he

started thrusting into me, holding me tightly to him, my back to the wall.

"This. Is. Amazing," I grunted, my brain not being able to process.

"Yeah," he agreed, keeping up the pace, his mouth on the top of my head.

My breasts jiggled with each thrust and our bodies slammed against each other. It didn't hurt. I loved it. It was primal and passionate.

Jake unleashed, finally.

Jake *fucking me*, finally.

In fact, I thought with surprise, that I could actually come in this position. I was so wet, so excited, so turned on, and he was so big, that every movement caused this chain reaction of pleasure racing through my body. All I could focus on was how good it felt, how everything in my body was tensing, how I was getting thoroughly fucked.

"I fucking love this," I moaned, "keep going, I'm going to come."

"Okay," he said, thrusting.

And he grabbed my ass and hoisted me up a little higher, changing the position and that did it, my body pulsing in pleasure, as the orgasm raced through me, making my pussy spasm, my fingers tingle, and my feet get hot. I held on to him, hoping he'd never let me go.

"What is *your* fantasy?" I asked him, once I recovered. "What do you want to do to me?"

"There's a list," he said, as the throbbing subsided, "and first on it is biting your luscious ass."

"Okay," I said immediately.

He stopped thrusting, pulled me away from the wall, and walked over and put me gently on the bed, staying connected the whole time. Then he pulled out, helped me to turn over, and pulled my hips back, so I was on my hands and knees.

His warm hands ran slowly over my ass cheeks, cuddling them, caressing them.

"You are so fucking hot," he said, and he leaned over and gave me a bite, just a small one, in the fleshiest part of my ass above where it hit my legs on the left side.

I liked the bite.

Then he did it again, on my right side.

And then he groaned and, hands on my hips, pulling me to him, drove his cock into me, hand on my pussy, rubbing my clit rhythmically.

And then I kind of lost focus with reality and entered *kairos*, that moment that everything happened at once, when all of time existed at the same time. That moment when you lost the sense of chronological time, *chronos*, and were purely existing. You didn't think about what happened before and you didn't think about what happened next. It was a moment of pure creation, of pure existence, and I was doing it with Jake, and *doing it* with Jake, and I did not want to be anywhere else.

Then the tremors began again. My legs quaked. He held me up with one hand and stimulated me with the other, and I shook, coming again, this time even harder, this time screaming.

Five more thrusts, and Jake was right behind me, embedding himself in me, and collapsing on my back.

After a moment, breathing heavily, he pulled out, ran his finger down my back, and gently helped me to flop onto my back. He got up, went into the bathroom, came back without the condom, and lay down next to me. He then leaned over and kissed my nose, looking me in the eyes.

"I'm not sure that was a quickie," I said, and he burst out laughing.

"It wasn't," he agreed. "But since I'm the boss and I set my own hours, I think it will be okay."

After a few moments, we both got up and got dressed, calmer. Back in his armor of a suit, my Jake still needed care. "Come over for dinner tonight."

He looked at me. "That means I leave the office before ten."

"Can you do that?"

He nodded. "Yeah. I'll be here at six thirty. Will that work?"

I beamed. "That will work." And I reached around his suit-clad body and gave him a huge hug.

18

CAN WE PUT IT IN TWO PLAYER?

"Lucy?"

"Yeah, Mom?"

"What happened today in court?"

It was later. Jake had gone back to work, I went over to my house, gave Rob a hug, told Sara everything, she left, and I worked. Then I started making dinner and my mom called. Grateful to have my mother in my life, I told her almost everything, meaning I didn't tell her about the sex. I did tell her that we had won in court, that it was just the first round, that Carlos wasn't watching Rob on weekends, and that I might have a new boyfriend and that could maybe get me in trouble.

"Oh, mija, Mister Jake couldn't get you in trouble. He told the truth. And he liked the tamales, no?"

My mom could be very cute. But the fact that she was completely supportive of me and my decisions—whether they were good ones or not—was something I tried not to take for granted. She didn't meddle too much and she didn't tell me what to do. She let me make my mistakes and then held my hand as I recovered from them. I was one of the lucky ones. By the accident of birth, I'd ended up with great parents. I was grateful for the fact that my mom and dad were in my life and were loving, reasonably well-adjusted people. A lot of people did not have that.

Like Jake.

No family around to speak of, no home, losing himself in the law, when he really had the soul of an artist. He was lovely, in a melancholy way, and not just because of his looks. It was the way he acted, thinking of me over himself. Mistakes? Sure, he made plenty, and I am sure he'd make more. But I couldn't wait until he came home.

Came home.

This wasn't his home but it might as well be. He said he didn't have one. Sometimes home is with a person, not a place. I loved my duplex and was proud of the fact that I bought it with money I earned from my writing, but at the end of the day, home for me was with Roberto.

But being in Jake's arms also felt like a type of home. I felt cared for, comforted, and secure. Sometimes, when I wasn't in his arms and he was being Mr. Distracted Businessman, I felt like shit, but when he touched me that never happened. His touch was strangely familiar—I felt completely at ease and really excited at the same time.

I'd never had an adult man to cook for besides my dad. With Jake living next door, he bypassed my previous dating rules. I'd hoped that Rob would think of him as a babysitter and a neighbor. It seemed like he did. I had to be careful, though. I didn't want Rob to get too attached to him and then have things not work out with Jake. It was hard enough to break up with a guy. I didn't want to get Rob's emotions involved in addition. I suppose with Rob knowing that Jake was only living next to us during the time that his house was being remodeled, he would understand that having Jake as our neighbor was just temporary.

I hoped.

As I talked with my mom, I assembled the chile relleno casserole that I'd told Jake about—green chiles, lots of cheese and eggs, and a whole lot of yum. It was Rob's favorite meal, and I hoped that Jake would like it. I made a salad too, and cut up some vegetables to steam to counteract all of the richness of the dish.

I hung up with her, and at 6:25, there was a knock on my door. I looked through the peephole. Jake, not a process server.

I was secretly thrilled that he was early. I'd worried that he would call and not show up, or be stuck at work, like the workaholic he was. But no, he came home.

And even though I'd seen him at lunchtime, he was still a treat to see. His suit was more wrinkled than usual, but he still smelled great and looked even better.

But Rob was right there as I answered the door, so I did not launch myself at my hottie.

"Hey, come on in," is what I said instead, being cool in front of my kid.

Jake looked tired, but perked up once he walked in. "It smells so good in here." I was amused. It was like it was the 1950s —*the way to a man's heart* . . . But I didn't care. I wanted to take care of him. He didn't have anyone looking out for him.

He leaned over and whispered in my ear, "I'm assuming no PDA in front of your son, right?"

"I'd appreciate that," I whispered back.

"Well, consider the thought," he continued quietly. "I want to kiss your adorable nose."

For some reason this made me blush. He touched my cheek and then called, in a louder voice, "Hey Rob, can we put it in two player?" Then he took off his jacket, loosened his tie, and walked over to Rob, who was sitting on the floor. Jake joined him, wearing his tie and suit pants, and began to play Minecraft with my twelve-year-old son.

He'd learned how to play.

He'd let my son teach him how to play.

And just like that Jake had my heart. Completely.

Seriously.

That did it. Hanging out with my son, doing something simple and everyday. I was already falling for my charming neighbor, I'd admit it, and I was falling fast. I didn't know what was going to happen with him and I didn't know what kind of secrets he was holding inside him, but I was at the point where not going further with him would break my heart. I was taken by this man, who paid attention to my son, and paid attention to me, even when he worked as if he had to. As if working was a compulsion for him.

I was going to find out why and see if I could fix it.

Now I knew this was dangerous territory. I know that you shouldn't try to fix another person, especially a man. People only changed when they were ready to change. You couldn't force it. But I was still guided by that saying that I'd heard before —*the busiest man in the world will make time for you if he is in love with you.* I didn't think that Jake was in love with me, but I knew that he was interested. Those drawings showed it. And I knew that he was trying to make time for me. So I was willing to risk it, willing to try a relationship with him. Yes, I knew I could get hurt. But I couldn't not do it at this point. And I was also willing to see if I could show him that he could work less and still thrive.

Maybe I could convince him to show his work in public.

I didn't want to think about what would happen if this went bad. I guess he'd move away and I wouldn't have to see him again. But it felt too good being with him not to risk my heart. So I decided to try it.

I gathered us all at the table, and we lit candles. The house was decorated for Christmas, plus the Minecraft things that Rob and Jake had made the other day, so I put a few of them on the table. It was funny, but it worked for me. And it felt right for Jake to be there with us, chatting, telling us about his day, asking us about ours, and talking about what he intended to do in Minecraft with Rob as we ate.

And, to be even more perfect, Jake rolled up his sleeves after dinner, tucked his tie into his shirt front, and helped with the dishes.

I wasn't sure where I'd found this guy.

Still, I knew, he had some demons that we needed to address.

But for now, it was enough just to do these simple, ordinary household things with him.

And since he didn't really have a home, I wondered—were they simple or ordinary to him?

19

I'M INTERESTED IN REAL

Later that night, after Rob had gone to bed, I sat outside with Jake on my little loveseat. He'd taken off his tie and unbuttoned the top button of his shirt. Because of a chill in the air, we huddled under a blanket, my feet in his lap.

"You could go change out of your work clothes," I suggested.

"Good idea." He lifted both of my feet over back to me, stood up, and said, "I'll be right back." He leaned over and gave me my first kiss of the night, a light one. And then he kissed my nose tenderly. "Thanks for dinner, Lucy. It meant more to me than you know."

He went into to my house through the patio doors, and I heard him open the front door and close it. A few moments later, he stepped out onto his patio, wearing blue plaid pajama bottoms and a black t-shirt. He vaulted the low gate between our patios and sat down next to me, rearranging my feet over his lap again, putting his arm around my shoulders. I cuddled into him.

"I like you in your suit, but I also like that I get to see you out of it."

He groaned and squeezed me with both arms. "You can't say sexy things like that to me when your son is in there sleeping."

"I meant it in a couple of ways, Jake. Not just the, you know, naked way, but also the private side of you."

Very slowly, he turned to look at me. His eyes darted up and down my face and then he looked crestfallen.

"What?" I laughed, giving him a tiny push.

"If I kiss you now the way I want to, I'm not going to want to stop."

"So talk." Frankly, though, the self-imposed restraint on affection was hard on me too. I couldn't get my fill of him. But I was enjoying his physical, comforting presence and for now, that would have to do. He put his chin on top of my head and held me.

After a moment, he started talking.

"I don't know everything about my parents because I wasn't around for some of it, obviously, but also as a kid, you don't know all that is going on. So I know this. My mom was from a wealthy family back east, in New York."

"Manhattan?"

"Westchester County. Back then, my dad was an artist. He did weird shit. Sort of post-Jackson Pollack. Throwing paint on canvas and seeing what happens. Mixed media too. They fell in love and when my mom announced to her family that she was pregnant by the stereotypical poor, starving artist, they threw her out."

"No!" I yell-whispered.

"I've never met my grandparents on either side. So I guess that there was something about my dad that my mom loved and my grandparents couldn't stand. They eloped and had me almost immediately."

I liked the idea of Jake being a love child, born from passion, but his background was incredibly heart wrenching.

He continued. "Three years later they had my brother, Ethan. I think at first, it was very romantic for my mom. Here she was, married to this artist, you know, who was unpredictable. He'd do things, like bring home a monkey, which was fun for us kids, but there was bad stuff too, like him not coming home for three days, leaving her with us. And that got old real quick.

"The poverty also wore her down. My dad didn't seem to care, but since she had grown up used to being surrounded by things, it hardened her. When I was little, she was so soft. And then she got rougher and more brittle, like she was going to break if we touched her. We eventually made it out here to California and you know, Santa Barbara is both great and tough if you are poor. The weather makes it so that you can live outside for most of the year. But it's expensive."

Didn't I know it. Santa Barbara was a place where people walked over the homeless to open the front door to Saks Fifth Avenue, not that I shopped at Saks. I'd never seen such a dichotomy between the rich and the poor as I'd seen in Santa Barbara.

Then I thought of something. "I thought you had said that your dad was a workaholic."

"He wasn't when I was really little. He just did his art and he didn't make much money from it. He was obsessed with all these weird, creative ideas. Meanwhile, I thought it was a good day when I got dinner."

I took his hand and squeezed it. What could you say to that?

"We got evicted often and I stayed in shelters sometimes. When that happened, normally I'd be with my mom and my brother. My dad had to stay in a different building, with the men. But the thing is, he had artist friends, so he'd just leave us, sometimes for days. He'd come back and I'd hear my parents fighting, and it was always about the same thing. Why wouldn't he work more and make some money so that we could have food and a home."

"Did your parents use drugs?" I was not able to comprehend people who wouldn't sacrifice everything to take care of their children and thought that was the only explanation for this behavior. But maybe it wasn't.

He nodded. "My mom especially. It was her way of coping. So I basically took care of my brother when she was out of it."

His story just kept getting worse and worse.

"So when my brother was killed in a car accident—a freak thing, coming home from school—everything collapsed. My mom went into this zombie state, where she was almost catatonic. When she came out, she left us. She went back home to her parents. I talk to her every once in a while, but she has a new family now, with two kids. She lives in Arizona. We're pretty much estranged."

"And your dad?"

"He couldn't paint any more after Ethan died. With my mom leaving, he checked out too, but he checked out by working. Finally, for the first time in his life, he got clean and held a steady job, working as a copy machine salesman in Ventura. But he does nothing but work now. I barely saw him in high school. I never saw my mom. Now I don't see either. So I got the fuck out of there as soon as I could. I got a job at a grocery store bagging groceries the minute I was old enough, and kept working, making money to go to school, to go to law school, and to just—" He paused.

"Yeah," I said quietly. "To get some security."

"So since I was old enough, I've spent almost all of my waking life working to make sure I had a place to sleep and food. Now? I'm fine. Doing well. I won a few big plaintiff's cases and I have plenty of money. But I can't seem to get away. I'm so used to being in the office. I'm never home."

It had to be a refuge for him. A safe place where this awful, unsafe, hungry childhood didn't come to haunt him.

"Do you think you could work less?" I asked tentatively. "I mean, if there were a reason to come home?"

He looked at me for a long time and it felt like he was analyzing me again, the artist taking a picture of the way I looked when I asked. "Yes," he said finally. "Growing up like that, the only dream you have, really, is to have enough money for a home and food and a family. The traditional shit. When you don't have it, you want it because it looks so nice that everyone has it."

"But no family is perfect," I started, but he interrupted,

"I'm not interested in perfect. I'm interested in real."

20

ANSWER THE QUESTION

"But what about your art?" I asked, wanting to know why it was so important to him and why he hid it.

"What about it?"

"Where does that fit in? In your life, I mean?"

"It doesn't."

That couldn't be true. No one could create art the way Jake did, have a separate room set up, even in a temporary house, just for it, and not have it be a major part of their life.

"Jake. It does."

He sighed and was a little grumpy when he spoke. "Here's the deal with my art, or whatever you call it. I've always doodled. I drew as a kid. But after Ethan died and my dad stopped painting, he buried himself in his work and I never saw him. Making a living off of art, in my dad's mind, was equated with him losing my mom to drugs and divorce, and losing my brother. So he freaked out, stopped doing his paintings and his mixed-media, and started being addicted to work."

He got the message that it was not safe for him to be an artist. Not with that background. "So your dad was your role model?"

"Sort of, yeah, I guess. I don't really have a role model in my family. I mean I have no idea how you make it, Lucy, being creative for a living. Writing? Seriously? I don't know how that works. I can't believe that you can do it and make money off of it. I couldn't do it, so I chose the law. Always wanted to be Atticus Finch, I guess."

"Really?"

"I liked that movie with Gregory Peck."

I snuggled into his chest. "It's a wonderful movie, but the art. I know you still do it, regardless of whether you get paid for it, regardless of whether it makes sense. You have to do it. Right?"

"Yeah," he said quietly, fingering my hair. "I have to do it. I can't stop drawing. I started drawing for real after Ethan died. I didn't want to forget him. I must have drawn hundreds and hundreds of pictures of my brother, so that I would remember everything about him. The way he put on his shoes. The way he rode his bike. The way he ate spaghetti. But between my dad working, and me working to get out of there, it was never something that I considered doing as a profession. Never something I could consider. It meant homeless shelter again and I needed to pay for school, a roof, and food."

I nodded into his t-shirt.

"But I still had to paint."

Pulling back from him, I hooked my hands low behind his waist. "Of course you did. It's a gift and a talent that you have and you have to do it. You have to share it. By not creating what comes easy for you to create, or what you want to create, you deny all of us the chance to see it and to know that we are understood. To know that there is a connection. It is basic human nature to create."

He looked skeptical.

"I can't live on the streets again," he said. "I can't just be all free and creative. Life doesn't work that way. I have no idea how you did it, but it's not the way it worked for my dad, and it wouldn't work for me."

"You don't know that," I challenged, pulling a hand away from him but resisting putting it on my waist. I settled for walking my fingers up his chest. Yum. "It sounds like you haven't tried."

He stared at me. "It isn't worth trying to do anything. It's just something that I do. It doesn't mean that I could make a living off of it."

Now my hand was on my hip. "It's more than that, and you know it."

"So what if it is? Like I'm going to be some sort of slacker artist, who draws all day long and gets nothing done? No thanks. I'll go to my office."

"Do you like your office?"

He paused. "It doesn't matter if I like it or not. It's my life."

"Jake, you said you have plenty of money. Think about it. Do you need to work so hard?"

"Yeah," he whispered. "I do. I have so many cases, so much responsibility. So many people counting on me."

I shook my head. "You need to do something for fun."

"These days I hang out with you or your kid. That's really fun." He smiled an adorable half-smile on the last one, some of the grumpiness from his earlier words subsiding. Oh, I wanted to kiss him.

So I did.

I leaned over and brushed my lips against his and he wrapped his arms around me, holding me to him, warm and comfortable. I broke apart and snuggled back into his chest.

"When is the last time you took a vacation?"

"What's that?"

"No jokes, guapo. When's the last time you took a vacation?"

"Does going somewhere for a work conference count?"

I rolled my eyes and looked up at him. "Answer the question."

He shook his head. "I don't think I've been anywhere since I made partner, and I don't think I've really ever been on vacation. Other than moving around a lot as a kid, I've never been anywhere just for fun."

Oh my poor nene. "We're going to fix that. For Christmas, I'm giving you a vacation. You and me. We're going away for a weekend. Plan on it. We'll pick a weekend when Rob's dad has him and we'll go."

He looked interested but also worried. "The office will freak."

"Your office will function just fine without you. You're just scared that they will think something got into you if you're not around. But they can handle it just fine."

"That's probably true," he admitted. "But it's going to feel weird to go somewhere."

"That's the point."

He nodded.

"It's also the point to get a really nice hotel room and make the most of it. Go get tested and I will, too."

"Done," he said immediately.

"I want to invite you inside," I whispered, "but I don't think it's a good idea tonight."

"Probably not. But Rob is with his dad this weekend, right?"

"More like with his grandma, apparently. But yes."

"We'll make up for it then."

A few minutes later, he kissed me, rubbed my cheek with the back of his hand, kissed my nose, and whispered, "Good night, honey." And then he hopped over the partition between our patios, and we both went in to sleep in our separate beds.

21

LEGAL RIGHT

"**O**kay, mijo, I'll see you Sunday night," I said to Roberto, very early Saturday morning, as we walked up the pathway to Carlos's house. As much as I wanted to keep Rob for myself, his dad had the legal right to see him overnight, every other weekend. I couldn't change it. I kissed him and watched him go into the house, then drove back home.

And if I was truthful, it would be nice to have a break from my kid to do some last minute Christmas shopping and to spend time with my neighbor. I also modeled later this morning—the class was halfway through the session—and my skin prickled with anticipation. That class now constituted serious foreplay.

Per the Saturday routine, at my usual fifteen minutes before class, I went into the anteroom and took off my clothes, putting on my robe. Today the class assignment was to use charcoal to draw my weight, making the drawings of my body darker where I weighed more. I tried not to think about this concept too much.

I hadn't been with Jake since our quickie the other day. He'd been back to his working ways, although I was starting to make up a dinner plate for him, and bring it over, so he had something to eat. He stopped by every night to talk, say hi to Rob, give me as much of a kiss as he could get away with, and take a plate of food home. I wished that he'd work less, but he explained that a case of his was blowing up, and he needed to be there.

Now, as usual, Jake sat at an easel in the back, watching me with increasingly lusty eyes. Clad, again, in a white t-shirt and dark blue jeans with a heavy black belt, he looked like the bad boy, not the buttoned-up lawyer. He kept running his hands through his ebony hair, making him look even sexier and with those dark blue eyes? Lordy.

Although he was working on his drawings, every time he caught my eye, I felt a throb go through my body. I was looking forward to tonight, since right now, my libido was going haywire. It was a good thing that women can hide their arousal. If an aroused man was the nude model, the whole class would know.

After class, I met him at his easel. He pulled me into him by my waist and wrapped his arms around me, not caring that anyone saw. Uh huh. Yes. This was major progress for the man who initially hid from others that he knew me. We got a few curious looks from two other students who were packing up, but I didn't care. I was seeing him, and I had the right to see him. Their opinion didn't matter. One of the remaining students left.

"Hey," he said, holding me to him. Then the other student took off.

"Hey."

He tilted his head. "Do you want to go out to dinner with me tonight?"

"I'd love to."

"Great. I need to go into the office for a while but we'll go after."

Engrossed by my guy, I think I registered that the professor was leaving, but I was mostly paying attention to Jake. *"Yay,"* I whispered. And then he kissed me, a soft kiss that explored and lingered, ignoring the fact that we were in a classroom.

This kiss got out of hand.

With such a gentle start, it ended fiery, with both of us moaning into each other's mouths, tongues tangling, hands exploring. We had to break apart, or we would end up naked on the floor in a few moments.

He put his forehead to mine, breathing heavy. "I got tested the other day. I'm clean."

"Me too. All clean."

"Good. Then tonight—"

"Yeah."

He kissed me again, lightly this time, and then kissed my nose, like he always did. "Good."

Walking me out to the car, we kissed and parted ways. I was headed to Target to get Rob some clothes.

When I got there, I saw a Minecraft shirt that I knew he would love and a pair of shoes that he needed. But I couldn't remember his shoe size. I thought I knew it, but I wanted to call just to be sure.

I called Carlos's cell.

When he answered, loud music blared in the background, along with a strange ringing noise, and the noise of tons of people. "What do you want, Lucy?"

"Can I talk to Roberto? I'm shopping and need his shoe size."

"Figure it out yourself."

"Carlos. Don't be like that. Just put him on."

"I can't."

Argh! My temper flared. "What do you mean you can't?"

"He's in the hotel room, he's not with me."

What did that mean? His words made my blood boil. "*What hotel room?*"

"He's in Vegas with me."

I shrieked, and all of Target turned to look at me. I tried to lower my voice. "You know that you are not to take him across state lines," I hissed. "That's kidnapping. It's illegal."

"Your boyfriend lied on the stand. That's illegal."

"He didn't lie, Carlos."

"I know what I saw. I told my attorney."

"Why are you in Vegas with my son?" I tried to control my breathing and say it calmly. I didn't succeed.

"I had to come here this weekend, and my mom couldn't watch him, so he came with at the last minute. He's fine, he's in the room, playing on the tablet."

"You left my child alone? In Las Vegas?" I shouted.

"Calm down. He's old enough to watch himself."

"No he is not! He's twelve!" I'd completely lost all sense of my surroundings. I didn't care that I was having an argument in Target. My son could not be treated like this. "I'm coming to get him. Where are you?"

"Jesus fucking Christ, calm down."

"I will not calm down. I am coming to get my son. Where are you?"

"Downtown. Fremont Street."

"Where, exactly?"

He sighed as if it was boring him to talk to me. "I'm only telling you this because there's a huge game on tonight, and I have a lot riding on it, so you can take him. Just for this weekend, though. I want him the rest of the time." WTF? Did Carlos have a gambling problem? Was that why he needed to modify child support? "I expect to get him back after Christmas and then weekends as normal you hear? This doesn't change anything. This will just work out better this weekend. We're at the Golden Nugget."

"I will be there in six hours. I am going to take Roberto back with me. And we will be talking about how this does change everything, or I will see you in court. Do you hear me?"

"Yeah, I hear you." He hung up.

I called Jake as I hurried out of Target, not buying anything. "Change of plans. Carlos took Roberto to Vegas."

"Across state lines? That's against the child custody order."

"I know. I'm getting him. I'm canceling tonight. Sorry my ex is such an asshole."

"It takes hours to get to Vegas. Even if we fly."

"He's left my son in a hotel room by himself so that he can gamble on some football game."

"I'm coming too. Come home, pack, and we'll leave immediately."

I raced home, packed quickly, and ran out the door into Jake, who held a duffle bag and his keys.

"Let's go," he said, without preamble.

We slid into his BMW and it purred into life. We raced to the desert.

Vegas was the playground for Southern California. I'd certainly partied many a weekend there. But it is not a place for kids. What was Carlos thinking? Was he just so arrogant that he thought he could get away with this?

"This isn't the vacation I meant to give you," I told Jake.

"No," he said, seriously. "But I've never been. How is Rob doing?"

When I'd talked with Rob, he sounded annoyed that I was coming. "Mom, I'm playing Minecraft. I'm fine." But he was not.

Turning to Jake, I said, "Just drive faster, please. Please."

22

EVERYTHING THAT'S RIGHT

"Vegas is everything that's right with America. You can do whatever you want, twenty-four hours a day. They've effectively legalized everything there."—Drew Carey

"I mean, what do you do in Las Vegas? You gamble—and you go to strip clubs."—Scott Caan

"Man, I really like Vegas."—Elvis Presley

As many times as I'd been to Las Vegas, because I loved the clubs, the dancing, and the fun, it still struck me as odd that a city like this existed. It just shouldn't. You drove for hours in the mostly barren desert, with basically nothing to look at, except for the periodic billboards advertising casinos in Vegas. When you approached the city, the buildings and the lights arose out of the ground, ringed by dusty mountains. The ultimate oasis.

My idea of a trip to Vegas was to get dressed up, go out with the girls, have fancy drinks on the Strip, ogle cute guys, and go dancing. But I only did this when Rob stayed with my parents. I'd never taken Rob here.

Instead of staying at a nice hotel on the Strip, however, Carlos stayed downtown. It figured.

Downtown meant old Las Vegas. It embodied everything that was right with Las Vegas, but also everything that was wrong—older, smaller, seedier. Dingier casinos, cheaper slots. While much of it had been redone and during the summers there were free concerts on Fremont Street, it was no place for a child to be left alone.

We arrived around eight o'clock, so when Jake and I pulled into the parking lot of the Golden Nugget, the massive amount of lights on the hotel shocked my system. Focused on my son, I sprang from the car immediately, impatient. All I wanted was my child. I ran into the casino, Jake hot on my heels, and went up the elevators to the room.

Could the elevators take any longer?

Finally, we reached the floor, I found the room number, and pounded on the door.

Carlos opened the door, smelling like cologne and wearing pressed pants and a button-down shirt. Dressed up to go out.

I put my hand on my hip and glared at him, all attitude. "Is Roberto here?"

He backed away from the door with a grandiose, "Come right in" gesture, and I barged in. Jake stayed in the doorway. Rob sat on the floor, playing videogames.

"Hey, mijo," I said quietly, crouching down next to him. "How are you?"

"Fine, Mom," he said, and I breathed a sigh of relief. He looked subdued but safe.

"You're overreacting," muttered Carlos in my ear.

"Outside," I hiss-hurled at him, with as much contempt as I could pack into two syllables. As always, I didn't want to argue in front of Rob. I grabbed a room key that was sitting on the dresser and opened the door. "We'll be right back, Rob."

Jake went out, and Carlos grabbed the other hotel key and followed me and Jake into the hallway.

The second the door was closed, I hissed, "What were you thinking?"

Carlos got in my face. "He's my son. This is my weekend. I had plans. We came here." Jake stepped forward, but I waved him back with my hand.

Oh, my baby daddy was an arrogant idiot. "Do you know what it means to really be a father? It means you don't make plans the weekend you have your son. It means you spend time with him. It does not mean that you take him to Vegas to sit in a hotel room."

Carlos made a disgusted, impatient noise. "He's fine. He's having a good time. He just likes to play on the tablet anyway."

It was all I could do to keep from screaming. "First, you took him across state lines. You don't have the right to do it. It's in the court order."

Carlos rolled his eyes. "Whatever. That's a technicality."

"Second, this is no place for a child." A group of college kids stumbled by loudly, clearly celebrating someone's twenty-first birthday with open bottles of alcohol. Illustrating my point.

"I have the right to have him on week—" Carlos started, but I interrupted.

"No you don't. You don't have the right to do this. You have the right to have him overnight, in Santa Barbara. You have the right to take care of him and to show him what it means to have a father who is interested in him. But you don't have the right to —" I stopped and started whispering fast. "I figured it out, you know. You're gambling all the time, right? That's it, isn't it? That's why you're running out of money. That's why you want to change the child support."

Carlos shifted his eyes and shoved his hands in his pockets but he didn't deny it.

So he did have something to lose.

I continued, "Well, you know what? You're never going to win any money gambling. You don't need to see Rob any more than you already do. You need to drop the case, Carlos. Keep everything the way it is."

"No," he said firmly.

"No?"

He stepped forward toward me, getting in my face. Jake hovered in the background, totally pissed. Carlos's voice lowered to a nasty whisper. "I'm not dropping the case. I pay too much in child support. My lawyer thinks I can win. I told him how your lawyer boyfriend lied on the stand and I saw you tongue-fucking him in the courthouse hallway. My god, Lucy, have some respect. First me in the car and him in the fucking courthouse?"

Jake stepped closer to us and I waved him back.

Carlos kept going. "The next time around? When we have the hearing in a few months? My lawyer thinks I'm going to win because it's a father's rights case."

"Then you better act like a father," I hurled back. Jake stepped closer, eyes blazing, and I waved him back, again. Then I got in Carlos's face. "What did you promise him? What did you tell Rob that he could do in Vegas? What promise have you broken?"

Carlos spat out the words right back at me. "God you talk too much. Just fucking shut up. You have no idea what is going on. There's a big game. It's important, and I'm gonna win. I always do. I have a lot riding on it." He looked around. "So I took my son to Vegas? Big fucking deal. You're totally overreacting. Typical. Fucking bitch. Were you always this much of a bitch when we were together?" Carlos got closer to me, spit coming out the side of his mouth, his nostrils flaring, eyes full of hatred.

"Knock it off, Carlos," I muttered, taking a step back. "This is about Rob, not me."

"Yeah, you were this much of a bitch. Dry fucking pussy got me into all this shit—" he started, but Jake grabbed Carlos by the neck and slammed him against the wall.

"Don't fucking talk to her like that," he snarled.

Carlos jutted his chin out and spat in Jake's face. Jake wiped his cheek and stepped back. "I can talk to her however I like, pretty boy. What are you going to do about it?"

"Show some respect to your son's mother," said Jake with disgust.

"Her?" jeered Carlos. "She's a mistake I made, and she wasn't worth it."

"Don't talk to her that way," Jake repeated dangerously.

"Ha. You're not gonna do anything about it, pretty boy."

Jake rolled his eyes to the ceiling.

Carlos shook his head, his eyes narrowed and mouth pinched. "Take that nasty cunt and go," and he lunged, fist raised to hit Jake's face, but Jake was too tall and Carlos hit him in the chest. As I cried "Stop, stop, stop," Jake reared his fist back and landed a solid punch right in Carlos's face.

Damn if Carlos didn't deserve it.

Carlos bent down, shoved Jake in the stomach with his shoulder, and tried to push him across the hall, but Jake was taller and more muscular, and didn't move. Then Carlos took a step back.

Blood beginning to pool out of his nose, Carlos started laughing. He jutted up his chin and wiped his nose with the back of his hand. "You just made a mistake. Go take Rob now, and do whatever you want. I'm gonna call my lawyer after I take a few pictures of my face and ask security for a copy of the tape of this hallway. I'll tell him that your pretty boyfriend is violent and shouldn't be around kids."

I felt like I was going to faint and Jake looked horror-struck.

"You wouldn't dare," I said. "You asked for it. You totally provoked him."

Carlos raised his eyebrows. "Don't know about that. Get your son, bitch." And then he sauntered down the hall away from us.

23

PART OF MY FAMILY

*W*hat *the fuck do we do now?*

Jake walked over to the side of the hall, leaned his forehead against the wall, and stayed there a moment. When he pulled back to gaze at me, the look of pain on his face physically hurt me.

"Lucy—" he started, but I interrupted him, shaking my head. "Give me a minute."

I moved next to him, my back to the wall, and then collapsed to sit down on the floor, my knees to my chest, my arms hugging my legs. I needed to regroup, to analyze, to think. So many thoughts and feelings at once. In this position, I looked defeated but I didn't feel that way. I just needed to pause.

The most important thing to me in the world was Roberto. This family law proceeding had turned Carlos, with whom I'd never had a good relationship, into a total dick and a total idiot. Well, he'd always been a selfish idiot, just now he showed it. But Jake hit him, which he deserved, but I still didn't like. I figured I'd start there.

"I thought you were the artsy type," I whispered.

"What?"

"What were you doing hitting him? Do you have anger issues? I didn't think you had that in you."

"Neither did I," he replied, bitterly. "I haven't been in a fight since high school."

Silence. Then Jake crouched down next to me, put his hands on my knees, and looked at me, sincerity radiating from him. "The last thing I want is to hurt you. I keep trying to protect you, and I keep fucking it up."

I reached over and touched his cheek. "Maybe I don't need protection. Maybe I'm fine the way I am."

He crinkled his eyes when he smiled. "You are more than fine the way you are. It's a lawyer thing. At work, I'll do anything to protect my clients. I want to protect you just as fiercely. Anything for you. I'll do anything to protect you. Even go away if I have to. I care about you, and I fucked it up again."

"You were protecting me," I said slowly, as I thought about his words. I loved that he cared about me.

"It was too much to take. I tried to stay out of it but it went too far." He paused and then looked analytical. "I don't know how this is going to play out. He clearly violated a court order by taking Rob across state lines. He also threatened you. His lawyer will spin it that I'm violent. The thing is, I'm not really. I can still testify, and so can you."

"There's the footage too, likely," I said, and he nodded and let out a breath. He sat down next to me, his back against the wall.

"Let's hope it shows Carlos in his glory."

"I don't know what to do with you right now," I admitted. "I'm grateful to you for coming here with me and having my back. And yeah, I was scared of Carlos. I'm both pissed and happy that you hit him. I don't ever want you to go. I'm a mess right now."

"I wasn't going to put up with that shit, Lucy, I'm sorry, but maybe I fucked up. Fuck." He looked so remorseful that I felt bad for him. But I needed to think about this from the perspective of what was best for *Rob*, not what was best for me or Jake.

Then I did think about it. And what would be better for Rob than someone like Jake, who was willing to stick up for his mom?

I leaned my head on his shoulder and reached for his hand.

"I'm glad you were here tonight. I'm not happy you got in a fight, and it scared me. I'm freaked about what's going to happen. But I'm just . . . I'm glad that you were here."

And we sat in the hallway, not talking.

"No judge will take Rob away from me," I said after a moment, willing myself to believe it as I said it. "Carlos is an idiot. He was neglecting Rob here, leaving him in a hotel room while he gambled away his child support money." Then I smiled a rueful smile. "Good thing for the case that Carlos has made some mistakes, but bad for Rob. Fuck, I wish his dad were different. But he isn't."

"Should we get Rob?" Jake asked after a moment.

I nodded. I opened the door with the key I'd grabbed.

Rob sat in front of the television. He hadn't moved.

"You okay, mijo?"

He nodded, and I let out a breath. Time to talk to my kid about what had just happened. I sat down next to him and looked him in the eyes.

"Look. Me and your dad, we don't get along. This has nothing to do with you." I reached over and stroked his face. "You are the most precious thing to me. Your dad and I fought just now, and I'm sorry you had to hear it. I can't promise you that it will all be perfect in the future, but I can promise you that I love you, I always will love you, and I always will fight to make sure that you have the best life you can. Do you have any questions? Do you need to talk about it?"

"No, Mom." He seemed quiet, but he was always quiet.

"You ready to come find our room?"

"I get to stay with you now?"

"Yeah," I said. "And we'll do something fun tomorrow."

Rob's eyes lit up. "Cool. I wanted to go to the Luxor. They have Titanic artifacts. I read it in the hotel guide."

"Then we shall, mijo."

We grabbed Rob's bag and left for the Bellagio. Much better.

Despite the sumptuous surroundings, I knew it was going to be awkward to share a room with Rob and Jake, but I didn't want to make Jake get his own room. I couldn't say why. I just didn't.

Perhaps it was because he was becoming part of my family.

We entered the room, which had two beds. Making an executive decision, I said, "Rob, you and I sleep here, Mister Jake on the other one. Are you hungry?"

He shook his head no.

"It's been a long day. Let's go to bed."

Thankfully, it wasn't awkward having Jake with us. We took turns getting ready for bed, and then I crawled into bed with Rob, cuddling him.

Jake came over to both of us, ruffled Rob's hair, and kissed my forehead, saying "Goodnight." And then he crawled into his own bed and turned out the light.

24

A FORM OF LOVE

S unday morning, I woke up early in the hotel room, squished into about six inches of bed, Rob curled up against me, pressed into my back. A vast expanse of bed lay undiscovered on his other side. I had forgotten how my kid took over the bed. One night of cramped sleep wasn't the end of the world, but I preferred to actually have space in bed. But when children are asleep, they are the most perfect angels and can do no wrong. His little nose was upturned and he made a soft, whiffling noise as he slept.

I felt kind of crappy, like there was too much air conditioning in the room. I hoped it was just allergies.

Glancing over at Jake, asleep in the other bed, my eyes widened. Damn. Now he looked fine.

When he was awake, he looked like the romance heroes that I wrote about—tall, dark, and chiseled. Asleep, he was all of those things, but there was a softness to him. His lips pursed when he breathed and his eyelids flickered slightly, his black hair sleep-messy. He was so tall, he reached the end of the bed. Resting on his front, his hands under the pillow, I admired his muscular shoulders. He'd worn modest clothes to bed, a dark blue t-shirt and striped pajama pants, and there was something both comforting and arousing about his presence.

Perhaps sensing me staring at him, he blinked and opened his eyes, the color startling in the morning light.

"Hey," he whispered, across the way from me, in his separate bed, just out of reach.

"Morning," I whispered back. And I realized that I could really, very easily, get used to waking up to Jake.

"You and Rob sleep okay?"

"Yeah, though he takes up as much room as a baby elephant."

He gave me a glorious, sleepy, morning smile. "Let's make it a good day for him."

We spent the rest of the morning visiting the Strip, going through the Titanic exhibit at the Luxor, and eating lunch where Rob wanted. Spoiled? Maybe. But he didn't get to leave the hotel room yesterday, so I wanted to give him what Carlos should have given him (if he'd had permission to take Rob out of state). Then we drove home to Santa Barbara.

I called Amelia first thing Monday morning and told her everything. Carlos's kidnapping, Jake's punch, all of it. She told me that she would subpoena the surveillance tape, take Carlos's deposition, and get a statement from me and Jake. She also said that because I had custody, she didn't see this as being something that needed to be brought to the court on an emergency basis, but that we could bring it up at the next hearing, which took a ridiculously long time to get before a judge. It would be months before I had to deal with Carlos in a courtroom. But she made me email her the whole story so that she had notes of everything that happened. It was the best we could do for now.

A few days later, it was three days before Christmas. Despite my planning, it had still snuck up on me. House? Decorated. Presents? Wrapped. Rob? Excited. Me? That slight cold that I'd hoped was allergies back in the hotel room had bloomed into full-blown illness. I woke up with a fever, chilled, sweating, and coughing. I felt horrible. Really, death sounded better. Well, not really, but I was very sick. Rob came in my bedroom, worried when mom didn't get out of bed, bringing me water and saltine crackers.

I needed to see a doctor. I didn't have time to be sick. It was Christmas! After going to Urgent Care, where they gave me a prescription and diagnosed me with a form of pneumonia—which I'd probably caught in Vegas—I filled it and went home to bed.

When Jake called me from work, as he often did, I must have sounded dreadful, because he said, "Lucy, honey, give me your mom's number, and I'll have her bring you over some soup."

Since Jake and I had gotten back together after the hearing, I'd continued to feed him dinner, although he had nevertheless been working a lot. He took the time to come over and see me, but still, he worked way beyond a nine to five schedule. Well beyond. That man needed to learn that he just did not have to do that anymore. But he'd taken to texting or calling me throughout his busy work day, which I loved. My man thought about me, he was taking the time for me, and he communicated with me.

Too tired to think or argue with him, I gave him my mom's number.

A few hours later, she appeared at my door with a tureen of homemade tortilla soup, the spicy, clear-your-sinuses chicken broth its own medicine. Homemade soup is a form of love. I managed some broth and went back to bed.

Jake came by that night, earlier than usual, and checked in on me. Even though I was practically comatose, I appreciated his concern. He stroked my forehead, brought me ice water, and straightened my bedsheets. Then I heard him talking with Rob in the living room for a long time, and I dozed before falling asleep.

By Christmas Eve, I could tell that the antibiotics were doing something. I felt vaguely human instead of like death.

We were set to go to my parents' house for tamales and a good Christmas Eve dinner. My sister Celia drove up from Los Angeles and Sara and Georgie were coming, too. My brother Gabriel couldn't make it.

Jake wasn't coming, even though he was invited, because he was going to visit his dad. But we were going to have Christmas together. I made it through the family dinner, barely, then wrapped up in a blanket and lay down on the guest bed at my parents' house. After a while, my dad drove Rob and me home.

Christmas morning, I felt like a human being. I was still sick, but now living and human. Jake knocked on the door early and made us coffee. He and Rob made muffins out of a mix and cut up some fruit for a salad. It was the best thing ever. While our celebration was tiny and subdued, it still felt special.

I curled up on the couch with a cup of coffee, wrapped in a blanket, and watched Rob open his presents. I gave Jake a card that said, *Good for one weekend trip away, my treat.* Careful of how to act around Rob, he reached over and ran his finger along my hand. "Thank you. We'll use this as soon as you feel better."

He stood up, went to the tree, and pulled out two identically wrapped packages. Handing them to me, he said, "These are for you from me and Rob."

Surprised, I slid my finger under the tape of the first one.

It was a framed drawing by Rob of me. Jake had clearly spent time with Rob helping him draw because the picture, although childish, captured me—my hair, face, clothes, expression. I was smiling in the picture and smiling in real life.

"Did you draw this, mijo?"

"Yeah, Mom."

"You did such a good job. I want to know when you did this, and I want to know all about it. First come here and let me kiss you."

"You sure you're not contagious?" Rob looked wary.

"The doctor says no."

"Mister Jake and I spent time drawing when he watched me and when you were sick. It's fun."

I shook my head. "It's more than fun, son. It's art. It's wonderful." And then I turned to Jake. "It's so wonderful I might cry."

He beamed. "Open the other one."

I opened another drawing of me, framed and matted identically, but this one was by Jake. In it I was looking over my shoulder back at him, my ass in a mini skirt, my feet in high heels, and my mojo all on display. It was totally me—at least me when I was healthy.

"I love it, guapo," I whispered. "Thank you. We'll put them up today."

Jake nodded, and Rob said, "We thought you might like a homemade present, Mom."

"Yes, mijo, I do." I didn't know how to express how much it meant to me that a man, not Rob's father, took the time not only to teach him how to do something but show that it mattered— by presenting his creativity in a way that gave it legitimacy. I was honored by the present, and I was honored to know him.

So instead of saying this, I leaned over and kissed Jake lightly, in front of my son. "Thanks. And Merry Christmas."

25

ANOTHER DEFINITION OF HEAVEN

The next day, I felt even better and took Rob to Carlos's house. The order required a twenty-four hour visit from nine in the morning to the next day at nine. Obviously I wasn't happy to leave Rob with his dad after what had happened the last time, but there was nothing I could do about it. Watching Rob walk up the pathway to the front door, my heart dipped down low and stayed there, even after I saw him wave at me and the door close behind him.

I drove back home, cleaned up the detritus from the day before, and then decided to indulge in a spa day at home. I gave myself a facial and a pedicure, took a long bath, and a nap. This was a definition of heaven.

Earlier, I'd heard Jake do his usual routine of getting up, going for a run, getting ready, and going to the office, even though it was the day after Christmas. I shook my head. He still needed to learn that it was okay for him not to work crazy hours. Easy for me to say, though, progress on my book was going well, despite an interruption due to my illness.

That evening, late-ish, he came over for dinner, dressed in

his suit and tie. As we ate, we chatted about his day and how I felt. Then I asked, "When are we going to take your vacation?"

He looked at me thoughtfully. "I don't know. I'll have to get out my calendar and check my work schedule."

"Seriously? Pick a weekend and we'll go. It's better if it's a weekend that Rob's dad is watching him, but if not, I'll ask my parents to watch him." It was too damn hard to convince him to take a break that wasn't an emergency.

He looked at me, his cool dark eyes registering an emotion that I didn't understand. "For you, I'll do it." And it felt like it was settled.

After dinner, he took off his tie and we sat outside on the patio, looking at the pool and drinking wine. At Christmas time in California, you had to put on the air conditioning to have a fire in the fireplace. Tonight was no exception—even though it was cool, it wasn't cold. You could go swimming.

That gave me an idea.

"Come in the hot tub. Time to get some warm water on us. I think it will feel good."

Unlike scheduling a vacation, on this he caved easily. "Alright. I'll meet you out there."

As Jake walked back into his home, I heard his cell phone ring. "Don't answer your phone, *cariño*," I whispered to myself, willing him to be stronger than it.

Dammit, he answered it.

So we still needed to work on that.

I headed into my house and changed into my bathing suit. I wore my navy blue string bikini this time, with high-heeled espadrilles. Toting a towel under my arm and taking my keys, I teetered down to the pool, set down the towel, slipped off my shoes, turned on the jets, and tiptoed into the hot tub.

Aaaaahhhhh.

The complex had quieted down and gone to bed for the

night, although you were allowed to swim until ten. There were a few lights on in rooms, but otherwise it was a silent night.

A few moments later, Jake strolled down, holding a towel, barefoot, shirtless, wearing black swim trunks that sat low on his hips, tied with a white string. I wanted to undo that string. Between his work schedule and my time with Rob, even though I lived next door to Jake, I didn't get to spend much time with him naked. But since shirtless Jake was yummy yummy, this would have to do for now.

He walked over to the side of the hot tub and hopped down next to me. In the cool evening air, the steam from the water lingered a constant foot or more above it, creating patterns in the night. A dim light lit the water beneath us, but instead of being clear, the stream of air from the jets made the water an opaque white.

I wrapped my arms around his toned tummy and put my legs in his lap, cuddling into his chest as he cradled me. He kissed the top of my head, and put his finger under my chin, lifting it up and kissing my nose. Leaning in, he kissed me for real, very softly, very slowly, and very deeply. "Um-yum-yum," I moaned into his mouth, and the tone of our kiss went from cuddling to erotic. We bit gently at each other's lips, tasted each other's mouths, caressed the inside of the other with our tongues.

As the water bubbled around us, I ran my fingers up and down his back and his torso, while he held my back firmly. I could feel the stirrings of his erection under my leg resting on his lap, which made me feel oh-so-turned-on. He broke apart from our kiss.

Then.

"You had public sex down as a fantasy in your book, right?" Jake let his lips brush my ear as he spoke.

"Uh, yeah," I responded tentatively.

"It's dark and there's no one around."

I shivered all over, even though I was bathed in the hot water, and shook my head in disbelief. Then I looked at him. "Are you serious?"

He nodded. "Yeah," he whispered. "Now." And he pulled me into his lap so that I was straddling him.

Okay, now this was naughty. We were out in the middle of a housing development, where anyone could open up their window, look out, and see. They probably wouldn't see anything but a couple making out, but still, it felt like we were going to go show everyone, and that felt über hot.

I ran my hand down his chest to his trunks, felt for that pretty white string, and tugged, loosening it. Then, under the water, I slipped his trunks down his hips, freeing his hardening cock.

"Yes," I whispered back. "We're gonna do his."

Reaching between my legs, I started stroking his cock, as the water swirled around us, getting him aroused, letting him grow. The soft skin of his hard tip felt extra reactive beneath the water, twitching at my touch. He reached a hand into my bikini bottoms, at first grazing my clit, then rubbing it for real as he slowly and gently fingered me. He slipped two fingers into me, and I moaned again into his mouth.

Even though we hadn't had sex with each other for a while, it felt like we had all the time in the world. Everything was slow —caressing, feeling, touching. After he was fully hard and I was bothered, he broke our kiss. "Ready?"

I nodded. He untied my bikini bottom and pulled it off of me, setting it on the pool coping. Then he held my hip with one hand, positioning his cock with the other, and guided me down onto him.

With pleasure, I sunk down onto him, enjoying the way it all felt, all of the sensations—the cool night air, the warm water, his strong arms, his big cock in me. Holding my ass, he held me down. Then he guided me up, slowly, and it was his turn to moan. Then slowly, down again, riding him. Repeated. Leisurely, but with focus, strength, heat.

He reached between us and resumed fingering my clit as I continued to ride him, measured, deliberate, and sensual. Heaven help me, this was hot. The water was warm, my pussy stimulated, and my feet began to get super-hot from the blood flow around my body. Down, again and again, and then up, slowly, quietly, I made love to Jake in public.

And then I felt it. The quickening that I was going to climax. "I'm going to come," I warned him. Still, he continued to finger me, filling me up from the inside and massaging me on the outside. With a hallelujah and an angel's chorus, my body shuddered and climaxed. I desperately reached for Jake's mouth to muffle my moans.

After I came, he held my ample booty with both hands, guiding it up and down, but this time faster. I angled my body, made more friction for him, and he threw his head back, then returned, looked at me, and with a burst, came inside me, pumping, a raw look in his eyes. He held me down as he thrust up, and this set off a chain reaction that made me come again.

This was another definition of heaven.

The timer for the jets turned off.

Wrapping his arms around my back tightly, he ducked his head onto my shoulder and hugged me tightly.

"Stay with me tonight."

"Okay."

He kissed me softly, and then kissed my nose, retrieved my bikini bottoms, and tugged his pants back up. Dripping in the cool night air, we hurried for our towels and headed back up to our homes. I looked forward to being in bed *with* Jake instead of *next to* him or *next door* to him. Not separate. Together.

26

A LOT OF GOOD THINGS GET CREATED
IN WATER

He stood in my bedroom doorway, still wet, shirtless, wrapped in a towel, as I retrieved a set of pajamas and underwear, also still dripping from the hot tub, now shivering. I walked up to him, and he leaned down and kissed my nose.

"Grab your phone and charger in case Rob needs to call."

I did, and walked out of my home, locked it, and went into his. This felt both normal and monumental. It felt like I had the freedom, for one night, to do what I wanted. As a parent, upon the birth of your child, you received a near-constant tightening in your gut that didn't ever go away. You could never fully relax, because you knew that you were in charge of another person until they were an adult, if not longer. But for tonight, knowing that I had a night off, the clenching in my body loosened slightly. A wonderful feeling.

Now certainly, I was concerned that Carlos was going to pull some other shenanigans, but I knew, just knew, that he wouldn't hurt Rob, at least not physically. Carlos was selfish, and this could cause emotional hurt. It would be okay tonight, though. I hoped. After all, Carlos had issues with me, not with Rob. I hoped, at some level, that Carlos loved his son.

If I cared to admit it, there were also some deeper parenting questions presented by Rob visiting Carlos, which I really didn't feel like analyzing. Like, what would it be like for Rob to have a real relationship with Carlos? Was Carlos even capable of that? Did I want to give him a chance to develop a relationship with Rob? Certainly he didn't deserve it, and I didn't want him to. Based on his history, it was a joke. But if he really wanted a relationship with his son, honestly and truly, then perhaps I shouldn't stand in the way.

The thing was, I just knew he wasn't genuine. All this stuff was to get him out of paying child support so he could feed a gambling addiction. I was sure of it.

Actually, I didn't know for sure. Yes, Carlos behaved badly in Las Vegas and recently. But years of visitation on the weekend meant that he had a lot of time with Rob.

I didn't want to think about these things right now. All I could say was that for tonight, I felt a sweet ease that I rarely felt.

When I stepped into Jake's home, I got suddenly shy. I'd barely spent any time here. Most of the time he came to my home. But I loved being a part of his private world. I knew that he didn't show his artistic side to people at work, and it felt special to be let in, be privy to it.

I set my purse and keys on the counter and plugged in my phone, turning to him. He tilted his head in a welcoming way. "Let's get the chlorine off."

Ooh. Bath time with Jake.

Holding my hand, he walked down the hall, turning the lights off as we walked, and setting my pajamas in his room.

We stepped into his clean but austere bathroom, and slipped off our wet bathing suits, putting them in the sink. He turned on the shower to warm it up.

And then we were on each other again, but this time with more passion than the slow, sensual lovemaking in the hot tub.

No chance of anyone watching us this time, my hands grabbed his ass and pressed him to me, feeling his muscles, making him start to grow hard again. He reciprocated, taking his big hands up my belly to my breasts, covering one entirely with his hand, palming it, then running his long fingers over my nipples, fondling them, one then the other.

So the thing about sex with Jake. While he was no alpha hero of my books, ordering me around and being all bossy, it was really freaking great to do it with him. He lavished attention on me, his artist's fingers playing my skin, whether gentle, soft touches, or a fierce and fiery clasp. For the most part, he communicated well, which was interesting, given our first terrible misunderstandings with each other. In bed, there was no separation. No door between us, no wall separating us. He let me in. He asked me what I wanted and gave it to me. And he let me know what he wanted. So incredibly healthy.

It was also hot.

The shower warmed, we stepped in, the water a momentary shock to our systems, and we took turns lathering each other up, washing off the chlorine from the hot tub. I ran my soapy hands all over him, feeling his body, enjoying it as the shower sprayed into his chest, his upper back. Then, of course, the shower got steamier, as I ran my soapy hands up and down his hard cock, and he reciprocated on my body, slipping first a finger between my legs, and then two.

"You're good for round two?" I asked.

"Yeah. You?"

I nodded. "Let's get out of the shower. There's a drought, you know."

"A lot of good things get created in water."

But still he turned off the shower, grabbed me a towel, and

started drying me off, but didn't finish. He hoisted me up so that I was straddling him, and carried me to his bedroom, still wet.

We smelled the same, like clean shower. He laid me down gently on the bed and lowered his body on me, kissing me with the same passion as before, body to body. Rolling so that I was on top of him, straddling him, he pulled my hips toward his head.

"What are you doing?" I gasped.

"This," he answered, and he wiggled under me and started licking my pussy in earnest.

Oh my.

I'd never done oral sex before in this position, basically sitting on his face, and it was really fucking hot.

While I hadn't had sex in the time between Carlos and Jake, well, I'd done other stuff. But not this.

I reached behind me and angled back, stroking his cock as he licked and sucked my clit, using his hand to assist. He kept going, and going, and then I knew that I was going to come and I gulped, "Oh my loiuhggyrdd." My body, tender from his ministrations in the shower and primed from the hot tub, exploded again.

Straddling his face.

So naughty.

So hot.

When I came down, he pulled out from under me almost like a car mechanic, and then flipped me on my back. In a second, he slid his cock into my primed pussy.

Now, at this moment, immediately post-orgasm, my body barely done shaking and shivering, I entered a place of *kairos* again. I lost all track of time, and I lost any rational thought. All I did was feel, and I felt the connection with Jake, both physical with his body, but also the way he looked me in the eyes as he thrust, willing me to accept him, showing me the parts of him that he didn't show to anyone else. It was also this period of synergy—being connected together, we were creating something new, bigger than us. Like his drawing or my writing, the creative process and sex were similar. One person taking energy and applying it to something else and making something new, without thinking, only feeling. I knew that we were creating something here, which was beautiful.

Looking at me the entire time, he thrust into me repeatedly, until, with a shuddering jerk, he rammed into me harder than he'd ever done before. It didn't hurt, it just felt like he meant it, like he released, with a groan, all of the tension in him. Collapsing on my body, he nuzzled my shoulder and kissed it.

After a moment, he lifted himself up onto his elbows, and then gently slid out of me. He padded down the hall, got more towels, and gave me one to finish drying off.

Then he tugged on his boxers, and I put on my pajamas, and I crawled into bed, sated, clean-smelling, and happy. He got in bed behind me, spooning me, kissing my shoulder, and I drifted into a restful sleep.

27

EVEN BETTER

O kay.

I liked this.

I really, really liked this.

Waking up in the arms of a warm, sleepy guy? The way his strong thighs felt, curled into mine? His toned arm across my waist? His face nestled in my hair?

I had all of the good things, all at once—cocooned in a fluffy, supportive pillow of comfort. When I thought the word pillow my mind started free-associating—it was like marshmallow sweetness, hot fudge sundae goodness, and a warm summer breeze that made you feel simultaneously alive and at peace. Above all, I felt safe in his arms, as if nothing could go wrong, as if I were finally at home.

Yeah, I was totally falling in love with him.

This damaged, complicated man. Protective of me, attentive, caring. And the way he embraced the fact that I had a son? Amen and hallelujah. His artistic talent, his nobility. And the practical stuff, too—he was pleasant to be around, chatty, help-ful. He didn't snore. He didn't kick. He just peacefully slept, holding me.

Love.

I was totally in trouble.

Because I coughed, leftover from my illness, I woke him up. He squeezed me, holding me closer, and muttered "Morning," into my hair. I flopped over to look at him, and brought my hand up to run my fingers along his morning stubble.

After a moment of leaning into my hand, he spoke.

"You are so stunning, first thing," he started. "And all day."

I turned my head away.

"No, really. No makeup. This nose." He kissed it then shook his head. "I'm just grateful. You in my bed? It's amazing." He paused. His eyes darting around my face. "I was thinking, do you want to go look at my house? See the progress on construction?"

Again, being invited into his world. Cool. "Yeah, I'd like that, but we have to be back before it's time to pick up Rob."

"We can take him with." Even better.

"You're not going to work?" I asked, and then immediately regretted it, because he stiffened.

"Shit."

"Does that mean cancel?"

"No. That means we do not cancel. But yeah, I will have to get to work."

I wiggled a little closer to him. "Do you ever think about what it would be like if you didn't work at your firm? I mean, what would you do if you didn't work these long hours?"

"Probably work for legal aid. Help poor people who can't afford it and need justice."

The part of him that wasn't an artist really was Atticus Finch.

"Why don't you do that now? Do you need the money?"

He looked at me. "The remodel is expensive, yeah, but I have money saved. I don't spend that much. And I work hard so I make a lot."

"I don't mean to pry."

Hand on mine. Eyes on mine. "Lucy. It's okay. I don't need the money. I'm good."

"So yes, you could do that now," I pressed.

He gave me a half smile. "Maybe."

"If that happened, you'd have to totally change your thinking about all this stuff, huh? That you don't have to always go into the office? That you could work part time? It might take some effort, but I think if we worked on it—"

"I'm gonna shut you up by kissing you," he said, and he did.

I knew that he liked to change the subject when he didn't want to answer a question. But eventually, we were going to get to a place where we could talk about it. Work on it. Make his life more balanced. I just knew it.

Jake ended up taking the whole morning off, spending it by first exploring my body in the most naked way possible. We then picked up Rob, who'd had a good time at his dad's house. He loved the Christmas presents from his dad and that side of the family. I couldn't decide if I was pissed they were trying to buy my son or grateful they were showering him with gifts. I decided to be grateful.

But then I looked at the presents. Carlos had given him a complete set of Minecraft gamer books. If that wasn't perfect for my son, I didn't know what was. And it made me wonder if Carlos really did want to be more of a father to Rob. I watched my son stick his nose in the first book in the series immediately, as we drove away from his dad's house.

Then Jake drove us to his house located by Santa Barbara City College, on the hill with a view of the ocean. Spanish-style like everything in Santa Barbara, the work would update it to be environmentally-friendly, but sensitive to the original design.

A remodel like that had to cost a fortune.

His house was spectacular, not because it was a huge mansion, but because it was ideally located and had everything you needed, done in a really nice way. Two stories, it had an outdoor deck on the second floor that looked out to the water.

I could spend an eternity there.

Rob seemed to like it, although, typical kid, he didn't say much. Things like the practicalities of expenses and time for remodel didn't register on him. As we walked around, looking at the construction progress, I really watched Jake, seeing what it was like for him to take a morning off. Half-expecting him to go into withdrawals and start shaking, he didn't. He checked his phone once we got to his house, but so did I. A step forward, perhaps?

"How much longer do they have until construction is finished?"

"About three weeks."

That news hit me in the solar plexus. In three weeks, Jake wasn't going to be my neighbor. It didn't mean I couldn't see him, of course, but it was easier to see him when he could stop by on the way over to his house. Having to drive across town? I didn't know what that would mean for our relationship. Now that I was completely head over heels for him, I didn't want him to go so far away. Across town felt like across the world with how busy he was.

After we went back home, Jake walked us to my door, and Rob made a beeline to his room to put away his new presents. I lingered for a moment outside, kissing Jake lightly, and then he headed to work, promising to be home in time for dinner. But he'd taken the morning for me and my son. Another step forward.

When I walked in my house, my phone sounded. It was Georgie. "You feeling better, mama?"

"Yeah, mostly. I still have a cough. The doctor said it would take two weeks or so until I felt all the way better."

"So are you going to be up for going out on New Year's Eve?"

I hadn't been dancing with the girls in a long time. It sounded perfect. We made plans to go out with Sara to State Street, and I got my mom to babysit.

Then I called Amelia. She'd prepared papers to have my child support direct deposited out of Carlos's paycheck, which the judge granted, so that I didn't have to worry about him doing something crazy in the meanwhile. And she'd told the judge that Carlos was a flight risk because he'd taken his son to Vegas illegally. The judge had ordered Carlos not to do it again.

God, yes.

Go get him, girl.

The hearing in a few months still loomed over my head but I tried to forget about it and instead focused on my writing that afternoon.

When it came time for dinner, I realized something. I'd lived my entire adult life as a single mother, without looking forward to anyone coming home to me. I had Rob, but he was nearly always with me. But now that Jake was in my life, I felt like I had something that I'd never known I'd needed—someone to appreciate me. And I had someone to appreciate.

And I instead of appreciate, I really meant love.

28

TWO TRUTHS AND A LIE

N ew Year's Eve, after I'd taken Rob to my parents' house and got myself dressed in a pale pink, tight jersey dress with long sleeves, a ballet neckline, and a mini skirt, I closed my front door and tottered over to Jake's in silver, strappy heels. As I raised my hand to knock, he opened the door, wearing a light gray long-sleeve, button-down shirt, and dark gray slacks. He smelled divine.

"Ready?" I asked.

"No," he answered, looking me up and down, and I laughed. "You look insanely hot. I don't wanna leave."

"C'mon." I tossed my hair back. "We're going out and meeting my friends."

Truth be told, I wasn't totally feeling it. Still sick, still tired, but I still wanted to go out. I'd just take it easy and drink more water than margaritas.

We took a taxi downtown, not wanting to deal with parking, and walked to State Street, a popular area packed with shops, restaurants, and bars. When we arrived at the still-quiet restaurant where we were meeting Sara, Georgie, and their dates, I did a doubletake.

My attorney, Amelia, sat next to a stunning blond guy who looked like he was out of a Billabong ad. At their table, a pretty but edgy girl with long, lavender hair, chattered away, totally animated about something. She sat next to a drop dead gorgeous cowboy, who looked dangerous in a black cowboy hat and had his arm around her. Jake did a chin lift at Amelia and walked over, holding my hand.

"Lucy!" chirped Amelia, getting out of her seat, and showing off her curvy figure in a classic, wrap-around, little black dress. "Come meet my friends. This is Ryan Fielding, my fiancé," indicating the surfer, "Marie Diaz-Austin, my best friend since third grade, and her boyfriend, Will Thrash," indicating the chocolate-eyed cowboy.

Wait. My attorney was dating Ryan Fielding? As in the famous bazillionaire? Holy shit. It was immediately apparent that Marie was a firecracker. And the country boy, Will? Wow. One look at him and you needed a new pair of panties.

As I shook hands with each of them in turn, they all stood up and towered over me. Sheesh, I was always the shortest in the room. Just then, Georgie, Sara, and their dates, Anthony and Jordan, walked in, and there were more introductions. Georgie got a good look at all of the men, and then pulled me aside.

"Team. Fucking. Switzerland," she breathed, gawking, shifting her attention from Ryan to Will to Jake.

"It's unbelievable," I whispered back. "Plus the two you guys brought? This is going to be a fun night."

"Okay, we'll make room," squealed Marie. Before anyone could protest, she shimmied her body, clad in a dark gray, metallic tunic minidress and stilettos, around all of us, and started pulling over chairs to gather everyone at one large table, calling over a waitress to order drinks. We all helped to set up. I caught Will checking out Marie's ass as she leaned over to pull the table toward her. The waitress brought our drinks. Marie sat down, and continued, "We all don't know each other very well—"

"—we just met half of them—" interjected Amelia.

"—so I think we should play a game," Marie finished.

Amelia groaned. "No body shots this time."

"No. That's later. We're going to play Two Truths and a Lie."

"Marie. They—just—met—you," Amelia argued.

"And now we'll *really* get to know each other. If someone figures out your lie, you have to drink."

Sara looked worried. Georgie looked amused. And the two guys with them plainly didn't know what to think. "And we all have to play," Marie finished. "I'll go first."

Will started, "Darlin'," but Marie shushed him with a quick kiss. He got a look on his face like, "She does what she wants, and I think it's funny."

Marie cleared her throat, looked everyone in the eye, delighted, and announced, "I have voted for a conservative. I eat bacon. I only own vegan footwear."

Amelia started to talk, then stopped and looked at her, and then started again. "Wait, I thought you said it was two truths and a lie, not two lies and a truth." Sitting back in her chair, Marie looked satisfied. Amelia continued, catching on. "Wait, you either voted for a conservative or eat bacon, and neither of those would happen and hell hasn't frozen over, so who are you and what have you done with Marie?"

"I'm gonna guess that Will got her to vote for something conservative, after careful discussion and persuasion," said Ryan.

"Ding, ding, ding," said Marie.

"Naked persuasion," muttered Will, and I stifled a giggle.

"Wait, shit, that means I have to drink," said Marie. "Okay, Ryan's turn because he got it."

"Fuck," said Ryan. "Okay. Let me think." He paused for a

second and then spoke. "I surfed a huge wave at Teahupo'o. I was Freshman Prince when Amelia was Homecoming Queen in high school." And then he grinned wickedly. "I've let Amelia tie me up naked and do naughty things to me."

"Ryan!" squealed Amelia. "Lucy is my *client*."

Jake burst out laughing. "It's gotta be Teahupo'o. That's a crazy wave."

"You got it," said Ryan, and he took a drink.

"Jake's turn," ordered Marie.

He shook his head slowly, like he couldn't believe he was doing this and fingered the label of his beer bottle. And then he looked up at everyone and spoke in a clear voice. "I go for a six mile run every day. I never want to be anything but a lawyer. I fell for Lucy the moment I saw her."

"Holy fuckballs," said Marie.

My body seized up. Did he just say what I think he said?

"Wait," said Amelia. "Those are all true. Aren't they?"

Jake looked at her and shrugged, saying nothing.

Now it was Sara's turn to talk. "I think the lawyer is not true. I think you have other dreams."

"That's it," said Jake, and took a drink.

"Mister Privacy, my ass," I said, whispering in his ear. "What happened to Jake-I-don't-tell-anyone-in-the-office-about-my-business?"

He looked embarrassed. "Figured I'd try on sharing for a change," he whispered back.

"It's a good step," I agreed.

As the night went on, our group got louder and louder, and drunker and drunker. Hilarious Marie was the life of the party, and I could tell that if I spent any amount of time with her, I'd become her new best friend. Will pulled her onto the dance floor when they started playing a slow song, and sheesh, watching them dance was mesmerizing, they were so good.

Still not feeling well, I took it easy. After we finished our drinks and ordered new ones, the music got louder, and I pulled Jake out onto the dance floor. He wasn't the best dancer I'd ever been with, but he also wasn't the worst. He held me close and smelled wonderful, a familiar scent, like he belonged to me. I loved it.

At midnight, we gathered to watch the ball drop on the television screens at the front of the restaurant. As we all counted down the seconds to the new year, I really felt excited for the new year with my new boyfriend. It was going to be a good year.

When the clock struck midnight and the restaurant played "Auld Lang Syne," Jake leaned down and kissed the hell out of me, lifting me up and swinging me around at the end. I saw Ryan catch his eye appreciatively, like, "Dude, nice one."

Getting tired, I made my way to the restroom to leave. As I left, I saw Jake pull his cell phone out of his pocket and answer it. The first time all night that I'd seen him do it.

When I got back from the restroom, I couldn't find him. I called over to Georgie, "Where did Jake go?"

"He said he had to go, it was an emergency, and he left you some money for a taxi."

Wait, what?

"What was so important that he had to leave?" I asked.

"I don't know," said Georgie, "but he looked panicked and said he had to go immediately, and to apologize to you."

There had to be an explanation for this, right? I hoped that he was okay, or that whatever had happened, was going to be alright. But if it was work-related, I was going to be pissed. I'd give him the benefit of the doubt, but I was seriously worried about whatever his emergency was, and how he had just left without saying goodbye. It was weird—I wanted a reason for his rudeness, but I also didn't want him to have a real emergency.

Ryan called a car for me and sent me home in style, and I

went to my bed and undressed, slowly. I'd texted Jake in the restaurant and in the car, to no answer. Finally, I just texted, "Whenever you get this, call me or come by. I need to see you." And then I tried to go to sleep.

29

THAT DOESN'T SCARE ME

My phone pinged, waking me up, at the same time that someone knocked hard on my front door.

Jake.

Grabbing my phone as I crawled out of bed, I glanced at the time. Five in the morning. And a text from Jake, saying that he was outside. Ignoring my robe and my sleepy face, I ran down the hall and flung open the door.

My boyfriend stood there, exhausted, serious lines etched on his forehead, his hair completely disheveled.

"What happened?" I asked. "Come in, come in." Instead of waiting for him to move, because he seemed to be made of granite, I grabbed his hand, closed the door and locked it behind him, then pulled him down the hall into my bedroom. He followed me, looking defeated, not saying anything. We got to my room and looked at each other. Poor guy was completely lost. "Are you okay, cariño?" I whispered.

He let out a breath. "My dad. He had a heart attack and went into cardiac arrest. It's bad. He was up here in Santa Barbara visiting friends, so he's at Cottage Hospital. Luckily, he was at a restaurant that had a defibrillator. They acted fast, and managed to save him."

"Oh no," I gasped. "I'm so sorry. Did you go see him?"

He nodded. "They made me wait. When I finally got to see him, they didn't let me in the room for very long, and he was asleep. I'll have to go back tomorrow, I mean today, at visiting hours."

"Okay." It was so late. He needed to rest. "Nene, come to bed." I started unbuttoning his shirt. "You need sleep."

He nodded and just stood there, tired and done, in my bedroom, letting me undress him, while he rubbed his eyes and ran his hand along the back of his neck. I did this simple act with as much care as I could, easing the clothes off of him, helping him with his shoes, getting him down to his light blue boxers. I got under the covers and made room for him.

He crawled into bed next to me and wrapped me in a fierce hug, front to front, shoving his face in my hair. He shook, and I held him, trying to squeeze all the pain out of him, let it transfer to me, let me help him.

"Lucy," he choked. "What's going to happen to him?"

"I don't know. But the doctors will take care of him. The thing you need to do is get some sleep so that you can be rested to go see him tomorrow."

He didn't respond verbally. Instead, he just held me tighter. He was struggling to keep it together.

"It's okay to let it out," I whispered into his chest.

Shaking his head into my hair, he refused to say anything. But that was okay.

After a while, his arms relaxed around me, and I could tell that he'd fallen asleep. I wiggled so that I was comfortable and fell asleep, too.

The next morning, I awoke with a start, coughing still, but Jake was already up and out of bed, putting on his pants.

"Sorry to wake you," he said.

"Where are you going? Stay."

"Visiting hours are soon. I gotta go."

I nodded. "Can I come?"

He paused. Then finally he said, "Yeah. But they don't allow kids. Rob can't come."

"I'll call my parents. They'll love a few extra hours with their grandson."

An hour later, we walked into Cottage Hospital, hand in hand. When we were finally allowed into Mr. Slausen's room, I was struck by how much Jake looked like his father. Even though he was sleeping, the elder Mr. Slausen had the same distinguished face as the younger. Something to look forward to.

"Hey, Dad," Jake said, reaching out and holding his father's hand. I noticed how Jake's artist's fingers looked next to his dad's older hand. They had the same shape, just Jake's were younger, the skin smoother.

His dad didn't respond. "I just wanted to come and say hi, you know. I hope you're feeling better."

He let go of his dad's hand and pulled over a chair by the bedside, then reached out and held it again. "Dad, it's incredibly rare that you survived what you went through. Incredibly rare. I am so grateful they got to you fast. So now you gotta do it, you know? You gotta get better. Because you survived it and it's like six percent of people who do. So don't let me down, Dad. I know you'll get better."

I'd never heard Jake talk like this. He sounded earnest, almost like a kid. He also had almost an East Coast accent that I had never picked up on before. Slipping into a pattern from his youth.

But then he looked over at me. "Dad, this is my girlfriend, Lucy. She's the best thing that's ever happened to me. You gotta get better so you can meet her, okay, for reals now."

We stayed until visiting hours were done. Then, instead of going home, I asked if we could go to the beach.

Once we got there, we took off our shoes and walked along the water, watching the waves crash and feeling the cool sand from the winter day. New Year's Day. A day of new beginnings.

Neither one of us talked as we ambled the entire length of the cove and then headed back, hand in hand, looking out at the water. But when we passed by a group of intrepid January sunbathers, Jake spoke suddenly.

"I'm not going to do it anymore," he declared.

"What?" I had no idea what he was talking about.

"I'm *not*."

"Not going to do what?"

"Wait until I have a wakeup call like him to do what I really want to do."

Yay, I thought. But what I said was, "Oh?"

"I'm not going to be a slave to my job anymore. I don't like it that much."

"No?"

"No. I like some parts of it, but no."

"'Kay." So happy he figured this out. So happy he did it without me pushing him too hard. So happy he came to this decision on his own.

He stopped walking and grabbed me. "You'll help me, right?"

"Of course. Help you how?" We stood on the beach, feet buried in cool sand, the waves crawling in. Then we didn't move in time, and a low wall of water got us. Feet all wet but we didn't move.

"Help me figure out what I'm going to do. You remind me of a dream I had. A dream that I could do my art, and, well, I don't want to scare you, but have a family, and just live. Alive. Not be holed up in an office. Not be so irresponsible that my family suffered. But just be able to have a normal life, the kind that I didn't get growing up."

"That doesn't scare me."

He moved his head to the side and his eye color flicked to a deeper blue than I'd ever seen it, like all of a sudden he was alive. And he looked at me with a passion I'd never seen before from anyone, let alone him. "Good."

30

MONOLITHIC PRIMORDIAL SOUP

Jake leaned over, wrapped his arms around me tightly, and kissed me on the beach, a desperate, giving-taking-needing kiss, the kind that you remembered afterward, not just because your lips were kiss-stung and swollen, but because you remembered the way it made you feel. This kiss made me feel essential to his life. Like I was a requirement for him to be able to breathe or to function. No other world existed except the world that I was creating with him.

A phenomenal kiss. I loved it.

And I admitted it—I loved him. I'd tell him soon enough.

The vast ocean spread before us, murky but nevertheless sparkly in the early January sunlight. I thought about the primordial soup that made up the contents of that water—all of the kelp and plankton and sea life living within it. So many creatures coexisted in the ocean, but we normally just looked out and saw water and surface waves, nothing more. The waters of this earth looked so deceptively simple and beautiful from above, almost monolithic, but underneath, and within them, one found peace and terror, creation and death, activity and entropy. It was complicated, but if you paid attention, you learned that within the waters, there was a constant source of growth and expansion and a whole lot of astonishing beauty.

I didn't want to leave the beach. We kissed more.

But then, becoming self-conscious of the sunbathers who watched us but pretended not to, we walked hand-in-hand back to his car, putting on our shoes when we got off of the sand.

"Let's get your son."

We walked into my parents' modest suburban house to pick up Rob, and my mother—who was no taller than me—reached up and pinched Jake's cheeks. Oh, for crying out loud, he wasn't twelve too. Then she looked at me and said, "Lucinda, he is muy guapo."

"I know, Mom."

My mom turned to Jake. "It's so nice to meet you. I like how you call me to bring my Lucinda her soup when she was sick. Mijo, how are you? How is your papa?"

He gave her his melancholy half-grin, which was nevertheless devastating, and I saw my mom, not immune to his charms, falter a second and recover. "It's nice to meet you in person, and thanks for asking, Mrs. Figueroa. He's not doing that well. I'm going to go back and get him after I drop Lucy and Roberto home."

"I'm so sorry to hear that," said my mom. "I will pray for him."

"Thank you," said Jake politely, and he looked around the living room. A bookshelf held copies of my books. Pictures of me and Roberto and other family members were framed and put on the walls and on shelves. Neat but cluttered.

Then I realized that Jake didn't have a family home like this and never would. I couldn't give him a different past. We'd have to work on a different future.

My dad had been in the den watching television, but he came out and sized Jake up. My dark-haired, mustached father wore a plaid, button-down shirt, jeans, and a large belt buckle. He looked like he belonged in the country, even though he was a mechanic in the city. Standing next to Jake it was immediately apparent that height was inherited. My father came up to about Jake's shoulders. Boy.

"It is nice to meet you, Jake. I wish your father a speedy recovery," said my dad formally.

"Thank you Mr. Figueroa, it's nice to meet you too. And yes, I hope he gets well soon."

"Now. You must eat. You need to keep up your strength to take care of your papa." My mom took his hand and pulled him to the dining room table. "Sit down, I will bring you food. I have *chile colorado, frijoles, arroz—*"

"Mom, he's not used to people fussing over him," I started, but she completely ignored me. I eyed Jake, and he looked amused. Oh well, he did need to eat.

And I supposed he needed to also get used to having people take care of him.

"Lucy, did you have lunch?" called my mom from the kitchen.

"No."

"I'll make you lunch, too." What was it with food being equal to love? I supposed that being fed meant that you were cared for. This was normal for me. My mom always took care of me like this. She worked in a grocery store, after all.

But I thought that even though this was normal for me, it was probably strange for Jake.

The more I thought about these things, the more I wanted to expose him to them, and make it so that they were his new normal. I was so glad that he was going to let me help him stop being a workaholic businessman and start being just Jake.

Then my son walked in the room, sock-clad, looking rested.

"What did you do today, mijo?"

"Watched the Rose Parade and football. Played games with abuelo."

"How much Minecraft did you play?"

"Some." Then he spotted Jake. "Mister Jake, you're here!" And he ran over and gave him a hug.

Well.

Now I wasn't jealous of my own child, but I noticed that he didn't give *me* a kiss, but Jake got a full-on welcome with a hug.

Interesting.

But Jake needed a full-on welcome from a child. And I loved that my son seemed to really like Jake. The next thing I knew, Jake had asked Rob about his science fair project, and was agreeing to help him make something. Glory and hallelujah, I didn't have to do it.

My mom served us plates of tacos and sat down with us. She turned to Jake.

"Do you read her novels? They are as spicy as my chile colorado."

"Mom!"

"It's true, mija."

"She likes to embarrass me," I told Jake.

"I'll have to read them," he said. "Priority."

Just then the door opened and my younger sister Celia walked in. "Hey!" she said. "Happy New Year!"

Because she lived in Los Angeles, we saw her on holidays and today was no exception. My brother was too far away to see often. My sister worked as a makeup artist at a high end salon and loved it. While she was two years younger, in all other respects, she was my twin—same looks, same body, same high maintenance, same attitude.

"Celia," my mom said. "Mija, how was the drive? Not too bad?"

"Not too bad. Lucy, you feeling better?"

"Mostly. I'm not all the way back to normal."

She turned and gave Rob a kiss, squeezing his cheeks, hugged my mom and dad, and then noticed Jake. She put her hands on her hip, all sassy-Lucy. But I guess it was sassy-Celia.

"Who's this, Lucy?"

"Nice manners. This is Jake, my boyfriend."

"How'd you get one of them to come to life?"

"Stop it! He's a real person."

Jake stood up. "I'm Jake Slausen. Nice to meet you."

"Celia Figueroa." Then she turned to me. "Jesus, Lucy, I know you waited forever to find one, but how did you find this one?"

I rolled my eyes. "Nice, real nice. And he found me." And I proceeded to tell her about how he walked in on me in my bikini. She laughed and pulled up a chair and had tacos with us. Rob sat next to his grandfather, talking his ear off about Minecraft. But I heard Rob tell my dad about how Carlos took him to a rock shop so they could look at all of the rocks that were in Minecraft, like lapis lazuli. And that's not what I expected Carlos to ever do. Huh. Meanwhile, my mom and sister peppered Jake with questions about art and photography and law.

"So what do you see in my sister?" asked Celia. "She's always got her head in the clouds, all these ideas in books."

"Oh my God," I said, and gave her a push.

"She seems pretty squared away to me," Jake replied. And I loved him for saying that because I'd worked hard my entire adult life to be pretty squared away for my kid. He'd noticed.

I was glad to give Jake some glimpses of my family, because when he was with me, I was at home, and I thought the same was true for him.

31

NEGATIVE SPACE

A few weekends later, Roberto went to his dad's, and Jake and I attended the final art class of this session. At the end of the class, after I'd dressed, I walked over to him at the easel, and he showed me what he'd drawn. With intricate, exquisite detail, he'd captured my body on paper—my small waist darting in from my booty, the strength of my legs, the tips of my nipples. Using a single line, he'd drawn my cheekbone, and with another, the under edge of my lower lip.

But the part of the paper where he hadn't drawn anything also mattered. I'd heard the professor talking about negative space from time to time—the idea that the seemingly empty visual space around an object, not necessarily the object itself, could be drawn. Rather than fill up the paper with clutter, Jake drew the essentials, just what was needed to convey the subject —namely me—and no more. This left a lot of blank paper, but it felt vibrant, not barren.

He needed negative space in his life too. We all did. We often went through life trying to fill it up with work, activity, noise, and busy-ness. And while all of those things could be fun—I loved the activity—we also needed quiet time to write, create, and live our lives. I thought that's what Jake had been doing—burying himself in his work and his busy-ness, so that he didn't have to really live. And who could blame him for being fearful of really living his life? His childhood had been super scary. For so long, he'd avoided the fear, and side-stepped his life, by filling it up with work. This way, there'd been no room for living. He slept, ate, exercised, and went to work, and filled up all of the space on the paper of his life. No art to it.

Now, finally, he was starting to live, to not pack so much work into his days. To instead trust that it was okay to be unscheduled. That was how I operated—I normally wrote when Rob was in school, but not on any particularly rigid schedule. With joy, I watched him start to get that roominess in his days, paring down his list of things to do to what was essential and allowing for free time on his calendar, so that he could live his life for real. So far, so good with keeping his vow to not work so much. He'd started coming home at six or seven o'clock, sometimes earlier. Since previously, his habit had been to come back at nine o'clock, this was major progress. I didn't say a word about it. Inside, though, I was dancing. *Yay.*

Things were looking brighter for me, too. Amelia had called me after New Year's. She'd successfully gotten Carlos's paycheck docked for child support. We had a hearing scheduled where we would hash it all out—the kiss in the courthouse, the trip to Las Vegas, the fight, all of it—but the court had ordered Carlos and me to a family law mediation process. This was where we met with a mediator and tried to negotiate a child custody settlement out of court. While I didn't want to talk to Carlos, Amelia assured me that I would be in a separate room and I didn't have to see him. Fine. That wasn't for a few weeks, though. If we didn't resolve it, then we would have a full-scale hearing. I was worried about the cost of all of this, and I hated having the uncertainty stress me out. So I'd go to the mediation.

Jake folded up his notepad and packed up his art supplies. Still perched on his artist's stool, he pulled me by my waist so that I stood between his muscular, jean-clad thighs. Then he looked at me, regarding me carefully. "I am so glad that I took this class. So fucking happy." And he kissed me on the nose with a smile.

It was important that he was smiling. While his dad was still in the hospital, he was recovering. I knew that Jake went there at lunchtime every day. But he was at my house for dinner. And we were starting to call my house his home.

And I'd also taken another step. After I kissed him in front of Rob on Christmas, since he was around so much and since Rob knew him and liked him, he'd taken to spending the night at my house. The mom part of me wondered if I was going too fast with it, but it felt right—Rob knew he was my boyfriend. I still worried about how Rob would take it if Jake and I broke up. Rob knew he'd be imminently moving, so I hoped that having him stay with us for now would be okay. Second-guessing myself as a parent was second-nature.

We left the art class and, instead of Jake going to work, as was his habit, we went to the hospital to check on his dad. After assuring himself that his dad was stable and recovering, we left and went to lunch. Then he looked at me, an unusual, impish, conspiratorial look on his face.

"Let's go do something."

"Sure," I agreed easily. Spontaneity was a good thing and something that I didn't often get as a single mom. The freedom that I had while Rob was with his dad was something that I could be grateful for, even if I had my problems with Carlos. I was still tired from being sick, but I was happy to go and play.

"I feel like I'm playing hooky. Yes, I know it's Saturday," he said in response to the *dude-are-you-serious?* look on my face, "but let's go down to L.A. and go to the Getty."

The huge Getty Museum perched on a hilltop, surveying all
of Los Angeles, its fancy Italian stone warming the modern
building. Jake's eyes lit up as we took the monorail up to the
museum. We wandered around the galleries, looking at a
photography exhibit that interested him and then at the illumi-
nated manuscripts, which interested me as a writer. I marveled
at how someone took that much time to decorate a single page.
When I wrote, I typed pages on my computer so quickly. Each
page of an ancient, hand-written manuscript, decorated with
ornate designs, must have taken days. It made me think about
how my words might matter more than the value I placed on an
easily delete-able electronic document. What if every word
needed to have that kind of artistic weight?

As we walked through the galleries, I noticed the reverent
way that Jake looked at art. He stopped, giving each piece attention, commenting on styles, subjects, artists, compositions.
Totally in his element. I enjoyed seeing it. My style at a museum
was more to go through quickly before heading to the gift shop.
But I loved taking this slower pace with him. It was a form of
negative space in our lives. Recharging at a museum for
inspiration.

He got naughty too, when we were looking at the nudes—
women with glorious curves lolling on chaise lounges, or in clas-
sical poses. "We need to get you back home, don't we?" he said in
my ear, coming up behind me.

"Why is that?"

"I think I need to see you naked."

"That's nothing new—you drew me today."

He laughed. "Okay, I want you naked, but bent over my bed,
Lucy, that glorious ass all mine. I want to use my tie. Then I want
you on top. All your beauty. Mine."

Uh huh. That. We could do that.

He continued. "Think your parents will watch Rob next weekend?"

"Yeah, they don't mind."

"Then we're going to go away. I'll take you up on my Christmas present."

Yay.

32

CONNECTIONS

"So, as I recall," said Jake thoughtfully, as he inserted the key into the hotel room door, "one of the items on your wish list—your list of things you write in your books—was sex in a hotel room. Correct?"

I nodded and grinned.

It was the following weekend. Jake's dad had been discharged from the hospital and was now home, on a slow but steady recovery. Roberto had gone back to school after winter break. I was almost done with my first draft of my new book. And Jake? He'd told me that he'd given a few of his cases to other attorneys in his office, so that he could have free time. Free time! After all, there was no law saying he had to single-handedly take care of all of the work in the office by himself. Instead of filling up his time with the office, he came to me. He helped Rob construct a papier-mâché volcano for his science fair project, complete with red-painted lava and well-contoured landscaping. And now he let me take him on vacation.

One of the few times that he'd ever been away for fun. So special.

I'd wanted to go to a place where we could drive away for the weekend, so we went to Palm Springs, which had lovely weather in winter. While, sure, it had the reputation of being a golfing paradise for the retirement set, it also had a thriving gay community, wonderful shops, and cool architecture. It was a whole lot of fun.

Deciding that we needed to have the whole mid-century modern experience, I booked us into a boutique hotel near downtown—a converted 1950s apartment complex with a retro-style pool and patio, a kitschy pink-tiled bathroom, and a bedroom that even had a record player with Frank Sinatra records.

We set down our bags, took a quick look around, put on a record, and collided into each other. In seconds, we were tumbling out of our clothes. First, my wedge heel espadrilles were off. Next, his shirt, buttons undone and thrown to the side. Then, his shoes kicked off. He didn't even bother to take his belt out of the loops, he just undid it, unfastened his pants, and they were off. My blousy lavender shirt? Off. My shorts? Off. And then I could feel him, his soft skin running under my fingers, his lips insistent, and his hands all over me.

With a flick, he released my lavender bra, pulled it off of me, and backed away from me, wearing only his boxers and socks. His eyes raced around my body, lingering on my nipples, my belly button. And then his socks were gone in a flash.

He did a little twirling motion with his fingers, wanting me to spin. As I was wearing just some little lavender panties, I knew that he would get a full view of my ample booty. So I stuck it out, smiled, turned slowly, and gave it to him, and I heard him groan.

"Dat. Ass. Lucy."

When I finished turning, his erection was no longer within his boxers, because his boxers had disappeared. And my man stood there naked, wanting me, and I wanted him back.

"Let's get you wet," he said and he walked me backwards to the bed. Perching my booty on the edge of the bed, he gently spread my knees and then kneeled between my legs. Next, slowing the frenzied tempo, he bent forward and let the tip of his tongue softly dance on my pussy, teasing it, teasing me. Darting around, his tongue made my whole body quiver. Ooh baby. Then he flattened his tongue, licking the whole length of me, which felt like I was on fire from my toes to my waist. So hot. And then he did it again. After a while I couldn't take it anymore.

"Come up," I moaned, "I want you inside me. Now, please, guapo. I want your cock in me."

Giving me a half grin, he stood up, put his hands under my ass, and moved me up the bed. He covered me with his body, embracing me, resting his torso between my legs.

"Now," I ordered. "*Now*. Move up. I need you inside me. Fill me up, Jake."

At my words, my frank begging, he positioned his hard cock at my entrance and slowly, carefully, slid in, and stayed there, enjoying the connection. Now this was what I wanted.

"Oh that feels so good," I groaned. "God, I love you inside me."

I didn't realize that I'd dropped the L-word until he looked at me quizzically. "Me too," he said and I wondered what he was referring to. And then finally he started to move, kissing me, kissing my cheek, my shoulder, the top of my hair, running his hand down my curves.

But then suddenly, he grabbed my ass and flipped us over, keeping the connection, so that I was on top, astride him. My hair reached down past my shoulders, and some of it covered my breasts. He swept that hair aside, brushing it behind my back, and lifted his hands up to rub my nipples, cupping my breasts.

"Ride me," he said. "I want to see you."

I began to move up and down on his cock, thumping him soundly, so wet, enjoying the way we were connected, enjoying the sensations of him inside me and under me, and I started to build my own orgasm. He reached out and stroked my clit insistently, letting me come. I did. Hard.

Once I came down, he gave me the little twirling motion again, with his finger. I looked at him, questioning. "Turn around, I want to see your ass," he urged. "Keep the connection."

Very carefully, I leaned and moved around, so that I was now facing away from him, and he reached up and fit his hands along my booty, massaging my cheeks, and spreading them.

"Oh yeah, baby," he groaned. "Win."

Moving up and down, I gave him a view of my booty. Suddenly he knifed up, wrapped his arms around my middle, and flipped us over again. This time, I was on all fours. I loved it this way.

Reaching down between my legs, he again massaged my clit until I climaxed. A few more thrusts and he pushed into me, letting go with a groan.

We collapsed on the bed, in each other's arms, sated and spent.

He nipped at my shoulders, oddly energetic. I still hadn't recovered totally from my pneumonia and felt tired. Maybe I needed a follow up visit.

"Was that how you'd write it, Lucy?"

"It was better."

He laughed and hugged me. "What do you want to do now?"

"Go swimming, of course."

That night, we went to an old-school steak house, and I ate the best steak ever. After dinner, we drove up along the foothills with the windows rolled down, enjoying the warm air and parked, looking out at the lights in the desert.

Saturday morning, I awoke to Jake gently pressing his finger up and down my arm. He always looked so glorious first thing in the morning, his black hair tousled, and his eyes piercing. Oh, and shirtless. That was a good look, too.

"Sorry to wake you," he whispered.

"S'okay," I answered, worn out from yesterday's sex and swimming. "I needed to get up. We have a lot to do today."

"Lucy, I don't care if we never leave this hotel room. I don't want to do anything but be with you."

And for some reason, his words made me emotional. I wasn't usually that hormonal, but they made me feel like crying. God, I'm not a crier but lately? I'd cried more than I had since Carlos originally left me. I didn't know what was happening. It must be that time of the month. "I don't ever want to leave you," I blurted. Then I admitted in a whisper, a secret thought that I had felt, but not vocalized, ever since the day I saw the construction on his new home. "I'm scared of what is going to happen once you move away from me back to your home. Are you going to go back to being a workaholic? When will I see you?"

Very seriously, he looked at me, then leaned over and kissed my nose. "Lucy, I love you." Chills erupted over my skin. "We'll figure it out."

As if it were that simple.

"You love me?" I whispered.

"Yeah," he whispered back. "I do. I fell in love with you when you brought me the tamales. Maybe before. When I brought you the panties. So strong. So beautiful, naturally. So wise."

"You don't mind that I have a son?"

"Of course not," he said. "You're a powerhouse, and you've handled everything on your own. I'm making room in my life so that I can help you. I want to be with you. I don't care where we live. That can be figured out."

"I love you too," I said, and a tear slipped down my nose. "I fell in love with you when I realized that you were protecting me and with the way you took care of Rob."

He smiled, his foxy toothpaste smile and wrapped his strong arms around me.

"Love making or breakfast?"

"Both, I think."

Later that day, we shopped in the antique and vintage stores, visited the art museum, loving the sketch books on display, which showed the thought processes the artists went through to create, went swimming in the vintage pool, and cleaned off together in the shower, which led to a few more orgasms. We went to sushi for dinner and, warm and sated, fell asleep comfortably.

The next morning, my head was in the toilet.

He came to the door of the bathroom and knocked quietly. "Are you okay, honey?"

"Yeah," I called, not feeling it. I'd been feeling bad since Christmas. "I will be." And I slumped up against the wall. All sorts of scenarios ran through my head of what was wrong with me. What it could be.

But all I wanted to be was home.

33

RECIDIVISM

Four days later, it poured rain in Santa Barbara. With our drought, we needed it. I walked into my doctor's office, checked in with the receptionist, and sat down on the one open seat. The waiting room was packed with people, and four of the women surrounding me had huge bellies.

Oh shit. I knew it wasn't contagious. But still, I felt unbearably uncomfortable being here.

The office attempted to have a personality with funky patterns on the chairs and piles of magazines. Regardless, it was an institutional doctor's office. I mainly focused on trying to avoid panicking.

Every morning since Sunday in Palm Springs I got sick. My boobs hurt. I was achy. And so, so tired.

No fucking way.

This couldn't be happening again. Right? *Right*?

The door opened to the waiting room and a nurse with a clipboard and purple scrubs called, "Lucy?" Gathering my purse, I stood up. Going to this appointment on my own was my idea. I'd made the appointment for a time when Jake was at work and Rob was in school, not wanting to tell anyone in case I was wrong. Now that I was actually here, however, I knew that I'd made the wrong decision. Some support would have been welcome. I always was surrounded by friends and family. And Jake. Bad idea to not have them because I knew deep down what I was going to find out today. I was sure that my suspicions would be confirmed. A woman knows. I just didn't understand why it had happened.

The nurse weighed me in the hall and then walked me into an exam room. I perched on the paper-covered examination table, the crinkle sound registering loudly in the quiet room.

I breathed in and out.

"When was your last menstrual cycle?" she asked.

I told her. "I'm three days late," I whispered. "I'm on the pill. It's always on time, exactly."

"Let's have you take a urine test." She opened a drawer, pulled out a cup, and handed it to me. I hopped off the table, and walked the plank down the hall to the bathroom.

It felt like a doomed trip, like I was headed for my sentencing date at my trial. What was the punishment going to be? Another eighteen years?

The hall closed in on me as I walked to the bathroom.

I peed in the cup.

I went back to the room.

The doctor came in.

Yep. Pregnant.

I was in a daze. I managed to ask, "How did this happen? I mean I know how, but I was on the pill."

"When you were prescribed doxycycline for the community acquired pneumonia, it lowered the effectiveness of your oral contraception for about five days."

I just stared at her.

She repeated in English, "The antibiotics made the pill not work. So, obviously, since you're pregnant, stop taking your pill, and start taking a good prenatal vitamin." She went on, giving me instructions and handing me pamphlets. Somehow I got out of there, with a follow up appointment scheduled. I left the building and, having forgotten an umbrella, managed to have the perfect luck to step outside when there was a torrential downpour. Then I stepped in a puddle.

Soaked, I got in my car and buckled myself in.

I was pregnant with Jake's baby.

And all I could think was that I did it again. Total recidivist. You would think that I'd learned from my past. But I was pissed because I *had* learned from Carlos. I'd learned so fucking much. I'm not stupid. I was careful. Since Rob, I'd been on the pill *and I hadn't even had sex for twelve years*. That's how careful I was. This was not fair.

But now I was yet again going to be a mother.

I started crying, my body chilled, sitting in my driver's seat, rain pouring down, not going anywhere. Raging hormones stirred up the memories of the abandonment I felt when Carlos had broken up with me and then refused to have anything to do with me after he'd found out I was pregnant. I'd made a promise to myself that I would never get into the same circumstance that I was in with Carlos, but here I was, a second time over pregnant, unwed woman.

Fuck.

I was collapsing on the inside, my brain resurrecting every negative thing that I had ever heard said, not just to me, but in general, about pregnant, unwed mothers. Years of being strong? Sassy? Wise? Gone. Now thoughts had found a landing space somewhere in my psyche in the form of shame and I started talking to myself in the most unhealthy way. My baby daddy was going to leave me. I was going to have to fight for child support again.

Tears streaming down my face mixed with the rain in my

hair, but I had to leave the parking lot. I needed to clean up my face so that I didn't freak out Rob when he got home from school. Thinking of a way to tell Jake was going to take some time, and I had no idea when to do it.

I made it home somehow, but when I got there I couldn't have told you how I did it, I was so lost in my thoughts. Toxic thoughts.

I opened my front door and an overwhelming smell of good food invaded my nostrils. What on Earth?

"Lucy?" called Jake. "I wanted to surprise you with making you lunch. I thought you would be here, but when you weren't, I started cooking."

Wiping my eyes, I set myself in the doorway, dripping, unsure of what to do. He rounded the corner from the kitchen, took one look at my face, and his smile disappeared. "Honey, what is it?"

I stood there, mute, unable to tell him. Tears streamed down my face again, and I held onto the doorknob for support. I dropped my purse and just looked at him.

He closed the gap between us and folded me into his arms, kissing the top of my head. He held me for a long time, not saying anything, just holding me. I could hear his heartbeat, my ear pressed into his chest, and it soothed me. His strong arms around me also soothed me. And his head cradling the top of my head, with his lips kissing my hair—that was the best part. I was sure I was getting his clothes wet but he didn't move, he just held me.

After a few moments, we broke apart, and neither one of us said anything. He stepped away for a moment, went down the hall, and came back with a box of Kleenex. I smiled despite myself. "Thanks."

Feeling hopeless, useless, stuck, I just stood there by my doorway, wanting to tell him, needing to get it off of my chest, but at the same time not wanting to tell him for fear that he would react badly. After all, I'd seen him react badly when we went through the fight with Carlos.

I was just so scared. The last time this had happened to me, it had not gone well.

But that was Carlos and this was Jake. Jake, who told me that he loved me. Who'd sacrificed for me and who had taken care of my child.

It had to be okay. It just had to. But I didn't know how he would react.

He brought a finger forward and trailed it along my jaw. Looking at me, straight into my brown eyes, he said, "You know you can tell me anything, right? Anything at all. It's okay, whatever it is, I'll help you with it. You'll be safe. I'll help. It's going to be okay."

And now it was my turn to rush into him, needing his embrace again, needing the assurances that everything was going to be okay. He let me cry into his chest not asking any questions, just letting it be.

"You don't have to tell me if you don't want to," he continued in a whisper. "But I'm here for you if you need to tell me something."

I took a deep breath.

And let it out.

And looked at him in his face straight out of one of my books. This guy who wasn't perfect, but who was noble, artistic, protective, and hot.

The best, most real man I had ever met.

Then I closed my eyes, opened them, and out came the words, "I'm pregnant."

34

SUSPENDED ANIMATION

He blinked.

I stared at him, a tear running down my nose, my blouse sticking to me, my feet cold and wet.

He blinked again and cocked his head to the side, holding up a finger in suspended animation.

I bit my lip. "It's true. I just got back from the doctor's office. The antibiotics when I was sick made the pill not work."

"You're pregnant?" he whispered.

I nodded. "Yes. Not just a little bit. All the way pregnant. With your baby."

"You're pregnant with my baby?" he whispered again.

"You're freaking me out here, nene. I haven't had time to process this. I didn't think you'd be here. I was going to plan a way to tell you, but I just found out myself. I am in total shock, and I don't know what to do. I am pissed that I did this again to myself. I'm a pregnant, unwed mother yet again," I spat out angrily and then started crying some more. "And I love children and I'll love this child and I love you and I don't know what you think or how you're going to take this and I'm scared," I finished, sobbing.

He leaned into me and his eye twitched a little and he started to shake his head back and forth.

Oh shit.

"I never thought—" he started, still whispering, and then he stopped.

"Never thought what?" I asked, now shivering. His reaction —or non-reaction—was going to be the death of me.

But I was at the emotional end anyway.

"Oh, Lucy," he choked out. He reached under my arms, wrapped me in a big hug, and lifted me off the ground, spinning me around, nestling his face in my neck. Then he started repeating, "It's okay, it's going to be okay." He set me down, but didn't let go, still keeping his face in my neck.

God, did I have to push him? What did that mean? What was he thinking?

He ran both hands through the back of my hair, a calming gesture. He stood there for a moment, looking at me.

Then he got down on both knees in front of me, pulling me to him by my waist.

And then he lifted up my wet blouse and kissed my belly tenderly, reverently.

He brushed his hand over my belly, gently.

"Our baby is in here?"

I nodded.

With a rush, he wrapped his arms around my waist and embraced me firmly. I leaned over and nuzzled his dark, thick, good-smelling hair.

"I'm so happy," he whispered. He pulled back to look at me, his blue eyes moist. "So happy."

"Yeah?" I asked, finally hopeful.

"Yeah. I am so happy. This is my chance. I always wanted a child. This is my chance to do it right. Our chance." He paused and stood up. "God, I love you. I'll do anything for you."

And now my tears started welling up again, but this time I was crying with relief.

"It's going to be okay?" I asked, quietly.

"Yeah," he said, just as quiet, smiling and reassuring me, "It's going to be okay." Then he swooped down and picked me up, under my knees and neck, my booty hanging down, and carried me to the couch. "Hang on a second."

Jake was okay with it.

Yay.

He went into the bedroom and came back with a clean t-shirt and yoga pants for me, dry, and a towel. Then he went into the kitchen, did something, and came back, looking sheepish. "I wanted to surprise you with lunch, so I enlisted your mom. She made you a tortilla casserole. I didn't want to burn it, so I turned it off."

"You came home for me?"

He grinned. "New to me, too. I mean, I work in town. It's not like I can't take a lunch break. I thought you'd be home. Then I thought it would be nice to surprise you when you returned from wherever you were, but you surprised me. This is so surreal. Get warm, here," he said, and he helped me change.

"So this is what happens when I give you keys, guapo? You surprise me with lunch from my mom? I'm good with that."

Once I was dressed, he wrapped me in a blanket and sat down next to me on the couch and gathered my feet into his lap. "I still need to process this," he said seriously. I reached out and ran my finger along his cheekbone.

"Me too."

"But you? How are you? How are you feeling?"

"Emotionally or physically?"

"Both."

"Emotionally? In shock. I didn't know how I could have gotten pregnant. Pissed that I am. Already in love with my baby.

Our baby. Scared as to your reaction. Panicked about being left alone again."

"Not gonna happen. You're it for me."

I looked at him gratefully.

Then he asked, "What about physically?"

"Crappy. Achy. I knew something was wrong."

"I'm so sorry." He paused. "Look. You're not going through this alone. I want to go to every doctor's appointment. Is that okay?"

I nodded happily.

"What else do you want? Anything. If you wanted to get married today, I'd do it."

What? I was taken aback. "Are you serious?"

He nodded. "That's not the way I wanted to do it, but yeah, I'm serious. Anything you want. We're in this together, you're not alone."

Did he just propose?

"I think we should wait," I said. "We're still new."

Jake went into problem-solving mode. "Think about what you want and need, and we'll do it. I don't want to move too fast, but you and Rob can move in with me, or I'll sell my house and move here. Want to be with you. For real, I mean. This speeds it up, but it's right, don't you think? I mean, you and me? I don't want to frighten you off."

"That doesn't frighten me. Being abandoned frightens me. It's fast, yeah, too fast."

"Okay," he said. "Think about it. Whatever you want to do, I'll do it." His voice softened and got a little dreamy. "I love kids. I never thought I would have a chance for one. It's the best news I've ever received. Better than passing the bar or anything having to do with work or school. The best." Given his past, this had to be true. I knew that he didn't have a lot of positive things in his past and it was a complete relief to know that he was on board about this. If he hadn't been? I didn't know what I would have done.

He leaned over and gave me a blistering kiss, probing, wild. And then his phone in his pocket sounded. God bless him, he ignored it, moving in for a deeper kiss, starting to run his hands down my neck, my breasts.

"I could take you now," he said against the skin on my neck, "under this blanket. Since we have a few hours before Rob has to be home."

"'Kay," I said.

We ate lunch late.

After, when we were cleaning up the dishes, I got to thinking.

This baby was something that Jake and I had created out of love, and while it surprised both of us, both of us wanted it. And I thought about how much I'd changed since I had Rob.

I wasn't a seventeen-year-old girl, still in high school, losing my virginity to a slimeball in the parking lot.

And that seventeen-year-old girl had a lot to be proud of. I was an excellent mother to my skinny, bookish son who I'd raised under not ideal circumstances. My job was my dream job, and I made money at it. I loved my job. I owned my own home, I had fabulous friends and family who surrounded me and supported me.

And now I had Jake.

As I thought about it, I thought that maybe I needed to forgive the seventeen-year-old girl who had unprotected sex. I was a strong woman because of it.

As I forgave myself, a lot of the emotional weight I'd been holding onto washed away with the dishes.

I looked at Jake, teary-eyed, yet again. "I think we're going to be okay."

"Yeah," he said, giving me a squeeze and drying off a plate, "I think we are."

When he gathered his keys to go back to work, he checked his phone and his eyebrows furrowed.

"Something up with work?" I asked, wiping off the counter.

"No. It's a text from my mom. She wants me to come to Arizona and meet my family."

35

DON'T WORRY

The next day, Friday evening, Jake, Roberto, and I boarded a plane for Arizona to go see his mom. Rob had never been on an airplane before, so he chattered away, asking all kinds of questions about planes and the airport, because he was so excited. I was grateful to Jake for answering all of his questions.

He always seemed to have patience for Rob and genuinely paid attention to him. Sometimes I didn't do that. But I wanted to not think about the things I did wrong as a mom. I wanted to think about the things I did right.

Since I had custody, I could take my son wherever I wanted, but I sent Carlos a text about what we were doing, just to be courteous.

I didn't receive a courteous reply.

Nevertheless, it was an adventure for all of us, not just for Rob as his first trip on a plane, but also for me as a trip to learn more about Jake, and for Jake because his mom had been vague on the details for the reasons that he needed to come. He figured it had something to do with money. She had told him that she needed to see him immediately, that he had to sign some papers related to his grandparents, and that she wanted him to meet his brother and sister.

A not-so minor detail.

His half-brother Shawn, twenty-one, and half-sister, Veronika, nineteen, were part of his mom's new family. Apparently, after Jake's mom left him and his dad, she went back to her pedigreed parents, then met a wealthy new man, a plastic surgeon, and started a family in Phoenix.

Jake had never met them. I couldn't believe that he had a brother, sister, and stepdad that he'd never met. It blew my mind. What kind of mother never saw her child? Never had her son meet her other children? Well, since he'd never met his grandparents, I guess that it wasn't surprising. He told me that he saw his mom on rare occasions, having invited her to his graduations, but she'd never brought his half-brother and sister along. I mentally shook my head.

Still, she meant enough to Jake for him to drop everything and go to her when she asked. Evidence that there was a binding tie between mother and child that could not be cut.

Or that's what I thought. But what he said was, "I want to meet my brother and sister. I need to know them. Even if this is about money, which I'm sure it is, I don't want to die without meeting my brother and sister."

Good.

My new condition had not really settled in for me. Besides the physical discomfort of early pregnancy, emotionally, I was raw. I still hadn't internalized it. I'd sworn off alcohol and started taking a vitamin, but that was it.

I hadn't told Rob yet either, although I planned on telling him soon. But I first had to have a talk with him about Jake. Yes, he knew that Jake stayed over, and yes, he had seen me kiss Jake. But I hadn't actually talked to him about it.

Further, I needed to have a talk with *Jake* about Jake. I mean it was a relief to know that he loved me and that he said he was going to stay by me, but we had a lot to discuss about our future. We were going to be parents together.

But then I saw Jake buying Rob a hot chocolate and a Minecraft magazine in the airport, leaning over to listen to Rob chatter about some environment you could create in Minecraft. And any man who paid that much attention to my son was going to be a good father.

We arrived in Phoenix late. By the time we got to the hotel room, it was after ten o'clock at night, way past Rob's bedtime.

When we walked into the hotel room, just like in Las Vegas, there were two beds. As a mom, this was yet again a minor crisis moment. Did Rob sleep with me like in Vegas or did I sleep with Jake the way I did now? While I'd been sleeping with Jake at our house, we were careful to keep it from Rob.

Taking a deep breath, I decided that it was okay for Rob to be in his own bed, and for Jake and me to be in the other. If Jake was going to be the father of Rob's brother or sister, he could see us sleep together.

It still felt like a big step.

After Jake had received the text from his mom on Thursday, and we'd hastily made arrangements to come to Phoenix, we discussed how we were going to share the news of my pregnancy. Because of the fears of something going wrong in early pregnancy, I wanted to wait. But we agreed we'd still tell my parents, his dad, and my friends, Georgie and Sara, after the first ultrasound.

It was going to be hard to keep it from Rob that long, however, with me getting sick every morning. While a twelve-year-old boy wouldn't pick up on the diagnosis, he was sensitive enough to know when Mom was sick.

But different than the last time I was pregnant, though, was the very fact of Jake in my life. In the short time since I'd found out, I caught him looking at me and smiling for no reason. When we slept that night, he spent an inordinate amount of time making tiny circles with his fingers on my belly. And while he showed me affection as he always did, everything felt a little sweeter—the kisses on my nose, the way he played with my hair, and the hugs he gave when he got home from work, were all more intense. More meaningful. All of this was new to me, but it was also gratifying. I trusted Jake and I wanted him in my life, in every part of it.

We set down our luggage in the hotel room, and I turned to him. "Can I talk to you for a moment?" I said quietly. He nodded and we went off by the front door, while Rob rummaged in his bag for his pajamas. "I want to tell Rob about us but *we* haven't really talked about us."

He reached out to hold my hand. "I want to be with you forever. However you need to tell him I'm your boyfriend, you're my girlfriend, that's fine." He'd said it to his dad in the hospital, but somehow, we'd skipped that discussion amongst ourselves. "Are you okay with that?"

"Yeah. You're my boyfriend."

"Okay," he whispered. "We agree. Do you want me to go get some ice?"

I nodded. *God. This man.* He knew to give me privacy with my son. My Jake. I let go of his hand, walked over to Rob, and sat down on the bed beside him, while Jake took a key and the ice bucket, and left.

I looked at my sweet boy.

"Mijo, Mister Jake is going to be around us more. Is that okay with you?"

"Yeah, Mom. He's your boyfriend, right?"

Of course he already knew that, but it was strange to hear it from my son's mouth. I'd never been close enough to any man for them to meet my son. This was huge.

"Yes."

"He's cool. I like him. Don't worry."

Step one, done. I'd worry about step two, telling Rob he was getting a sibling, later. When Jake came back, we got ready for bed and went to sleep—me, cuddled platonically with Jake, my son sleeping in the next bed. Again, it felt like we were creating our own little family.

I wondered what it would be like in the morning with Jake's other family.

36

SILLY HUGE

"Jacob!" cried a raven-haired woman, striking in designer jeans, a peasant blouse, and turquoise jewelry. She ran out of the silly-huge house to greet us. And now it began.

That morning, Saturday, I'd woken up in Jake's arms, nauseous but so warm and comfortable. Rob slept peacefully in the other bed. Turning over, I wriggled into him and looked up as he opened his eyes. First thing in the morning, sleepy, stubbly, hair wonky, in bed? My Jake was a superb guy.

"Morning," he said, and kissed me lightly.

"Morning, guapo," I returned, happy to have this quiet moment with him, before what was sure to be a day of . . . something. Revelations? Connections? Boredom? Drama?

I think the fact that we had no idea what to expect made us both agitated.

He rubbed his fingers on my shoulder and started talking. "I dreamed last night that I had an art gallery, all my own. It was white, airy. It had good lighting and it was in a nice part of town. I had a room for myself, and all of my pictures were up." He looked wistful. "There was a whole wall of portraits of you." I rubbed my nose into his chest, snuggling harder. "That would never happen, though, because they're too intimate. They're just for you and me."

I tilted my head to the side, thoughtful. "Maybe. But I'm a professional, remember. I don't mind. I think that intimacy makes them really good."

He shook his head. "No, I'm not sharing those. Anyway, I don't really want to own an art gallery, I don't think. But it would be nice to have a show and feel like a real artist."

"You are a real artist."

"Well, one who puts work out there."

"When we get back, let's look at that art space collective in Ventura. The one that's housed in an old school."

He looked interested. "Yeah? I've never been there."

"I bet we could get you some show space."

"I'd like that." He sighed and looked up at the ceiling. "It still stresses me out to not be at work, you know. Hate to admit that. I worked those crazy hours for so long. Before we left, I gave away a bunch of cases to other attorneys in the office so I could let go of it. I had to."

"*Yay*," I whispered.

"I keep expecting things to go wrong or to be asked questions about it. I keep thinking of what's going on in the office. And I'm trying not to, but it doesn't feel right."

"We're not talking about making you a slacker. We're just gonna go for balance. When you ease up off of total workaholism, it's gotta feel like you're doing nothing. But in reality, you're just getting to be healthier." I leaned over and kissed him. This time, instead of the chaste morning kiss, he kissed me back for real, a hot kiss, hotter than we should be kissing in the morning, lots of tongue, hands engaged, running down my lower back and holding me to him. He looked over at a sleeping Rob. I giggled and sighed. "I hate to wake him, but I think we have to if we're going to get there on time."

I nodded. Torn, as usual, between parental responsibilities and a little somethin' somethin'. But plenty of Jake for me later.

"I just know it's gonna be about money today," he muttered. "That's all she ever thinks about, and it's gonna piss me off."

"Brother and sister. That's why you're here."

"Yeah."

We ate breakfast at the hotel, and as we drove in a rental car to his mom's house, he was uncharacteristically quiet. I never had trouble talking with him and he could be a real chatterbox. But right now? Silence.

The pale morning sky here in the arid Southwest looked bigger and wider than in Santa Barbara. There it was edged by the hills on one side and the ocean on the other instead of a whole grand dome over our heads, extending in every direction. We pulled up to the gated community of new, huge houses on big lots, separated from each other by a ton of land. Adapted to the Southwest, the adobe-style McMansions had xeriscaping— rocks instead of lawns and drought-tolerant plants like cacti, yucca, and mesquite. But the houses were ostentatious. This was serious money. Rob looked around, wide-eyed.

The guard at the gate let us in, and I immediately noticed that there were no sidewalks. The roads curved here and there, without a sense of being connected to the landscape.

Arriving at a house toward the back of the development, Jake parked the car and we got out. A tall, thin woman, with striking long black hair, came out to greet us.

"Jacob!" she exclaimed. "You're here." She wrapped him in a hug and he hugged her back, awkwardly.

"Hi, Mom. It's been a while."

"Oh, my, you're so handsome," she said, and pinched his cheek like my mom. I stifled a giggle. Guess all moms could act like that, even if your kid was six foot something and a chiseled hottie.

"This is my girlfriend, Lucy Figueroa, and her son Roberto. Lucy and Rob, this is my mom, Linda."

"You didn't tell me you had a girlfriend," she said. She shook my hand warmly.

I heard Jake say under his breath, "That's because we don't talk." I raised an eyebrow at him, and he took my hand.

"It's nice to meet you, Lucy, and welcome, Rob. Come, come inside." Her body was nervous and twitchy, but her face didn't move. Botoxed. She looked very young to be his mother. Everything about her was stylish and coiffed.

While I expected the house to be nice, I hadn't expected this level of grandeur. Jake was so down-to-earth. He didn't go for fancy, although his house was nice. But this level of showing off was not his style.

Jake tightened his grip on my hand and I could hear his shallow breaths, nervous to meet his family. I could feel the anxiety going through him. We walked into the adobe palace— really, there was no other way of describing it—and his mom showed us into an enormous great room with a huge television and lots of places to sit.

Sitting on one couch was, apparently, his brother. Perched on the ottoman, his sister.

Jake smiled, but it didn't quite reach his eyes. "Hi," he said, waving. "I'm Jake."

"Veronika," said his sister, standing up. Tall, very thin, with the graceful carriage of a ballet dancer and the energy of a teenager. She went over and gave him a quick hug, then stepped back and shook her head, looking pleased. "I can't believe I'm finally meeting my brother, after all these years. It's so cooool!"

I instantly liked her.

"I'm Shawn," said his brother, who looked like he played football, all brawny and short-haired. They shook hands firmly.

After introductions all around, Linda bustled about getting everyone coffee, even though everyone said that they didn't want it. Jake fidgeted on the couch, and I perched close to him.

Rob sat quietly in a corner. I'm sure he was hoping for a book or his Minecraft, but not today. Some days were like that, kiddo. I was proud of him for being polite, however.

There was no way around it. It was *awkward*. Jake, who could talk about anything, was mainly reduced to one word answers about our flight, the hotel, the trip over, how we found the house. Rob didn't say anything. I tried to talk, but found I had nothing to say.

Ugh.

I resisted the urge to check my phone and see what time it was. Now I was the one with the cell phone problem, not Jake.

Finally, we all left to go to a country club to join Jake's stepdad for lunch. A slight man, good-looking, wearing a nice tailored suit, he seemed quiet and introspective. Not a flashy plastic surgeon. And food became an icebreaker that was sorely needed. Over sandwiches, Jake started talking with his siblings. Shawn played community college football and talked with us about his studies. Veronika studied ballet. They exchanged phone numbers. Jake was amiable, but I could see the tightness in his smile and the wariness in his eyes, especially when talking to his mom.

When we returned to their house, after we were all seated in the living room, he looked at his mother and said directly, "Mom, you asked me to come for a reason. What is it?"

She came over and sat across from him, crossing her legs at the ankles, elegantly, with the excited air of someone heady with good news. "I wanted to tell you in person, Jacob." She took a breath and looked dutifully sorrowful. "As you know, your grandparents, my parents, have both died."

"I didn't know that," he interrupted. "I never met them. They never wanted anything to do with me."

She kept her poise, pausing for a moment, then continued. "Your grandparents started a trust for their grandchildren when you were born. They never told me about it, and they never changed it. It was for you and Ethan."

Jake stared at her.

"The lawyers contacted me right before I got in touch with you. There is a question about it, whether it is only for you, or whether it is for all of the grandchildren, meaning whether Shawn and Veronika are included as well."

"So you're asking me to—" Jake started.

"I'm not asking you to do anything right now," she interrupted. "But we need to deal with this. It's a lot of money."

He stood up. "I don't want it. God, Mom. I'd hoped it was something else. I really did. I wanted to meet my brother and sister. But this? God. I'm blaming myself." He shook his head. "Guess I'm crazy because while I knew it, I just knew it would be like this, I had this hope you'd be different, Mom. A kid always wants his parents to want him. But you never did, you just wanted money. I'm glad to have met them." Then he turned to me. "Lucy, Rob, let's go. We're done."

37

AN ARID ENVIRONMENT

"Wait!"

Jake's mom stood in front of him, her hand pressed to his chest. He looked at her with a mixed expression on his face—a combination of pity, disgust, and pain.

"It's always been the same with you," he said in a low voice. "And you and Dad taught me well. From watching you, having to survive the way we did when I was a kid, I learned that money matters more than anything. More than happiness. More than family. More than love. Work, work, work, even doing something that you hate, because you need it to survive."

His mother opened her mouth to speak, but he put his hand up.

"You were wrong, though. I've learned a few things that matter more." God bless him, he looked over at me. "And I'm not gonna take anything from people who were embarrassed that I exist. So no. Give me the disclaimer. I'll sign. It's theirs." And he pointed to Shawn and Veronika, who looked chagrined. His mom started shaking her head.

"Son, don't be rash. That's not what I'm talking about. All I'm asking is that you consider splitting it with them. It's all yours right now. We're talking about enough money that you'd never have to work again. You could live comfortably for the rest of your life. I thought you'd be happy."

He rolled his eyes to the ceiling, feigning patience.

This was happening too quickly. While I understood his pain, I wanted him to not make a rash decision. He was reacting, he wasn't thinking about it. And for someone who had been in fear of being poor for his whole life, to turn it down flat was a big decision. I wanted him to think about it, that's all, and not just react because of his shitty history with his mother and her side of the family.

Veronika stood up. "Can I show Roberto where the Wii is?"

My son nodded enthusiastically.

"That's a good idea," I said. He didn't need to be around this adult conversation.

"I'll go play with him," she said. "I rule at Mario Kart." Rob followed her happily down a corridor.

Shawn looked at his mother, with a weird look on his face. "Mom, don't you think you want to talk about this with Jake, by himself? Not in front of everyone?"

"But it's something that affects all of you," she started.

"Mom, we just met him."

"We don't have to talk about it right now—"

Suddenly, Jake interrupted. "My nose is bleeding. Can I use your restroom? I need a tissue."

"It must be because it's so dry here," said his mother. "Do you get them often?" She pointed him to the bathroom.

"No," he said, blood dripping into his palm. "I never get them."

"Let me help you," I offered, knowing full well that Jake didn't need any help, but wanting to talk with him. I called back to her, "I'm going to make him sit down for a few minutes."

We walked quickly down another corridor and ended up in a huge, plush bathroom, with a teak bench to sit on. Looking around at the oversized bathtub and separate shower, I thought that the square, LED-lit shower head, was particularly ostentatious, given the drought conditions. There's not enough water around here for that kind of indulgence. I locked the door behind us.

"Sit. Squeeze the soft part of your nose," I ordered, handing him a Kleenex.

He obeyed, holding the tissue up to his nose, and sitting on the bench while I hovered over him. He started muttering, only partly to me, "I hoped it wouldn't be like this. It's awful out there. I can't handle it. Too many memories. I guess I reacted that way because—" He paused, took a deep breath, and kept talking. There was pain in his voice, and he sounded funny, holding his nose as he talked. "You hope that your parents change. But they don't."

"No one changes if you ask them to. People only change if they want to change and it comes from within."

He looked at me and sighed. Then he nodded.

"I never get nosebleeds," he said. "It's so dry here. There's no water. It's like there's no life. I couldn't live here."

It's not like the watery, beachy views of Santa Barbara. Home. The place where Jake and I create.

"It's pretty, though," I said, feeling the need to acknowledge the dry majesty of the area. "I like the desert."

"Some get inspired by it, I know," he allowed, "but give me water any day." I handed him another tissue, throwing away his old one. "I realize that I'm being completely stupid, but they didn't want anything to do with me when they were alive. Why would I want anything to do with them when they're dead? I just can't accept it. I'll give it to my siblings. They can buy another wing for this house."

I sat down on the bench next to him and put my head on his shoulder.

"I'm not going to tell you what to do, but think about it, okay? Just hold off until later this weekend. It could mean that you are set for the rest of your life."

"What's a workaholic going to do except work?"

I shrugged. "Maybe you want to find out."

He looked so pathetic sitting there, holding a tissue to his nose, hunky as ever, but upset. I gave him a little nudge. "How are you doing?"

Shaking his head, he admitted, "Not good. Not good at all."

"Mentally or physically?"

"Other than the nosebleed, which seems to be drying up, it's all mental." I got up, threw his tissue in the trash, and got him another one. His nosebleed seemed to have stopped.

Then I sat next to him, his warm body next to mine, just quiet. Then he turned and wrapped his arms around me, giving me a big hug, saying "C'mere, you. I don't know what I would do without you." I cuddled into his arms.

Then, as we were leaving the bathroom to rejoin the others, he turned to me and said, thoughtfully, "You know, I have an idea."

38

BREAK THE CYCLE

"I'll do it," announced Jake, firmly but quietly, standing in the hallway.

"Do what?" He didn't seem angry now, or disappointed, like before. Instead, he looked calm, thoughtful, and determined. Taking my hand, he lightly traced a circle on the part of my hand between my thumb and index finger and bent down and kissed me lightly.

"Accept the money. And give equal shares to my siblings."

"Great," I said, whispering. Problem solved. I was confused, though. How did he resolve that so quickly, after he was pissed enough to want to fly back to California less than a half hour ago?

But then he took my other hand, drawing both of my hands gently behind my waist. And then he pulled me to him, holding me in the hallway, making me crick my neck to look up at his pretty face. His eyes were crinkling at me, and he looked at me very intently.

"Lucy, you don't understand."

I looked back at him, puzzled, not getting where he was going with this.

"I don't want the money for me. I want it for our children."

Involuntarily, my eyes widened, and I sputtered out a gasp. My stomach, already on a queasy, pregnant roller coaster, dipped. And I shivered, even though it was not cold. "*What?*"

"I don't want to touch the money. I couldn't do it. I can't do it. No matter how much it is. Those people were not family to me, and I'm not going to accept it for me. But I could create a trust for our children. I'll do it for our baby and Rob. And if we have others. I mean, we haven't talked about that . . ." he trailed off.

Oh, sweet heavens.

There were no words.

I figured this out when I opened my mouth and then closed it again. Like a fish.

"I'm gonna give the money to our kids. I'm going to break the cycle. I'm going to pass it on to our children, with love, not with guilt, and I'm going to make sure that they have lots of attention from me." He grinned. "And you."

Suddenly, a tsunami of emotions flooded my body—relief, giddiness, happiness, wariness, wonderment, shock.

And intense love for this man.

Between this announcement and the pregnancy hormones, I couldn't help it. I burst into tears, and he smiled and tugged me back into the bathroom, closing the door and sitting me back on the teak bench.

"Now it's your turn for a tissue." I nodded and took one gratefully. He sat down next to me and put his arm around my shoulders, resting his head on top of mine.

"It's going to be okay," I whispered.

"Yeah," he said. "It is."

And he kissed my tears and held me until I stopped shaking.

I'd learned before that Jake had a serious protective streak when he refused to see me, for the sole purpose of helping me with my court case. And I knew that his moral compass was set to true north because he refused to take a fortune that would make him feel inferior, or whatever it was that he was feeling. But I had also learned that he was caring, and this showed it. Ten fold.

After I calmed down, we went back out.

When Jake told his mother that he had changed his mind and would not only accept the money, but also give two-thirds of it away to his siblings like she wanted, she looked ecstatic—or at least as much emotion as her face could show. It figured. I tried not to judge, but was unsuccessful.

I also tried to like her. But I didn't. I felt sorry for her. I never wanted to find out what it was like to lose a son. Indeed, no one should have to experience that. The loss didn't excuse her behavior, however. Before the death of her son, she'd been irresponsible and that seriously messed Jake up. All parents mess up their children. But this was beyond the pale.

And then their estrangement. Watching them interact, watching how she looked at Jake, I understood it now. It was just too painful for them to spend much time together. I think that they reminded each other of hard times, all of the poverty, all of the problems, and their tragic loss. She seemed so fearful that it would reoccur. To prevent getting hurt, she'd put up walls—living in a gated community, marrying a high-earning plastic surgeon, flitting about socially, protecting herself from the past. She seemed frozen, Botoxed, scared, thin, perfect.

Never calling her son.

But it didn't really work. Even in her fortress, she was still scared. And I hoped that I never did that. I hoped that I stayed curvy, creative, and *real*, not perfect. And a part of my son's—and new child's—life. Forever.

The rest of our visit was fine.

Fun, even.

We learned that Veronika had a wicked sense of humor,

kicked butt in videogames, and was an all-around delight to be with.

Shawn was quieter, thoughtful. Jake pulled me aside at one point, telling me that it was uncanny how much he looked like Ethan. I think it was harder for Jake to be with Shawn than Veronika.

Jake reviewed the documents that his mother had her attorney prepare, and said that they were fine. He made a few changes, but signed them. And he told me that he would draft a trust for the money when we returned to California.

When he signed the papers, he turned to his mother and said, "I don't live in fear any more, Mom. I have all that I need. I'm going to be fine."

She didn't say anything in response.

We said our goodbyes the next day. Jake had finally met his family. He hugged his siblings and his mother goodbye.

On the return trip in the plane, we held hands, not saying much. Just processing the weekend. Seeing the waters of the Pacific Ocean, the waters of the Earth, I felt like we were coming home.

When we got back, I tucked Rob into bed and then sat on the couch with Jake, talking quietly. My head was in his lap, and he gently stroked my arm, meditatively. All of the lights of the house were turned off, and we sat in the dark, enjoying the quiet.

"I realized something today," he said, "during the flight. I told you that my childhood was shitty, and it was. But the thing about it is, it's the past. I don't have to dredge it up now, every chance that I get. I look around and see my girlfriend who I love, and her awesome son. I have a baby on the way. I'm employed. I have a roof over my head, food in my belly, clean water, and I woke up in the morning. And I have a lot of joy doing my art. Counting my blessings.

"At some point, you move beyond your parents' limitations. And part of being an adult is realizing that you aren't blaming them anymore for what happened. The past happened, that's all. Maybe it's someone's fault, but you can't go back and change it. So why bother complaining about not being able to change something when it's impossible?

"I think I was blaming them for not being able to live the life I wanted. I blamed them for everything: not being able to do my art, for all of the work I had to do to live, to go through school. For all of the crappy past.

"But I don't need to blame them now. That's old news." He tilted his head. "It wasn't my fault. My childhood wasn't my fault. Growing up the way I did, I was just a kid. I did the best I could. Everyone did, I think.

"But I'm going to do it better for Roberto and for our baby. And you and me."

39

EVIDENCE

I sat my booty down in a cushy lawyer's chair, in a cushy lawyer's conference room, wearing a professional skirt suit and heels, feeling like the inside of my stomach was going to bubble up, exit my body, and keep going out of the building.

Time for family law mediation with Carlos.

This was just a negotiation, I told myself. Amelia had told me this, too: It was voluntary. I could leave at any time. It was just to see if we could settle out of court. That would save time, money, heartache, and stress.

So, fine. I was here. I didn't want to be here. But I was here. And I felt queasy from being pregnant and queasy from worry.

Looking around the room, I noticed the coffee that I shouldn't have because of the pregnancy, bottles of water I didn't want, because I already had to pee all the time, and assorted office supplies stacked neatly in the corner of a side table. In other words, nothing comforting present in the room. I felt so out of place. And alone.

Amelia had left the room to talk with the mediator and the other attorney in private. Carlos and his attorney had their own room, so at least I didn't have to look at him. And I'd told Jake not to come.

Bad idea. I needed him.

No. "Need" wasn't the right word. I was beyond needing anyone, except for Rob. I could deal with my life on my own. I'd done so since I'd been pregnant with Roberto.

But I had come to a realization about Jake. Maybe it was a burgeoning trust that he wasn't going to leave me. I just knew that he wasn't going to abandon me and our child the way that Carlos or his mother had. Maybe it was simply the comfort in understanding that I had someone with me for once, who had my back. Not the way my family and my friends supported me, but as a partner. I'd never had one before. Since Jake was our neighbor, though, he'd snuck in. And I was keeping him.

Right now, he was tethered to me by my cell phone. And for once I didn't begrudge his attachment to the thing. I took comfort in the fact that his cell was an extension of his arm, attached to him at the palm. He'd promised that he would come immediately if I asked.

I absentmindedly turned the screen of my cell on and off. On and off. Waiting. Nervous. Bored. Tense.

Gah.

The door opened, and Amelia walked back in, looking brisk and professional. She had a knowing look on her face and sat down right next to me.

"Well?" I asked.

She paused. "You're right that Carlos has a gambling problem. And that's part of the reason why he's seeking to avoid paying child support. He's been searching for a quick fix to his money problems and keeps getting deeper and deeper in the hole. That's part of what's going on. I'm glad we got those emergency orders docking his pay."

"What's the other part?"

"He's going to have another child to support."

Say what?

"What?"

"He's been dating a cocktail waitress in Vegas. Apparently she's pregnant, and he wants to marry her. She's trying to get him to quit gambling. And he's worried about paying for this child in addition to Roberto."

"Oh, he's a fucked-up mess."

Amelia nodded. "Yes, but it looks like he wants to do this right with the new girlfriend. He wants to be a dad for real."

Maybe. I'd noticed Rob talking about Carlos more, which meant that Carlos had been spending more time with him. Rob had a few more books from Carlos and even came home with a story about how his dad had taken him fishing on the pier and to an amusement park.

I'd noticed over the past few months that he had, indeed, tried more to be a father. That said, twelve years of being a snake does not change in months. But for now, I just looked at her, resisting putting a sassy hand on my hip.

Amelia looked back at me, thoughtful. "Lucy, I don't trust him either. But I do get the sense that he really does want to behave differently with this new child. The way his attorney is talking, it feels very sincere."

"Is he going to move to Vegas?"

"No. She's going to move here. So Rob is getting another sibling."

Two siblings. We still hadn't told Rob or anyone about my pregnancy, but now that it was getting near the end of the first trimester, we needed to do so. Jake had moved out of the unit next to mine and back into his house. But he didn't live there. He lived with me and Rob.

We still hadn't figured out what we were going to do. Living in limbo-land, he came home to me every night. He almost never went to his house. And while we'd talked about it, about what we were going to do, we hadn't made any decisions.

Instead, we were just assembling evidence, so to speak, that we were together. Stringing together days and moments, I could look back and see the pattern of our relationship. Every night we were together, making love quietly. Every morning he woke me up with a hug and a kiss, before going for his run. Every afternoon, he'd either come by for lunch, bring me food, or meet me somewhere as a treat. He texted me in the middle of the day. He helped Rob with his homework. And while he stayed late at work sometimes, it wasn't every night.

Yeah, Jake was amazing. I was in love with him. I didn't know where it went from here, but being in the middle of this relationship was the best thing that had happened to me in twelve years.

"So what does he want from me? Does he really want more time with Rob? Or is this just a ploy to have to pay less in child support?"

"Both, I think," answered Amelia.

The thing was, Jake and I had talked about strategy for this mediation. If I moved in with him and rented out my duplex, I wouldn't need as much child support for Rob. But that was a super huge step, not just for our relationship, but also because I was Rob's mom and moving him out of my house and into a boyfriend's house wasn't something that I was going to do without careful thought. Having Jake stay over? Well, that was a natural extension of him being my neighbor and staying over so much. It didn't require Rob to move everything out of his room.

"He wants to talk with you, Lucy."

"I don't want to talk with him," I responded immediately.

"You don't have to, and I already told them you wouldn't want to. If you don't talk to him, then we will go forward with the hearing, and we will bring up all of it—that his mom was watching Rob, that he took him to Vegas and left him in a hotel room by himself, all that. But maybe talking to him is the way to finish this. They're threatening to bring in Jake for perjury and assault and battery. They are threatening to take away Rob. Talk to him. You've got something to lose if you don't."

Ugh. Enough already.

"Fine," I huffed. She raised an eyebrow. "Yeah, fine, whatever. I'll talk to Carlos." My reaction was to shut down and protect myself whenever he was around. But I had serious stakes here that I could not afford to lose. Neither could he. And occasionally, we were civil to each other.

I stood up and followed her out of the room, down the hall, to the conference room where Carlos was camped out. She let me in and closed the door behind me so that I was alone with him. It was the same as the room that I was in, only mine was bigger and had a better view. That was oddly comforting.

"Lucy." He stood up and crossed over to me, and I flinched. "Relax. I just want to talk to you."

"So talk."

"Rob's a really great kid."

"No thanks to you."

He blew out a breath. "Will you let me talk, please?" Goddamn, Carlos said please. I just stood and stared at him. "I am getting to know Rob, and he's a good kid. Smart. Real smart."

"Thanks to me."

"Fuck, Lucy. Yes, thanks to you. Can you take a compliment?" Gah.

He continued and looked sincere for once. "I can't afford it. I keep getting further and further in the hole."

"That's your problem—" but he interrupted me.

"Let me talk."

"Fine."

"Can you give me a break? I have a new kid on the way. A

girl. Rob's sister. And I don't want to fuck it up this time. I fucked it up with you—"

"You did—"

He sighed, exasperated, and shoved his hands in the pockets of his slacks. "I want you to agree, temporarily, that you'll accept less in child support. Trial run. I want to spend some more time with Rob."

"No you don't."

"Don't tell me what I want to do."

I rolled my eyes to the ceiling. "Carlos. This is bullshit. When you said you wanted to spend more time with him, you left him with your mother. You left him in a hotel room with a tablet. You left him with me for twelve years. You've never been interested in your son. Why are you starting now?"

He gave me a weird look. Almost like he was embarrassed. "Yeah. That's how I've been. It started with just the money. But I've been hanging out with him, and he's a cool kid."

"You haven't been hanging out with him, your mom has been watching him while you worked."

"Not the whole time."

"Whatever," I muttered.

"Give me a chance. One extra day. And this much in support," he said, shoving a piece of paper into my hand. I read it.

I could live with that amount.

Ugh.

The legal test was the best interest of the child. But that was also how I should act. What would be best for Rob? Not what was best for me. What was best for me was to never see Carlos again as long as I lived. But while Carlos was an asshole to me, and he'd been stupid in Vegas, he'd never hurt Rob. Actually, I think the hurt that he'd done had been through abandonment, not through attention. If Rob spent more time with him, well, maybe that would be healthy.

Fuck.

Fine.

"Okay," I said.

He did a double take. "Okay?"

"Temporarily, okay. I want your paycheck still docked. I want all the hearings to go away. I want Rob to tell me all the wonderful things you do with him, because I'll ask. We'll try it this month. And we'll take it one month at a time. Do. Not. Fuck. Up. Your. Son."

He looked down at the ground. "I don't think that I can fuck him up, Lucy, because you've been his mother. No matter what I've done, he'll always have you."

What?

Something nice out of Carlos's mouth. True, he wanted something out of me, but for now, I was going to take it.

Like the evidence that I was building with Jake, one day at a time, building a relationship, I'd give Carlos that chance too. One day at a time, he could build a relationship with his son. And I was going to be vigilant to make sure that he really was doing that. But if he did, I think it was in Rob's best interest to have a relationship with his dad.

I nodded at Carlos. "We're done here. The attorneys can write it up." And I left, going back to Amelia.

When I left, later, after signing the papers, somehow, I felt lighter.

40

MORE THAN THAT

R eaching up, I cradled his shoulder blade with my curved hand. It jutted out at an angle, covered in soft skin and muscle, and I yet again appreciated the strength of his upper body. From this position, as he looked me in the eyes, one arm hooked around my neck, the other arm holding him up over me, hand next to my ear, I enjoyed the sensation of his body against mine, the way his torso felt over me. Warm. Solid. Comforting. I slowly ran my hand from his shoulder blade all the way down his side. The edge of his torso spread wider than my hand, even though he was a lean guy, so I took my time and explored. Again, stroking his skin, no clothes on, noticing the way it felt to run my hand all the way down him, slowly, from just under his arm to his hip, reveling in being able to touch him, uninhibited. I pressed my hand into his gorgeous flesh, feeling his muscles, holding him to me.

Rob had spent the night at Carlos's house. Jake and I got naked and stayed that way. And now, his hard cock filled me and he gently moved inside me. My twelve-weeks-pregnant belly rounded slightly, meeting his trim waist.

He closed his eyes, and I watched the look of agonizing pleasure come over his face, as he slid out and in, out and in, and then he opened them again and brushed his soft lips against mine. He'd already made sure that I'd come. Three times. It was his turn.

"Do it," I whispered.

He nodded and kissed me again, this time wilder, wetter, more passionate, and he changed the angle that he was thrusting.

My breathing got heavy, because God that felt good.

"Come, lover, do it," I whispered, and with a shudder and a quiet groan, he climaxed, for a moment out of control, out of the world of cell phones and time and into a world where only he and I existed.

And then he collapsed onto me, lips against my neck, his thick hair all that I could feel of his head, and stayed there.

A moment later, he hoisted himself up, pulled back and pulled out, and went back on his knees, so that he could kiss my belly. Staying there for a moment, running his hand lightly around my navel, he rubbed his nose on my skin and then peppered it with kisses. Then he came up behind me, my back to his front, and he drew me in his arms, spooning, kissing my neck.

"We need to tell people," he said against my neck. "Your belly is starting to show."

"Okay," I agreed. "Rob first."

"Yeah," he whispered. "Definitely first."

We lay there for a moment and he spoke again. "What do you want to do about us?"

I shrugged. "I want to be with you."

"I am with you," he answered. "But don't you want more than that?" I could feel the pulse racing in his body. His breath got shallower and his voice was huskier than normal.

I started to shrug again, and then changed my mind. Nodding, I said, "Yeah, I do."

Because I did. I wanted to be with him forever. Yes, this pregnancy was unplanned, and yes, we were still in a new relationship, but it wasn't so new anymore, and with each day I spent with him, I fell in love with him deeper and deeper. I'd never felt this way about anyone before. I had no idea how I'd been able to write romance novels without experiencing the way he made me feel—like I was a precious treasure that he had to care for. Bringing me presents, spending time with me, and making sure that I had what I needed. He never missed a doctor's appointment. The workaholic in him was winding down. It wasn't a linear slow down, but he wasn't working anywhere near what he used to. We were talking about what he was going to do to transition even more from the craziness that he had hid himself in for so long. Soon. He was changing, and he told me that he planned on making a bigger change, once he figured it out what it would be.

And the way he was with Rob made me fall for him even more. He listened to Rob chatter and went to the effort to make sure to read the same books that Rob was reading so that they could talk about them.

I was sure.

"Do you want to marry me, Lucy? Before the baby gets here?" I turned over and looked at him. He looked completely sincere and a little scared. I felt my heart race, and I was just as scared as he was. "I love you," he continued, "and I want to make sure that you know that."

"I do know that," I whispered.

This wasn't the first time that we had talked about it. It wasn't the first time that I had thought about it. But it was the first time when I knew, I just knew, that I wanted to make our relationship formal and show the world. We were together.

"So will you marry me?" he asked again.

And I lost it. Pregnancy hormones. The release of good sex. Being secure in his arms and knowing that this not-perfect, but real guy wanted me. Yes. I wanted it forever.

"Yes," I whispered, a tear coming down my cheek. "I will."

"You will?" he said, sounding shocked.

"I will," I laughed, and he wrapped his arms around me and held me tight as I sobbed into his neck. "We'll tell Rob all of it at once." And then I paused and breathed and said in a rush, "Oh my God, we're getting married."

He laughed and kissed me, then turned me over on my back and started kissing me down my neck, down my breasts, down to my belly. "Wipe away those tears, honey, we're getting married. Go get a dress." And he climbed off of the bed, went to his jacket, and pulled out a small box. "I got you a ring," he said shyly, and pulled it out.

It was a square cut diamond, big, with two blue sapphires on either side. Like his eyes.

My stomach dropped. Not a far journey.

"If you don't like it, I can return it and we can get a different one. I just thought that it reminded me of you and me and Rob, with the three stones. And the ring is our new baby, holding us all together." He climbed back on to the bed and pulled me up to sit next to him, and gently took my hand.

I let him slide the ring on.

It fit. I'd never worn a ring there.

It was too much. Too beautiful. Overwhelming.

But I opened up and decided to let it in. The good. The amazing. The wonderful.

"I love it and I love you."

He looked giddy with relief. "Is it too soon to get married this week? I can make an appointment with a judge I know. Or we can go to church, whatever you want."

"Judge. Maybe after the baby comes, we'll do something bigger."

He nodded and kissed me.

I took a deep breath and thought about what had just happened. And mixed with the excitement, I felt an even bigger peace than I'd felt in my whole life.

41

SOMEONE TO HOLD ONTO

he End.
Delete.
Ugh.

I rapped my fingers on my desk.

Was I done? I never really liked to write "The End" on my stories, because in my mind, they were never done. There was always something else that the characters could do. My characters took on a life of their own, and I never liked to say goodbye.

I thought about it for a moment.

Yeah. I had finished my new novel. On deadline. And I was pleased with it. I started typing again.

The End.

Time to finalize and send it off to my editor.

After the birth of this creative project, I felt relieved and sated. But there were other things that I needed to do.

Like tell Rob that he was getting a new sibling.

And a stepdad.

I got up from my desk, my body achy from pregnancy, rubbing my fingers on my gently protruding belly. Having made it through the first trimester, I couldn't wear my fitted clothes anymore. Since I normally wore yoga pants to write in, so far I'd been able to hide my condition, but it was at the point where I needed to tell everyone. I'd managed to hide it from my friends and family by saying that I couldn't go out since I needed to finish my book. But now that it was done, I needed to show my face and start telling people. It was time to tell Rob about the baby.

I also needed to tell him about Jake and me.

Wandering down the hall, I walked into his room. It was the sweet spot of time after he'd arrived home from school and had finished his homework, but before dinner. I knocked on his open door to politely announce my presence. Rob sat inside, reading a book, his skinny frame draped with a t-shirt that hung from his frame, ankles hanging out the bottom of his pants.

Yes, that was my son, nose in a book.

"Can I talk with you?"

"Okay." He reluctantly set the book down.

Again, that was my son.

"I have a few things to tell you and they're important." His dark eyes got big, and I took a deep breath and continued. "First of all, you need to know that I love you, and I have always loved you, and I always will love you."

He looked at me suspiciously and said, "Yeah?"

"What do you think of Mister Jake?"

"I like him."

"Me too, mijo. Me too. He is very special to me. In a different way than you are special to me."

"Are you going to marry him, Mom?"

Smart kid. It didn't surprise me that he'd figured it out. Kids know.

"Yes," I answered. "I am."

"Does that mean we're gonna live at his house?"

"Yeah, it does."

"Do I have to switch schools?"

"No. I checked it out. You don't." He visibly relaxed. "What do you think, mijo?"

"Okay, I guess." He shrugged his narrow shoulders.

I gave him a smile. "There's more news." Looking back up at me blankly, he set his hand on his book in a comforting gesture. "There's going to be a new brother or sister."

"Yeah, Dad already told me."

This surprised me. "He told you he was having one?"

He nodded. "He says it's a girl." Rob grimaced. "Great, a sister. Guess that will be okay, though."

"Roberto, I'm pregnant too," I said quietly.

My son's lower lip started to quiver and he visibly grayed under his tan skin. "No. *No.* You can't."

"What? Why?" I asked before I could help myself. Then I recovered. "Tell me what you're thinking, mijo." He shook his head and a tear stuck at the corner of his eye. I reached over and held him in a big hug, which he didn't return, his arms held limply down. "C'mere," I muttered into his hair. "Just because we have big changes coming up doesn't mean that my love for you will change." He nodded into my torso. "Are you scared that the baby is going to get all of the attention?"

"Both babies," he whispered.

"You're a smart kid," I said. "To figure out how you feel and to tell me. Babies do take a lot of time and things will change."

I leaned back so I could study his face and watched the tear threaten to escape his tear duct. But he wiped it away with the back of his hand.

"It's a big change," I repeated. "I am scared too. And it surprised me too."

"It did?"

"Yeah. But it's a good surprise. It just takes some getting used to." I pulled him back to me in a hug.

Rob nodded, and I continued, "Just think about it, mijo. Jake and I are going to get married by a judge next week."

"Okay. Can I read my book now?"

"Yeah." And I ruffled his hair.

Just then I heard the front door open. Jake was home. He knew that I was going to tell Rob today and he'd wanted to know if he should be there or not. I'd told him that I wanted to tell Rob by myself and he'd stayed away, even though he was in the habit of coming home earlier these days. I got up and kissed his forehead. "We can talk about it more if you want, okay?"

He nodded.

Pausing a moment at the door to look at him, I steadied myself. I hadn't realized it, but my pulse had been racing the whole time and I'd felt flushed—not from the pregnancy. I'd been nervous to tell him. Things were going to change, and I was scared, too.

It was hard to be a parent when you wanted someone to hold onto yourself. I leaned my head against the door and heard Jake call out, "Lucy?" Some of the fear evaporated when I heard his baritone.

Righting myself, I went to the front door and got a kiss on the mouth and then a Jake kiss on my nose. "What's up? How was your day?"

Wrapping his arms around me, he lifted my chin and looked at me intently. He was my someone to hold onto. "How did it go telling Rob?"

"He needs to get used to it. But good."

He nodded and his eyes were dancing. I wondered why. "I'm glad you told him. Keeping secrets is stressful. It's a relief now." He paused. "Still gonna be an adjustment for us all."

"Yeah it is, but now we can tell everyone else." Like my parents. And my friends. The same feeling that I'd felt when I told Rob returned. I wasn't done with my uncomfortable announcements by a long run.

Then Jake spoke. "And I've got some more news."

42

PROMISES

"We had a meeting at work."

His eyes seemed to get deeper, a blue that was almost black. He looked like a kid dying to tell the answer in class, but who knew that he had to wait until he was called on. Well, a kid in a dark gray business suit with a blue and silver striped tie.

"What? Tell me." I gasped.

"A few things," he said, teasing me, making me wait. I put my hand on my hip in my classic sassy-Lucy posture. "We voted to make Amelia Crowley a partner in my law firm."

I squealed. "That's great! She totally deserves the promotion."

"She does. She's already taken over most of my cases. She put in her time. She's due."

I did a little dance, shaking my booty. *Amelia, breaking the glass ceiling.* He watched me dance until I stopped moving, and then I smiled saucily up at him. But I thought of something.

"She's not going to work too hard is she?" I asked, suddenly worried about my lawyer.

"No. We hired another young attorney, a woman, to help her."

Excellent.

"There's more," he continued, eyes still dancing.

I pushed his chest. Oh, yum, his chest. "Oh yeah? Hit me with it."

He leaned over and got right in my face, a beaming smile on his marvelous one. I almost expected him to do a happy booty dance. Heck, I wanted to see that. "I have a new job."

Awesome!

"What? Where?"

He wrapped his hands around my waist, pulling me to him. "The court has a program for helping people who don't have attorneys and a staff position opened up. It's got limited hours—ten to four—and I'll be helping people directly. People who can't afford lawyers."

"That's fantastic!"

"It's a pay cut but I have money saved. I think we'll be fine."

I squealed again and jumped up and wrapped my arms around his neck. He swung me around, as jubilant as I was.

"I'm gonna have time, Lucy honey. Time for you, for Rob, for our baby." He paused. "Time to paint."

"*Yay,*" I whispered, and he kissed me again, this time pressing me against the wall, his legs between mine, caging me in with one arm on the wall next to me and the other one on my ass, pulling my leg up.

When we broke apart, I wasn't breathing.

"That's too hot for right now," I said, whispering again.

"It's a promise for later," he replied, whispering back.

Just then Rob came out of his room, thankfully when we weren't entangled, and we set to work making dinner.

The next week, on Friday morning, Sara and Georgie sat on my bed, watching me dress.

"I still can't believe you didn't tell us you were pregnant," Georgie charged, a sassy-Lucy hand on her hip.

"I told you I was sorry, chica, but I needed to get things squared away with Jake before I could tell anyone. And then I wanted to get through the first trimester."

"But we could have helped you," Sara said sensibly.

I kissed the top of her hair. "You're helping me now."

My parents camped out in the living room with Rob, who I'd taken out of school for the day. My son had his hair slicked down, slacks and a dress shirt on, and his shoes shined. He looked sharp. Jake had already left for the Santa Barbara court-house, bringing his dad with him. His mother, stepdad, brother, and sister were going to meet us there.

I slipped on my dress. It was a bigger size than usual, but still fitted, strapless, knee length, and very me. Simple. Elegant. And white. Sara zipped me up the back and fastened the buttons.

Shoes on, hair down and straight, lip gloss applied. I was ready to get married.

Teetering, as usual, in high heels, I walked out of my bedroom and looked at my parents. My mom, dressed up in a navy skirt suit, came over to me with tears in her eyes. "Lucinda, you are a beautiful bride and you make your mama very proud."

I mock-complained, "Don't make my mascara run."

My dad came over and without a word, wrapped me in a hug. "Dad, not you too," I said, this time fighting tears for real. He took my hand and walked me outside, all of us leaving. I locked the door and then we all climbed into a black limo that waited at the curb.

Walking into the courthouse, I had an entirely different feeling than I did the last time I was here. Last time, of course, I was nervous with anticipation. This time, yes, I was also nervous with anticipation. But it was the delicious, happy kind.

We found the courtroom and walked in, the door unlocked for us.

My handsome Jake was standing up front, talking with the clerk. He wore a well-tailored black suit, black skinny tie, and looked like a Tom Ford ad.

Mine.

My dad held my hand and walked me up to Jake. My eyes locked on his, I held onto my dad for support, but I discovered, as I got closer to Jake, that I didn't need it. My mom, Rob, my friends, and Jake's family found seats in the audience. I held Jake's artist's hand, which was warm, firm, and comforting. As usual.

The clerk called the judge, who came out and spoke to us about how marriage was not to be entered into lightly, but with careful thought. And how the most important things in a relationship are love, communication, trust, honesty, respect, and understanding.

I looked back at my parents, holding hands, my mother daubing her eyes with a handkerchief. Those qualities were what my parents had and what I had with Jake. Glancing around, I saw Rob holding Georgie's hand, looking serious. And Jake's family, all with pleased looks on their faces. We had everyone's support.

The nervous anticipation disappeared. I was in the right place with the right people. I wanted to do this and I was so, so happy.

The judge continued.

"Do you, Jacob Slausen, choose Lucinda Figueroa to be your lawful wedded wife? Do you promise to love and comfort her, and to honor her and keep her in sickness and in health, in prosperity and adversity, and hold her needs above all others, so long as you both shall live?"

"I do." Jake's words rang out, filling the courtroom with authority. My statesman lawyer in the courtroom.

"Do you, Lucinda Figueroa, choose Jacob Slausen to be your lawful wedded husband? Do you promise to love and comfort him, to honor him and keep him in sickness and in health, in prosperity and adversity, and hold his needs above all others, as long as you both shall live?"

"I do." And as I said the words, I knew that all of that was true and would be as long as I lived. I would love this man who loved me back, who sacrificed for me, and who put my needs first before his. He'd done so already, in every way possible.

Rob came up and handed us our rings. I kissed him on his cheek and then watched him sit back down. And Jake and I exchanged rings.

The judge continued. "The groom has informed me that he has something to say."

"I made a promise to Lucy today, but I am also making a promise to her son, Roberto." He turned and looked at him. "Rob, I promise to care for you and put your needs above mine. I promise to read with you, play with you, and guide you. I love you."

And the nerves and the tears that had been in check came bursting out of me, and judging by the rustling noises behind me, out of others. Jake loved me. But he also loved my son. He had drawn his way to my heart.

"Inasmuch as Jacob Slausen and Lucinda Figueroa have thus consented together in marriage; by virtue of the authority vested in me by the State of California, I now pronounce you husband and wife. You may kiss your bride."

And my husband very gently, very slowly, and while looking me in the eyes, kissed me in front of our friends and family. And he was mine.

43

ALL THE WATERS OF THE EARTH

"Jake, my belly is getting too big," I protested, while at the same time I wanted him.

Pregnancy made me horny. Sorry, I had to admit it. I mean, just Jake's physical presence alone, most of the time, made me want to strip him down and touch him all over. But with the added natural aids during pregnancy? I was unstoppable. I found myself getting turned on all the time. He didn't seem to mind.

I discovered a love of all of the positions that didn't put weight on my back or belly. Doggy style. Standing up. On my side.

In the bathtub.

My joints were getting loose and achy and even though it was warm out, it still felt good to soak in the tub. Sometimes Jake would join me. Like tonight.

We'd been married for six months, honeymooning briefly in Mexico, and planning a bigger reception after I gave birth. We were in his house, which was now our house. I'd rented out mine, which brought in some extra income. But now, Rob was at Carlos's house and I was ready.

But I mean, my God, my belly was so big right now. "I don't know how we can do this."

Stripping quickly, his athletic body graceful, he sunk into the filling tub and called me to him. "Come in the water, Lucy honey." I took off my yoga pants and my cami, wanting to feel him and the warm water around me.

Reaching out his hand, he carefully pulled me into the bath. I stepped into the water, feeling it swirl around my feet, looking down at him for once.

Short girl gets a new perspective. Nice. It felt very different to be the one above him, almost like I could see new things about him. His eyes looked so arresting in the sunny, lit room.

There wasn't that much room, but I managed to kneel down and straddle him, setting my knees on both sides of his belly.

Running his hands up slowly up my body, over my swollen abdomen, caressing my breasts that were now perkier than ever, pausing at the hollows in my collarbone, and sliding one artistic hand behind my neck, he appraised me with his eyes. "I don't know that you have ever been lovelier," he whispered. "Carrying our baby." And he knifed up and kissed my belly.

Splashing a little bit in the water, I leaned down to kiss him, my belly in the way. He sat up, his cock hard below me, my need for him inside me increasing.

We kissed, a loving, total, passionate kiss, the kind of kiss that makes you forget about aching joints and knocking knees and just focus on the fact that you were getting some lovin'. Because heck yeah, Jake gave me some lovin'.

He reached around, gripping my ass, firmly but gently, then pulled me down, allowing me to guide myself onto him.

And now I was in charge. This was exactly what I needed— connection with him, release of tension, the warm water of creation all around me.

Enjoying our last days or weeks of being a couple without a baby.

Jake had learned, over the years of his life, that it was not okay to dream, that his art was not safe, that he had no family support, and that life was not certain or secure. But we had set to work undoing that.

He'd carried through and switched his job. While he spent a lot of time with me and Rob, he also spent time drawing, painting, playing, doing art. He'd rekindled a connection with his dad, who had recovered from his hospital stay and was working reduced hours. And every day that we were together added evidence to our relationship, proving that we were committed to each other and that life was secure when you were honest and open with the ones that you loved. Whatever the opposite of abandonment was, that was how we were. I spent my nights cuddled with him. My mornings in his arms. He came with me to every doctor's appointment. When we heard the baby's heartbeat go thuwump on the machine, every time, both he and I cried. And we talked all the time.

For he had learned that I couldn't read his mind and told me what he thought. He asked questions, he made mistakes, and he told me what he was thinking. And, be still my heart, he paid attention to Rob, too.

He had walked out of a romance novel and into my life, but he wasn't the hero of a romance novel. He was just my Jake.

Now, making love to him, in the water, with the baby that we'd created growing in my belly, my novel out there, doing well, and him finally taking his art seriously, I knew that this was bliss. In the arms of my lover, who cared about me. With the knowledge that I was loved. And doing what fulfilled me.

All of life existed in the waters of the earth. We needed water to exist, to create, for gestation, and for survival. Every single person on this planet was created from almost nothing—a tiny egg and a sperm. Then cells divided in the waters of the womb and there we were. Every single thing on this planet, from laptops to toothpaste, was created from nothing—starting with an idea and making it real. And the art, music, stories, movies, and dance that made us swoon? That wouldn't exist without all of us either.

As I arched my back, shuddering in ecstasy, I looked down at him, head thrown back, chiseled torso shaking as he came too.

After he recovered, he wrapped his arms around me, and then cleaned us off.

"I love you," he said, drying me off with a towel.

"I love you, too," I replied, nestling my head in his arms.

It is in our very nature to create. And it's the only way to live for real.

EPILOGUE—FOUR YEARS LATER

"Come here, girl," I crooned, as I plucked my daughter gently out of the stroller. Three months old, she fit in the crook of my arm, right on my bicep. As she liked to do, Lucy had decked her out in pink fluff, a pink band around her head taming her mass of dark hair. My wife liked to dress up our daughters. Lucy treated baby Natalie like a doll. With pretty brown eyes like her mama, my little baby girl sleepily rested her head on my shoulder.

Chelsea, my four year old, had run ahead of us and was now swinging on the swing set, free and wild. Her hair was up in two ponytails on the side of her head. She wasn't as pinked out as her sister, wearing a comfy dress over striped pants. She didn't let Lucy dress her up these days, because she liked to dress herself. Pumping her legs, going higher and higher, she giggled in delight.

I'd left the house—and taken everyone with—to give Lucy some quiet time to write. She had a new idea for a book and was excited to get going. I'd read everything she'd written and she still surprised me with her creativity and intelligence. Even though she had a string of major successes with her latest writing, she still pushed herself to try new things, to challenge herself. So I'd taken the kids and a diaper bag (it was amazing how much crap they needed) and walked down to the playground at the beach. She'd said that she would come and join us later so that we could get a ride back up the hill.

I'd settled on a bench where I could watch Chelsea and hold the baby, while talking to Roberto, who had come along.

"Dad?"

I looked over at Rob. Sixteen years old, he normally was too cool to hang out with me and Lucy and his sisters, wanting to spend time with his friends. But today they weren't picking him up until this later afternoon and he'd decided to come with. I was glad he did. Today was a tough day for me—the anniversary of my brother Ethan's death. I was glad to not be alone any more. The more people around the better. I was done with being by myself.

Losing Ethan didn't get any easier. His memory just got a little quieter. And I learned that celebrating his life was important, but it was also important to be here now, present, with the ones I loved—and that didn't take anything away from his life.

Over the years, Rob and I'd become pretty close. Now he called me Dad.

I loved that.

"Yeah?" I answered.

"How do you know when a girl likes you?"

He'd grown from a skinny, gangly kid to a classy young man, still bookish, but now with some serious style. Taking after his mom, his hair was always very cool, his clothes sharp, and he looked good.

The fact that he trusted me enough to ask was everything. "You got me, son. I have no idea. They're mysteries." My eye caught Chelsea's, who'd hopped off the swing set and was now headed to a slide. "But they're worth it."

"I want to take her to the movies, but I don't know if I have enough from my allowance." I shifted Natalie to my other arm. Rob didn't know yet that he was taken care of. The money from my grandparents sat in a trust to be divided equally between him, his two sisters, and also his half-sister Ella, Carlos's daughter. Lucy had asked for that, not wanting Rob and his sister to be treated differently, and I'd agreed. Rob was part mine now, if not legally adopted, definitely in spirit. And now he saw his dad too, regularly. That seemed to work, too.

"Who is she?" I asked.

"A girl at school. She's quiet, but I like her."

"I'll give you money to take her to the movies," I offered. "Will you babysit the girls so I can take your mom out?"

He nodded. "Deal."

We sat on the park bench, watching Chelsea play with a little boy who looked about her age and a little girl who looked a little bit older. It was the weekend, but these days, I had plenty of time to spend with my family. My job at the courthouse suited me. I helped people, but I didn't work crazy hours. And I had time to paint.

My first show at the schoolhouse collective in Ventura went well. I actually sold all but one of the paintings. With that success, Lucy persuaded me to do a show of pictures of her. I'd been worried that they were too intimate, but she was right— the intimacy gave them the spark they needed.

It's amazing that I'd worked so hard for as long as I did. Before, I didn't know how to live. I just existed. Now? This was living—watching my kids play at the park and talking with my son.

And then Lucy pulled up in her car.

Emerging from the car, I gazed at my wife.

She was so fucking hot.

Compact, yes. Curvy, fuck yes. So, so beautiful. She took good care of herself.

But more, she was wise. She was sassy. She loved deep, and she gave herself to me.

I loved her. More each day.

Lucy always wore high heels, today at the park was no exception. She had on some sort of sandals, along with little shorts and a pretty top. School would be out soon and it was warm out. She smiled and ruffled Rob's hair, which he protested, then leaned over and kissed me. Sitting down on the park bench next to us, she picked up Natalie, cradling her.

"All good?" she asked me, rubbing her nose into Natalie's hair.

I looked around.

"Yeah," I said. "All good."

ACKNOWLEDGMENTS

My thanks and love to:

My family and friends.

Kristy Lin Billuni, www.sexygrammar.com, for holding my hand.

Maxine Donner, for endless Skyping to plot this baby.

Little Dude, www. ... nah. I can't do a link here of his NSFW Tumblr site (thingsmydickdoes). Well, thanks to him for giving me a list of positions for one of the—SPOILER—sex scenes in this book.

The Wattpad community, including early readers Liz Madrid, B.G. Davies, and Amanda Cheairs-Cabral, along with many others I only know by username, for comments and feedback.

Mary Carr, www.romazingreads.com, for being the most amazing beta reader ever.

Deb Markanton, Temitope Awofeso, Melanie Martin, Catherine Bibby, Maria Monroe, and Margaret Provenzano for very helpful feedback.

Jerica "no comma for you" MacMillan, www.jericamacmillan.com, for a whole lot, including proofreading, although all errors are mine.

Heather Roberts, www.obsessedwithmyshelf.com, for being my spirit animal and my stripper pole of sanity to cling to.

Mitchell Wick, Wong Sim, Jennifer Watson, Michele Catalano (michelecatalanocreative.weebly.com), Shanoff Formatting (www.shanoffformats.com), and Social Butterfly PR (www.social butterflypr.net), for making everything better.

The Mariposa County Superior Court for verbiage.

And Wild Child for writing the song, "Break Bones," which was the only song I listened to while writing this.

ABOUT THE AUTHOR

Leslie McAdam is a California girl who loves romance and well-defined abs. She lives in a drafty old farmhouse on a small orange tree farm in Southern California with her husband and two children. Leslie's first published book, *The Sun and the Moon*, won a 2015 Watty, which is the world's largest online writing competition. She's gone on to receive additional literary awards and has been featured in multiple publications, including Cosmopolitan.com. Her books have been Top 100 Bestsellers on both Amazon and Apple Books. Leslie is employed by day but spends her nights writing about the men of your fantasies.

Website: https://www.lesliemcadamauthor.com

M/M-only newsletter: http://eepurl.com/hD9a4r

ALSO BY LESLIE MCADAM

Sarina Bowen's World of True North (m/m)

Undone (audio narrated by Iggy Toma and Tim Paige)

Unmanageable (audio narrated by Jacob Morgan and Teddy Hamilton)

IOU Series (m/m)

Ambiguous (audio narrated by Hamish Long and Kirt Graves)

Studious

Oblivious (coming soon)

Contemporary Romance (m/f)

All American Boy Series

Boy on a Train (audio narrated by Desiree Ketchum and James Cavenaugh)

Romantic comedies with Lex Martin

All About the D (audio narrated by Stephen Dexter and Ava Erickson)

Surprise, Baby! (audio narrated by Jacob Morgan and Muffy Newton)

The Giving You ... series

The Sun and the Moon (audio narrated by Tor Thom and Charley Ongel)

The Stars in the Sky

All the Waters of the Earth

The Ground Beneath Our Feet (audio narrated by Tor Thom and Charley Ongel)

Love in Translation series

Sol

Sombra

Standalone novella

Lumbersexual (audio narrated by Tor Thom and Charley Ongel)